SO-AXK-817

LP   8580
Est   Estleman, Loren

           Stress.

DATE DUE

JY 30'95			
SE 05'96			
OCT 0 1 '96			

North Webster – Tippecanoe Twp. Library
North Webster, IN 46555

DEMCO

STRESS

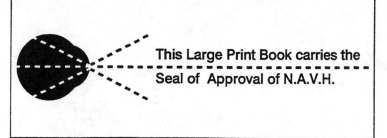

This Large Print Book carries the
Seal of Approval of N.A.V.H.

STRESS

Loren D. Estleman

Thorndike Press • Thorndike, Maine

North Webster - Tippecanoe Twp. Library
North Webster, IN 46555

Copyright © 1996 by Loren D. Estleman

All rights reserved.

Published in 1996 by arrangement with Warner Books, Inc.

Thorndike Large Print ® Cloak & Dagger Series.

The tree indicium is a trademark of Thorndike Press.

The text of this Large Print edition is unabridged.
Other aspects of the book may vary from the original edition.

Set in 16 pt. News Plantin.

Printed in the United States on permanent paper.

Library of Congress Cataloging in Publication Data

Estleman, Loren D.
    Stress / Loren D. Estleman.
        p.   cm.
    ISBN 0-7862-0695-0 (lg. print : hc)
    1. Large type books. I. Title.
    [PS3555.S84S74 1996b]
    813'.54—dc20   96-10419

For Louise A. Estleman, my mother

It became necessary to destroy the town in order to save it.

— Anonymous American officer, Vietnam, 1968

PART ONE

The Crownover Killings

Chapter One

If being rich meant having to listen to live music all the time, Kubicek would just as soon take his three hundred a week and an eight-track player.

Always conscious of his Hamtramck background in the company of that Grosse Pointe crowd, he'd felt low-brow at first for being bored by the string quartet playing in one corner of the half-acre living room, but as one show tune treacled into another and the conversation of the guests continued to drown them out, he realized *no one* was listening. Even the musicians — a fat bald guy, a pair of faggots in ruffled shirts with their hair curling over their ears, and a pasty-faced girl in her twenties dressed in black who looked like the female half of Boris and Natasha — wore expressions that said they'd rather be home watching Guy Lombardo. He wondered if this was typical, and for the first time in his life he didn't envy the wealthy.

The house was a fucking museum. Murky old religious paintings leaned out from the

9

walls in gaudy gilt frames and glass cases stood in inconvenient places showing off stone axes and bits of rusted armor. He'd shit a brick when told the cost of the Oriental rug in the dining room and had avoided the room ever since, terrified of tracking something into it. He couldn't imagine growing up in a place like that. It did a lot to explain the behavior of the spectral six-year-old girl who had appeared briefly when the party was just getting started, hiding behind the architecture and looking out with huge haunted eyes.

Kubicek looked at his watch, a Waltham with a heavy steel case and a Twist-O-Flex band. Quarter past nine. It seemed later. He was bushed. Some last-minute paper fuck-up had kept him at 1300 past his shift and he'd had to abandon his plan to stop off at home and shower and change before going on to the party. He felt sticky under the shirt he'd had on since six o'clock that morning, and out of place in his sturdy gray suit among the tailored tuxes and poofy low-cut gowns. The sight of all those bony spotted bosoms did nothing to lift his fatigue. Rich women were by and large sixty years old and looked more like men than their escorts.

The White Rock club soda in his glass had gone flat. If the party didn't pick up by ten, he'd treat himself to a bourbon and branch,

10

and to hell with his reflexes. It didn't look as if they were going to be needed anyway.

"Having a good time, Sergeant?"

Ted Ogden's sudden appearance from the crowd of chatterers startled Kubicek. That irritated him. He was paid to be alert. But Ogden was a small man, easily overlooked. He might have bought his white 007 dinner jacket in the boys' department at Hudson's.

"Not my job, sir. I'm here to make sure *you* have a good time. You and the guests. Nothing breaks up a party like a heist."

Ogden showed a set of beautifully bonded teeth that made the other man want to check his own for spinach. He had a head of tightly coiled auburn hair — a tribute to the wig-maker's craft — and large moist brown eyes that looked as if they would soak up details like twin sponges. "Relax, Sergeant. You're only here to keep the insurance company happy. One of the advantages of living in a depressed area is no one expects to see this many diamonds in one room. All the jewel thieves are in Palm Beach this time of year."

"I didn't know Grosse Pointe was depressed."

"I mean Detroit. Drive five miles down Jefferson and you're in the Third World. Can I get you a drink?"

"Thanks, I'm fine."

A woman who was taller than Ogden by a head and looked older by several years came up behind him and slung an arm around his neck, dribbling green-tinted liquid from the tall glass in her other hand. Her hair was dyed bright copper and the glittery blue dress she wore left a trail of sequins on the parquet floor, reminding Kubicek, disloyally, of a snail. Her eyelashes were long enough to erase a blackboard. "Teddy, you're marooning our guests."

"I am not. I'm talking to the sergeant."

Her oyster-colored gaze skidded past Kubicek's face without stopping to focus. Caryn Ogden, born Caryn Cooper Crownover, was already a furlong ahead of everyone present when it came to swamping away the year 1972 with buckets of alcohol. "Bullshit. You're paying him to be here, so he can't go. When people start asking after their host, they're this far from calling for their hat and coat." She released her husband's neck to hold up a thumb and forefinger. "Hank and Christina have to leave soon. I don't want them to go home thinking you're upstairs banging one of the caterers."

"Don't be coarse." Ogden shook Kubicek's hand, squeezing hard. "Make yourself at home. In case I don't work my way back through the mob before midnight, happy new year."

"You too." He watched his employer being dragged into the high human tide, thinking, *Poor pussy-whipped bastard.* If this was what life was like married to Crownover Coaches, a city salary and a part-time security job were looking better all the time.

Having disinterred the entire scores of *Man of LaMancha* and *Jesus Christ, Superstar*, the quartet had turned to the theme from *Love Story*. Sweet holy shit. He set his glass down on a convenient ring and opened a sliding glass doorwall leading to the terrace: terra-cotta tile enclosed by junipers trimmed into perfect domes and a sweep of winterkilled lawn to Lake St. Clair. He drew the door shut behind him. The air was cold but not biting. The surface of the lake, not yet frozen, was graphite-colored under a spray of dusty stars with Canada a zigzag of lighted windows on the far side like a jagged line on a business chart. From somewhere in the darkness the chainsaw whine of a motorboat drifted his way. At any hour of any day or night some idiot was out trying to extend the previous season. The spring thaw would find him dodging patches of thin ice at the wheel of a snowmobile, if he didn't hit a stray floe tonight.

Kubicek ran his fingers through his thick graying hair, missing the springy feel of his brush cut. It had been his wife's idea to let it grow out after twenty years. "You look like Goldwater," she'd said, and although that didn't sound half bad he'd sensed her disapproval and stopped going to the barber as often. At forty-eight it was the small changes that nettled. There were so many of them. Before long they piled up like driftwood, forcing the current of your life in strange new directions. Longer hair, reading glasses, a sudden intolerance for caffeine — friend of a thousand stakeouts and three all-nighters cramming for the sergeant's exam — and suddenly you were flouting department regulations and applying for a private detective's license to finance your divorced daughter's education in law. In his mind it was all connected. He went back inside. Absently he checked the time. Twenty-eight minutes past nine.

Questioned by the shooting team later, he would say he went for his piece when he spotted the guy with the shotgun, but that was just for the record. He'd testified a hundred times in court and had learned early that the gutty tingle shared by cops everywhere was a mystery to lawyers and judges. He felt the change in atmosphere before he saw anything. The musicians were still playing, unaware of the wave of unease washing their way, when Kubicek reached inside his jacket and unclipped his .45 automatic from the speed holster strapped to his ribs. It was already cocked when he located the first weapon.

It was a Remington pump shotgun, chopped down from both ends to a length of less than twenty-two inches. The gunner swung it up from under his quilted army fatigue coat, jostling the partygoers nearest him, and leaped onto a three-hundred-year-old trestle table, kicking over dishes of pastry and shouting for everyone to kneel.

But it was that jostling and the guests' reaction — outrage over this breach of the social contract — that rippled through the packed room before anyone was aware of the man or his threat.

The bottom half of his face, below mirrored glasses and a navy watchcap pulled down to his eyebrows, was caramel-colored, and his afro rolled out around the bottom of the cap. He spoke with a delta twang, either real or inherited; but by the time he spoke Kubicek was looking for his partners.

He knew where to find them. One, dressed similarly but without glasses, had stationed himself at the arch to the dining room. He held a short-barreled revolver twitchingly between both hands, extended at arm's length. The third, evidently proud of his natural — an impressive eighteen inches in diameter — or unable to contain it, had dispensed with headgear and coat, preferring a macramé vest that brushed his hips and a gray sweatshirt hung tail out over bell-bottom jeans. Hampered by the press of bodies, he was heading for the door to the terrace. His right hand was in his pants pocket.

Kubicek couldn't believe rich people. You had to be really caught up in yourself to miss three black guys in street duds entering a house in Grosse Pointe.

The man with the big hair was closest, but shotguns took precedence. Kubicek turned sideways and sighted along his arm at the man crouching on the table. The heavy automatic bucked twice in his hand and he saw the soles of the man's tennis shoes. He turned toward Big Hair.

But the scenery had shifted. The guests were moving now, scrambling to clear the line of fire. He lost his man.

He spun and shot the gunman standing in the dining room arch. The man doubled over, wobbled back two steps, and sat down on the Oriental rug. His revolver played spin-the-bottle on the slick parquet on the living

16

room side. Then a scurrying guest kicked it away.

The music had stopped. There was shouting and squealing and a long shivery splintering of crystal.

A *whoosh* and a spray of cold air brought him back around to the sliding door and Big Hair's macramé back on the terrace. Kubicek gave him three yards, then spread his feet and took two-handed aim through the handy frame of the doorway, just like on the police range.

Three times between the shoulder blades, his best group in years, in or out of qualification. Ruptures opened the size of poker chips. The man was still falling when the nasty ripping howl of a four-cycle engine climbed the scale close to the dock below the terrace and faded away. The wake of the retreating motorboat, an indistinct dark wedge, glittered in the reflected light from the house.

Kubicek glanced at his watch. Nine twenty-eight and thirty seconds. Less than half a minute had passed since he'd come in from the terrace.

The shotgun lay across the stomach of the man who had fallen off the table. Kubicek put the weapon on the table and removed the man's mirrored glasses. Only the whites

17

of his eyes showed.

The man in the dining room looked up as Kubicek entered, then sagged sideways. Kubicek felt the last throb in the big artery under his jaw and went outside.

There was no mistaking the position the man there had fallen into, all arms and legs like a pile of Lincoln Logs, but Kubicek kept the .45 trained on him as he pushed him over onto his back with a wingtip. Instinctively his eyes went to the man's hands, then searched the surrounding tiles. Finally he squatted and patted the body from chest to ankles.

He took the automatic off cock, lips pursed. This one wasn't armed.

Chapter Two

"What's wrong with the gun business is there's too many cowboys in it, and more coming in all the time," Joe Piper said. "Dealing in absolute shit, pieces from Norway and Czechoslovakia — Prague, I'm serious, that great firearms capital of the world — where the blueing comes off in your hand. Not that it matters, because you won't have one after you pull the trigger the first time. They got no *esprit de corps*."

He knew he was talking too much and too fast. It was a family failing; when a Piper got nervous you couldn't shut him up. Like his Uncle Seamus, a clam all his fucking life who ran guns to Ireland in the twenties with the dough he made shoving booze for the Machine mob, then at age seventy-one turned into a canary, all because his prostate blew out and he thought he had to dump all his sins before he scaled the rainbow. So far as Joe Piper could tell from the little he knew of Gaelic, the worst of these to Seamus wasn't the smuggling or the killings or the partner

19

he'd abandoned in Galway Bay and for all he knew was still rotting in some English prison, but the six-month marriage that had ended in divorce in Cleveland in 1930, and that he'd kept a secret from his children, his wife of forty-two years, and the Catholic Church. Fortunately Joe Piper's father, Seamus's brother-in-law and a partner on the American end of the old enterprise, had brought in a Polish priest who didn't know the language to hear the confession. Quinn Piper didn't care how many wives the old man had had as long as the source of the capital behind the family cement firm remained family knowledge.

Joe Piper's case of nerves had nothing to do with the prospect of dealing some guns. He'd been doing that all his adult life. Even before that, he'd fetched and carried for his father when the Edsel went bust in 1959 and the Detroit housing market fell down the same hole, and Quinn took up the slack by performing as go-between on a transaction involving surplus Korean War ordnance and some characters from Bolivia or somesuch shit place, who wore dark glasses indoors and handled English as if it weighed a hundred pounds. Nor was he agitated by the identity of his customer. In his line, a slot on the FBI's Ten Most Wanted list just meant a higher ante. Anyway, he'd done business with Albanians, and those guys scared Mao Tse-Tung.

No, it was the venue that put him on edge.

He hadn't been down Twelfth Street since before the riots. In the living room of his house in Pontiac he'd watched its neighborhoods burning on television, paratroopers trading automatic-weapons fire with snipers in windows, and tanks — Sherman and Patton *tanks,* for chrissake — trundling along the pavement, all those great blind pigs and rib joints boarded up, and thought for the first time of moving to California. He'd thought martial law would put an end to the local gun trade; forgetting that this was Detroit, where the answer to a recession was to make more cars and the solution to widespread insurrection was to arm everyone who was big enough to haul a gun uphill without training wheels. The social order had broken down. When you couldn't count on the cops to protect you, you heeled yourself. Within two years his orders had doubled, and he could have doubled them again in the next three if he wanted to trade in the shit peddled by his competitors. A Joe Piper piece never misfired or blew up in your hand. That was what kept him above ground and out of jail in a business not known for its loyalties.

But he didn't delude himself. To the majority of his clientele he represented The Man, growing fat off his customers' need, and he might as well have put on a pigeon suit when he ventured into the Detroit Black Community to work deals. For six years now his only contact with the DBC had been through buffers whose skin pigmentations matched his buyers'. The first time this particular buyer had asked to deal directly with him, Joe Piper had refused. When he found out how big a shipment was involved, he'd suggested a meeting in Pontiac. Told the customer's name, he'd realized why that was impossible, and after sleeping on it agreed to the Twelfth Street location.

He'd regretted the decision the moment he left his Buick Electra in Redford and boarded the DSR to downtown. The bus was loaded with black passengers, and in his fur-collared overcoat and doeskin gloves he'd felt their suspicion instantly. He was Black Irish, but not nearly black enough, pale-skinned under his rebellious shock of black hair, blue-eyed, pug-nosed, and built like a retired heavyweight fighter spreading into his middle years. Freezing on sidewalks in the Michigan March they'd seen his kind capering in the St. Patrick's Day parade when Cavanagh was mayor, green-hatted and swinging a shillelagh, and it might have been a peek at life on Pluto for all it meant to the way they lived.

The building, an apartment block with common walls built early in the century, looked vaguely familiar. It could have been any one of the places Joe Piper had stopped for a drink after hours or a barbecue sandwich in the days when he'd stepped back and forth across racial lines without having to think about it. The bricks and Edwardian gingerbread were charred and crumbling. He could just make out the ten-inch-high SOUL spray-painted on the plywood in a window beneath several generations of increasingly profane graffiti; an old attempt to forestall destruction by proclaiming the owner's race brotherhood, fruitless in the swirl of the tempest. The funereal black CONDEMNED printed on a notice tacked to the wood looked faded and chalky. It stood as much chance of being fulfilled as the building of which it had become a part. Most of the damaged blocks were still standing, a ghost town in the center of the country's seventh-largest city.

Someone who thought the place was worth finding had hand-painted the address Joe Piper was looking for on a door with a tarnished brass handle. When he pushed it open, a metallic crackle answered from the gray darkness inside. He obeyed the command to enter with his hands away from his body.

Although he had been around guns most of his life, he never carried one. The man inside frisked him, uncocked and belted his revolver, a short nickel-plated .357, and pulled a six-foot steel cabinet away from the door to a staircase leading to the upper stories. He was short, but he was as strong as a horse. His shoulder-length black hair, beaded headband, and the sweatshirt he wore with tribal designs painted on it under a quilted vest gave Joe Piper the impression he was an American Indian. It seemed an odd association, but then nothing had made much sense downtown since July 1967.

The Indian motioned up the stairs. He walked that way, accidentally kicking a piece of debris across the floor. The place appeared to have been a laundromat. Twisted and broken-off pipes stuck out like tentacles from the walls and there was a smell of detergent and mildew beneath the smoky stench.

At one time the second floor had been divided into apartments, but the walls had been torn out to make room for a single enterprise. Joe Piper knew where he was then. Before the riots he had come there on occasion to shoot pool and seal bargains over an unlicensed drink. A room without character at the best of times, now that the tables and fixtures were gone and the windows blocked it felt empty even of ghosts. The only light came from a Coleman lantern hissing on a square Formica-topped table and a kerosene heater on the floor. The flames cast more shadows than light and warmed little besides themselves.

Having delivered the visitor, the Indian made for the far wall facing the door and leaned against it. No introductions were made. They were unnecessary. Joe Piper assumed the man seated behind the table knew who he was, and even in the hollow illumination of the lantern he recognized the man's features from his FBI circular.

Wilson McCoy. The narrow dusky face, black beret, Fu Manchu moustache, and straggly chin-whiskers reminded Joe Piper of the young Dizzy Gillespie, but he was implicated in the daylight ambush of mob boss Patsy Orr and three associates in an elevator of the Penobscot Building in 1966. That had been at the time of the Kercheval Street Incident; although that dress rehearsal for the full-scale rebellion that took place the following summer had pushed the assault off the front pages, McCoy's connection with the Black Panthers brought him to the attention of J. Edgar Hoover, who had been searching for thirty years for another John Dillinger to touch up the Bureau's image. McCoy now occupied a spot on the list just below Jane Alpert, the woman sought for the 1969 New York bombings.

Unimpressive in person, with eyes set too close together and a sickly, hollow-chested look that Joe Piper suspected was congenital, McCoy had one habit that fascinated him: He chain-smoked marijuana. There was no mistaking that scorched-grain smell or the noisy way he sucked in air along with the smoke, but Joe Piper, a sometime indulger, had never before seen anyone round over an ashtray with hand-rolled butts, or light a fresh reefer off the stub of the last. The procedure was expensive and should have turned his brains to cornmeal, but there was nothing mushy about the way he opened the conversation.

"I know a smoke shop on Michigan where I can score all the pieces I need for half what you charge. How come everyone says call you?"

That was when he told McCoy what was wrong with the gun business.

Teeth shone on the other side of the table. Whether it was a smile or a grimace was anyone's guess. "I'm off the tit a long time. I guess I know a good gun from one that's going to blow off my own dick."

"You'd be surprised. I've seen some pretty guns, museum quality, that I wouldn't fire without a long string and a brick wall to squat behind. Automatics are the worst. They're the knock-off Rolexes of the gun trade. They gut them, part out the actions, and stick in any old Mickey Mouse works. You think you bought a Beretta, but what you've really got came from a boiler factory in Seoul. A real melting-pot piece. And there's something else to consider besides quality of merchandise." He started forward, intending to lean across the table. The Indian straightened and rested a palm on his .357. Joe Piper put his hands in his pockets.

"A gun can kill you without ever going off," he said. "Last month three guys got stopped for busting a light on Woodward. The cop turned out the car and came up with three unregistered S-and-Ws. Okay, that's a Class A felony, but any kid with a degree could plead that down to a fine and time served. Only come to find out one of the pieces killed a clerk in a Seven-Eleven in Dearborn last Thanksgiving. None of these guys was even close to Dearborn that day, but they're nailed for felony homicide. Now they're singing, taking everybody down with them, including the guy that put them on to the guy that sold them the guns. Not the guy that sold them the guns, though. Cops in Wyandotte snagged him out of the river three days after Christmas. See, that's another reason you can trust a Joe Piper piece. My balls are on the block. No fuck-ups. No history. Better than General Motors."

"There's another way." McCoy chain-lit a joint. "Don't bust no red lights."

He ignored the remark as irrelevant. "Someone told me you were asking about grease guns. That's a wide field: Uzis, AK-47s, BARs, M-16s. The whole alphabet. Maybe you better nail it down."

"I heard shitty things about M-16s."

"They're shit, all right, but they get the job done. Plastic stock, banana clip. Low velocity. Fucking bullets tumble end over end. Sometimes they go in sideways. Make a hell of a hole. I can cut you a deal now that the war's winding down. In six months they're going to be a drug on the market."

"What else you got?"

He hesitated. It occurred to him that he was dealing with a man who faced serious time. Joe Piper had a nose for such things as informants and wires. He wondered if the FBI's priorities had shifted to the supply side. He had contacts in the Bureau of Alcohol, Tobacco, and Firearms, and none of them had reported a thaw in the cold war between ATF and the Justice Department; still, Hoover was dead. "I'm not saying what I've *got*," he said. "We're just talking. Why don't you tell me what you have in mind and we'll figure out what's best for the job."

Again he saw teeth. "Last time I told whitey what I was thinking, I got six years at Whitmore Lake."

"Maybe you should tell me what you have to spend. If you were buying anything and I had anything to sell," he added.

"I might go fifty large for twenty pieces. Depending on the pieces."

Joe Piper never showed surprise. He had learned the art of dissembling early, when he had continued in the weapons trade on his own after his father had gotten over the hump and returned to the cement business, without the father ever suspecting what the son was up to until he was out of the house for good. Yet the amount quoted by McCoy rocked him. He did some fast mental arithmetic, and in his professional interest forgot to be cautious about terminology.

"For twenty-five hundred apiece, I can put you behind twenty Ingrams."

"What the fuck's Ingrams?"

"Machine pistol, folding stock. U.S. made, if you're patriotic, only I guess you're not.

29

Comes in two calibers. Thirty-eight's easier to handle, but the forty-five pokes holes big as a champagne cork."

"I like big holes. What's the ROF?"

He measured out a small smile. "Eleven hundred and forty-five rounds per minute. I'm telling you, you can't flutter your lips fast enough to duplicate the sound."

There was an impressed silence. Joe Piper broke it.

"For hard cash I'll throw in the suppressors and fifty thousand rounds of ammo."

"What the fuck's suppressors?"

"Well, silencers."

"Don't want no silencers. I like to make noise. Keep the silencers and make it a hundred thousand rounds. When's delivery?"

"I got the guns if you got the cash."

McCoy dragged in a lungful of smoke. When he spoke his vocal cords were constricted. "I ain't. I expected to, but something went bad. I call you when I got it. You box up the guns meanwhile."

The son of a bitch. Drag him clear down here just to listen to the Rotarians speech. It was lesson time.

"Thing is, this is perishable goods. If you don't have the pony, I know three other guys who do."

He didn't believe any living organism could

move that fast, much less one with so much marijuana in its system. The Coleman lantern tipped off the table, the Indian lunged forward to catch it, and McCoy caught Joe Piper's unruly hair in one fist and drew a thin edge of fire across his Adam's apple with the other. Released suddenly, Joe Piper started back, and only then saw he was bleeding, bleeding bright strawberry all down the front of his coat. He felt himself turning to water below the waist.

"It ain't cut." McCoy wiped the edge of the straight razor clean on the heel of his hand. "Not through. Not this time. Box up them guns like I said. You'll get paid."

Downstairs, the Indian, who seemed prepared for everything, dressed the five-inch slice with peroxide and a bandage that looked like a clerical collar and sponged the worst of the mess from his coat with a towel soaked in distilled water. Minutes later Joe Piper wobbled out into the bright sharp air of a January afternoon on Twelfth Street.

Chapter Three

Charlie Battle wondered at what point a squad lieutenant decided to transfer his forensic skills from unraveling the riddle of urban crime to solving the mysteries of nautical rigging.

Sweating a little in his winter uniform — the steam heating system at 1300 Beaubien had been designed for a building much taller than seven stories — Battle stood without fidgeting while Max Zagreb threaded thirty-pound-test fishing line through the tiny loops on the plastic main yard of Old Ironsides. The green blotter on the big gray steel desk was a litter of polystyrene masts, hatch covers, and able-bodied seamen frozen in mid-duty, from which the historic battlewagon was rising in 1/24th scale like a ghost ship from a miniature scrap yard. In time, Battle supposed, it would take its place among the *Mayflower*, the *Santa Maria*, the *Bonhomme Richard*, and the rest of the toy fleet that sailed atop every file cabinet and shelf in the corner office. Throughout the twelve precincts Zagreb, who spent most of his lunch hour driving to and from Rider's Hobby Shop in Ypsilanti, was referred to as Cap'n Crunch, but never to his face. As skipper of Special Investigations he drew deep water in every bureau.

He was a slight man with a balding head and enormous sideburns like the ones on the deceased city leaders whose pictures walled the corridors of the City-County Building where Battle worked. With the Bicentennial still three years away, a number of local notables were already cultivating such exotic adornments in the spirit of the shaggy greats of the past. It was the young officer's observation that most of them lacked training in the care and nourishment of facial hair; Henry Ford II and Senator Philip Hart especially looked as if they had hooked on false whiskers for a school play.

Zagreb tied the line to a halyard on the deck, snipped off the extra inch with a pair of pinking shears, and peeled aside his gold-rimmed reading glasses. "Know anything about ships, Officer?"

"I know they float. Sir."

"Under ideal conditions, yes. The only time I was ever on one — a real ship, I mean, not a rowboat or the ferry to Mackinac — I got sick as a dog. Haven't been on the

North Webster - Tippecanoe Twp. Library
North Webster, IN 46555

water since. So why do I build model ships? I could say it's good for manual dexterity, but there are other kinds of models I could put together, cars and movie monsters, and they don't interest me. I guess I'm fascinated by sailing craft because they're entirely self-contained. Maybe that's why I joined the police force. It's the only government body that cruises along independent of the rest."

"I guess us cops are all sort of in the same crew."

"Horseshit. I didn't call you in here to give you the don't-rock-the-boat speech. How are things at City Hall, by the way? Is Gribbs figuring to re-up?"

"I don't know, sir. The mayor doesn't confide in me. I only see him in the lobby and he's usually surrounded by TV crews."

"Well, if you do talk to him tell him I don't recommend it. The Democrats are grooming Young. That son of a bitch does his electioneering with a pipe wrench."

Battle, who thought it was high time the city had a black chief executive regardless of what tools he employed, said nothing. He wished Zagreb would invite him to crack a window. But the lieutenant didn't seem uncomfortable at all in a double-knit suit that might have been painted aluminum for all it wrinkled or draped or gave any indication that there was a body underneath.

He sat back, Old Ironsides forgotten. "We know now why I became a cop. Why did you?"

"To serve and protect."

"That's what it says on the cruisers, and it's horseshit. This isn't the academy finals. What made you decide to become a cop?"

"It isn't wrestling."

"Explain."

"There's a story involved."

"I don't have anything to do until this cement dries but listen."

"I was raised by my Uncle Anthony. He was born in Biloxi. Down in Mississippi a black man picked cotton or nothing. When his father had enough of that he came up here to make Model Ts and brought Anthony with him. Anthony didn't want to work for Ford, so he boxed. Only when he got to the Golden Gloves he found out he wasn't Joe Louis and went to work carrying a hod. When he got tired of that he became a professional wrestler."

Zagreb snapped his fingers. "Anthony Battle. I should have guessed. He took the U.S. championship away from Percival E. Pringle, two falls out of three."

"World, U.S., it was all the same thing. The same outfit held all the wrestlers' contracts and decided who won what. I didn't see any future in that. Hod-carrying doesn't pay much better than it did in 1953, so here I am."

"By default."

"Not really. I like the job."

"You like getting coffee for the deputy mayor?"

"Tea, usually. And it beats sticking my face in Dick daBruiser's crotch at Cobo Hall every Friday night."

"I've got something better than either of those," Zagreb said. "You know Paul Kubicek?"

"Not personally. I see his picture." It was pretty hard not to, unless the TV was broken, the subscription to the paper ran out, and something blew into his eyes every time he passed a newsstand. The scowl and crooked necktie Sergeant Kubicek had worn for his ID photo had appeared in every edition and on all the noon and six P.M. broadcasts since New Year's Day. The eleven P.M. too, probably, although Battle was usually in bed by then, resting for the six A.M. turnout.

"Yeah, the pricks in the press are really busting Division's balls over this one, as if one dead black ex-con more or less made any difference in this town."

"I don't guess it matters what color you

are once you're dead," Battle pointed out. But the lieutenant went on as if he hadn't spoken. In his twenty-two years the officer had encountered both extremes, raw uncut racism and white liberal bend-over-backward sympathy, and knew how to respond to both, but the unthinking impersonal bigotry that ran throughout the Detroit Police Department was something he didn't think he'd ever get used to.

Zagreb said, "It's a good shoot any way you stand it up. This Harrison character that went down on the terrace had a record and a gun in his hand. So did the others, Nampula and Potts, but their bulletholes were in front so nobody's raising any stink over them. This ain't the fucking Old West. When one of the perps in a robbery makes a break for it with a piece, it's a cop's job to put him down."

"No one at the party heard him identify himself as a police officer."

"He claims he did. There was a lot of screaming and yelling, so who knows what they heard or didn't? Only this citizen's group, this Afro-American Congress —"

"American Ethiopian Congress."

"As if any of them could find Ethiopia on a map at gunpoint. Anyway, this Junius Harrison turns out to be an office boy or something at the firm where one of the lawyers at Caryn Crownover's party works and he's got a message for the lawyer in his pocket, so the Congress says he was there on legitimate business. To me, that makes him the inside man, but they've filed a complaint and it looks like the N.A.A.C.P. is backing it up, so we've got to run it out. How'd you like a spot on the shooting team?"

Battle wasn't expecting anything like the question. Before he could frame a response, Zagreb held up a hand.

"It's not a promotion. You're still assigned to the City Hall Bureau and there's no raise and no guarantee when it's over you won't be right back asking the fire marshal if he likes one lump or two in his orange pekoe. It's a chance to work with Special Investigations and get out of the blue bag for a while."

"Why me? Sir."

"You can lay off that 'sir' horseshit. Whatever you may think of me and my toy boats, I'm a lieutenant, not an admiral." He leaned back in his chair, peering at Battle through the rigging. What he saw, or what Battle imagined he saw, was a tall young black man in a crisp uniform with the crudely blocked-out facial features of an ebony carving. His afro was modest even by department standards, an almost grudging acknowledgement of brotherhood with the types who decked themselves out in dashikis and named themselves after rivers in Nairobi. He had inherited his uncle's musculature but not his bulk; were Zagreb to enter the locker room while the officer was changing into his civvies, he might have been surprised by the hard-planed shapes that combined to form his slender build.

In fact the only thing remotely soft about him was his eyes, tender, brown, and luminous. Although he considered them a detriment to his life's work, his wife of six months told him he ought to be grateful for them, because without them she might never have seen anything in him to love.

"I've been over your file," said the lieutenant. "I see you were on the debate team at the U of D. That means you can talk. A couple of years ago that wouldn't have meant crap, but the department's changing. Police work's changing. When I joined up, the entire detective division operated out of a swamp on the seventh floor under the command of a real piece of work named Kozlowski. He didn't have one knuckle he hadn't broken at least twice on some poor sap's jaw down in the basement. And he had company. Back then you couldn't have rounded up enough cops with more than an eighth-grade education to play a game of touch football. They were tough, but they couldn't have stood up to a ninety-eight-pound reporter with a TV camera. You'll be doing plenty of that if this thing keeps heating up the way I think it will."

"How much does this have to do with me being black?"

"Damn near everything. The American Ethiopian Congress is pushing for an all-black team to investigate the shoot. They won't get it, one, because I'm being paid to run this bureau and with a boy in college who can't play basketball for shit I can't afford to split my paycheck with them, and, two, as fast as we've been stacking the ranks with black officers since the riots we still don't have any in Special Investigations. This business of detecting detectives is thorny as hell even without a bunch of rookies tripping over their own feet. Your record is clean, you can handle questions from the floor without drawing your service revolver, and according to your turnout sergeant you don't make a lot of enemies. If you've got reservations about being chosen for this duty on the basis of your race, sing out. Nothing? 'Kay."

He opened a rumbling drawer mounted on ball bearings, lifted out a thick gray cardboard folder, and held it above Old Ironsides' main-mast.

"Read it. Kubicek's report, eyewitness statements, autopsy records, paper trail left by the guns involved, etcetera. It should bring you up to speed on the official end."

"Can I take it home?" Battle hefted the file. He had never been in on an investigation and was surprised at how much paper a case could accumulate in just ten days.

"No. You're meeting the rest of the team this afternoon. Take your lunch hour and go over it in that corner. I'll leave you alone with it. If you have to go to the john, take it with you. When you're there don't put it down. Piss one-handed. The last time a file from an internal investigation left this floor it wound up in the Metro section of the *News*. The man who was behind this desk at the time is in Florida now, running a two-man police department and making just about as much at sixty as you make now. I'm forty-nine. I can't take humidity."

"I'm not much for beaches myself, Lieutenant. I can't swim and I don't tan."

"Be grateful you don't. In today's climate it makes you the only officer connected with this mess who doesn't have to watch his own ass." Carefully, Zagreb folded the scattered scraps of plastic inside the assembly instructions and transferred them to the vacant drawer. Pushing it shut, he rose.

"Take your time. The chair's more comfortable than the sofa, which is where I seat reporters. When you're through I'll introduce you to the men you'll be working with. They'll tell you what *isn't* in the file."

Chapter Four

Russell Littlejohn smelled the Indian from the landing.

The Indian, whom he knew by no name other than Wolf, was partial to Brut, and although he seemed to have rules about not wearing cologne before evening, splashed the stuff on promptly at six P.M. at what must have been the rate of a bottle a week.

Detecting the thick musk as he fished for his key, Russell felt a stab of panic and thought of leaving. But the stairs, built recently along the side of the house by his father from new lumber, made a lot of noise. Wolf would know he was there, that he'd run away, and if he and Wilson had any doubts at all about Russell's performance in Grosse Pointe, their minds would be made up from that time on.

It wasn't that the Indian would run after him. He knew he wouldn't. The implication, that they could lay hands on him whenever they felt like it, disturbed him more than the thought of being chased. The doorknob turned without resistance and he went in.

The tin-shaped floor lamp directed light downward only, leaving the room's top half and all but one corner in shadow. Nevertheless he found Wolf's short dark bulk without having to search for it, seated in front of the painted table where Russell had done all his homework since he was six years old. The Indian's long hair gleamed like a wet galosh.

"You need a good lock," he said. "You'd be surprised what people steal."

"There ain't a thing here I'd want back."

Seeing the place through the eyes of a visitor, he realized he meant what he'd said. The Jimi Hendrix albums, posters from *Superfly*, *Shaft*, and *Sweet Sweetback's Baadasssss Song*, and unmade iron-framed single bed clearly belonged to a spare room over the garage of a house paid for by his parents.

He hated them more than ever then: Dwight Littlejohn grubbing around in the ductwork at Redford High and his wife Elizabeth shuttling the little white pissants to and from school in a big yellow bus. Sometimes, stretched out on his bed blowing hash and letting Jimi's guitar licks wash over him like a big electric tongue, he pictured himself boarding the bus, spraying its passengers and his mother with automatic fire, then driving the bus to school, through the big front doors, and carving a gory swath studded with spent cartridges down the halls; finishing with his father, who would go down trying to defend himself with a wrench. Come the revolution there would be as little mercy for the collaborators as for the oppressors.

Wolf seemed to have trailed his thoughts. "It's not such a bad place. You ought to see the cells at Alcatraz. Six by eight and a view of the next cell."

"You were at Alcatraz?" He'd followed the accounts of the occupation by Indian activists with interest.

"Not for long. I bailed out after two weeks, stole a launch and went back to Frisco. They didn't call that place the Rock for fun. The white man can have it. If we were going to claim an island it should've been Catalina. Where'd you ditch the boat?"

Russell had to run to catch up to the new subject. "I didn't. I returned it to its slip. I even replaced the gas I burned. Nobody knew it was ever gone."

"Wipe your prints off the wheel?"

"No need. My prints are all over the marina. I work there."

"I know. That's why we used you. That and what Kindu Nampula said about you. Kindu isn't saying much now. A slug in the

45

liver will do that."

"I hung around as long as I could."

"How long was that, till you heard the first shot?"

"Hey, I hung tough even when a brother I didn't know come running for the dock. Pig shot him three times and I split."

"Cop see you?"

"No. Too dark."

"Any cops call on you?"

"*Hell*, no. Why should they?"

"Why? Shit. You're right. The only street out from the house dead-ends at the lake. Cop wastes Kindu and Leroy and some poor shit, speedboat takes off right after. Why should they check out every fucking power boat on Lake Saint Clair? Hell, there must be a half-dozen marinas with someone working for them pulling a record for Robbery Armed."

"That was juvie. P.D. pled it down to simple assault and I folded sheets and pillowcases for six months. I been talked to by pigs before. You think I don't know how to talk to pigs?"

"Maybe you do," Wolf said. "Maybe that's what worries me."

"What about Wilson? He worried?"

"I worry for Wilson. He can't leave that neighborhood. The feds know he's there but

46

they won't go in without artillery because of his friends and they're scared of touching off '67 all over again if they go in hard, so they're waiting him out. You can't go the same places all the time, talk to all the same people, and know what's going on. That's why he keeps me around. I know. What I know worries me. What I don't know worries me more."

"Oh, man." Russell looked to Richard Roundtree for support, but Shaft was more interested in Gwenn Mitchell. "Kindu was here, he tell you how good I am with the pigs. Customs stopped us coming off the bridge from Canada, strip-searched us, tore his LTD down to the fucking frame. All the time saying they got a tip, we was going to Marion till we was white-headed. They separated us, told me it was Kindu they wanted, all I had to do was tell them where to find the shit and I could walk, they was going to find it anyway. I say, you going to find it anyway, what you need me to tell you for? Well, we didn't walk. We fucking *drove* home after they put the car back together. Us and the eight kilos of smack we had hid out in the muffler. Stupid shits never thought to check and see if it was hooked up to the exhaust system."

He was shaking. He did the trick, stretched

out his arms and spread his fingers, the punctures showing in the tender flesh between them. He felt the tension going out the ends. That would work for a while. He hoped the Indian hadn't been through his drawers, helped himself. He lowered his arms. "Kindu, he tell you all right. Only Kindu ain't here. Kindu's dead, man. So's Leroy Potts, and all on account of your man inside don't even know the party's a cover for a fucking STRESS operation."

"It wasn't STRESS. If it was cops they wouldn't have planted just one officer without any back-up."

"Since when does a pig sergeant start rubbing butts with Grosse Pointers?" He was feeling aggressive. The shadows had found a crease of uncertainty in Wolf's forehead when Russell mentioned the inside man.

"Just be stupid when the cops come around," said the Indian. "Whatever he was doing there, they'll be asking questions extra hard. They never serve the taxpayers so good as when it's one of theirs on the hook. And stay clean. Go easy on that shit; it isn't hash. No more dope runs across the border. No dope runs, period. If you need cash, call."

No shakes now. What had started out as a ball-busting for Russell had turned into

48

something different. He sat on the edge of the bed, bracing his palms on his knees. They were big hands, large enough to cup a basketball. He had played all through high school and had only recently abandoned his life's dream of going pro. Something about his reflexes, a congenital defect. One more thing to thank Dwight and Elizabeth for. "Something going down?"

"Maybe. You don't need to know about it yet."

"Marina involved? 'Cause if it is I need to know when. I don't work every day but I can trade off if it goes down on a day I don't work."

"I thought it was closed till spring."

"Only boat rentals. We paint and repair in the off-season. When the lake freezes over we rent snowmobiles."

Wolf was silent for a moment. "We won't need snowmobiles," he said then. "This doesn't figure to happen before spring. A speedboat won't do it, though. Can you get hold of a cabin cruiser?"

"How big?"

"How big do they come?"

"Pick a number. Twenty, thirty-five, sixty; Henry Ford got him a hundred-foot retired navy minesweeper on the Canadian side. Can't get that, it's a different marina. They miss it anyway. Also it takes a crew of ten to run it."

"Thirty-five feet is big enough. We're not ramming the *Queen Mary*."

Russell felt energized. "Wilson figured we'd score fifty K at the party. If we needed a twelve-foot boat for that, this one must be good for a hundred and fifty."

"Leave the arithmetic to Wilson, okay? Just keep your dick clean, and for chrissake don't get fired." Wolf stood. When he reached inside his quilted vest, the shiny magnum in his waistband twinkled. The envelope he took out of the inside pocket was so thick the flap came loose when it struck the painted table. Some of the bills fanned out. "There's enough there to support all your bad habits till we call you. Don't hide it here. When the cops come they might bring paper." He went silent again. Russell could almost see the ribbons of Brut floating around him like in a cartoon. "I sure hope Nampula wasn't blowing smoke up our asses about you. Wilson trusts me because I've got nothing to lose. I trust Wilson because I've got nothing to lose. But I look around here, I see a place that's not so bad. More comfortable than the Wayne County Jail by a long shot. I'm thinking when it comes to a trade, revolutionary ideals may not look so good after all. I don't care about me. I don't want to think about Wilson sleeping and shitting in a room six by eight because some little puke found out life's not like *Viva Zapata.*"

"I said before there ain't a thing here I want."

The Indian left. Russell got up and went to the door to watch him descend the stairs, swiveling his big Geronimo head to take in the dark spots where anything might hide. He wondered where Wolf came by the almighty bullshit. Man's people lost a *continent.* How reliable did he have to be not to fuck up as big as that?

Chapter Five

NAME: *Geary, Jr., Atticus Virgil; a/k/a Kindu Nampula, Mohammed Habib Mohammed, Nirvana Mahayana, Moses Ben Solomon, Luke Matthew*

Crises of faith like clockwork there. Man couldn't make up his mind.

DOB: 7/3/48
RACE: *Negro*
NATIONALITY: *U.S.*

Battle skipped the physical description. Everybody's the same height lying down, and only the pallbearers care what you weigh. He took another look at the front-and-profile clipped to the sheet. If afros kept growing at their current rate, the turnkeys at Receiving were going to have to invest in a wide-angle lens.

CRIMINAL RECORD:

conviction, ADW, sentenced three to eight yrs Southern Michigan Penitentiary Jackson 4/11/67, released 9/20/68; conviction, R/A, sentenced fifteen to twenty yrs Southern Michigan Penitentiary Jackson 12/9/68, released 11/25/71; arrest, R/A, F/H, 1/3/72, no conviction; arrest, possession narcotics, 6/12/72, no conviction; arrest, CCW, 10/4/72, no conviction

A sweetheart. Assault with a Deadly Weapon, Robbery Armed, Felony Homicide, drugs probably heroin, Carrying a Concealed Weapon. No time on the last three meant he had more friends with records like his than eyewitnesses at the show-up. Judgment call on whether Parole's cutting him loose on the ADW after seventeen months cost the taxpayers less than keeping him in meals and denims until 1975; not to mention the poor bastard offed in the robbery last year. Letting Geary/Nampula fly just short of three years on the fifteen to twenty was beyond comment.

Charlie Battle, who liked to play around

with numbers, had calculated that the six hundred murders that took place in the city in 1972 averaged out to forty killings per 100,000 Detroiters, outstripping automobile accidents and heart attacks. Without poring over all the reports — he was a dabbler, not a fanatic — he surmised that if repeat offenders were removed from the equation, in particular suspects arrested and convicted for previous violent crimes and released early, the total would fall closer to two hundred, or thirteen per 100,000, bringing homicides down around Midwestern earthquakes and random strikes by lightning. The cops were popping the perps, all right. It was the parole-board appointees who weren't following through. So of course the city's answer to the statistics was to beef up police patrols and create a plainclothes commando unit, STRESS (Stop The Robberies, Enjoy Safe Streets; he still couldn't say that one without grinning painfully), endowed with all the stop-frisk-and-clobber privileges of the KGB. Now the holding tank at 1300, the Wayne County Jail, and the two state penitentiaries in Jackson and Marquette bulged with new inmates, obliging Parole to disgorge an equivalent number of their predecessors before their time to clear space. Nothing changed except the faces, and even that was just a rotation. There were more guns on the streets than cars, and in the Motor City there was a shitload of cars.

Leroy Potts, a/k/a Leroy Potts, DOB 9/14/52, was darker-skinned in his photo than Nampula, with a bad complexion, and his natural needed a once-over with the pick. He had two priors for armed robbery, one early conviction for Breaking and Entering, probation and time served. He'd been maybe fixable, should've done the max on the B-and-E, if for no other reason than to learn the highway he was on ended in forty feet. Battle looked for the judge's name in the case. Del Rio. That explained a lot. He turned to the sheet on Junius Harrison.

Age twenty-four, no aliases, one prior with conviction, a three-year pop for possession for sale of marijuana. Nineteen sixty-eight, The Year That Gave Us Nixon, bad time to be caught peddling reefers. Served the full count at Jackson. Battle wondered if he'd had much time to become acquainted with Nampula during the couple of weekends Nampula spent there for sticking guns in people's faces and threatening to blow their heads off their necks.

Harrison's mug shot had been taken before he grew his afro. He'd cropped his hair short back then. Medium-dark face, full lips, eyes like a deer's caught in headlights, normal for an eighteen-year-old arrested and processed for the first time. Aside from that, put him in a jacket and tie and he could have posed for the United Negro College Fund ads. Certainly his face lacked the sullen cast of the others. Nothing in that; Charles Starkweather looked like a kid who delivered groceries. Thirty-six months on a kiddie drug charge was enough to sour anyone on the system. Battle was sour on it himself, and he had a job and a clean shirt.

Trouble was, so had Harrison.

In addition to the dead men's rap sheets, the file on the killings at the Crownover-Ogden New Year's Eve party contained statements signed by eyewitnesses, one of whom, a lawyer named Chester Dalgleish, claimed that Junius Harrison had been employed by his firm as an intern since October 1972; that according to Dalgleish's associates, Harrison had been sent from the office with a message for Dalgleish of a nature considered too confidential to trust to the telephone in a crowded house with seven extensions. The maid who had admitted Harrison through the front door corroborated, reporting that he'd told her he had a communication for one of the guests. That was two or three minutes before all hell broke loose. Stapled to the lawyer's statement was a photocopy of a hastily scrawled bit of legalese on a sheet of notepaper displaying the company letterhead, found by Forensics in the dead man's pocket.

The message, something about an offer of a ten-thousand-dollar settlement in a MacNeil case, meant nothing to Battle. Its presence bothered him a lot. It didn't go with the cheap Romanian-made .32 revolver found on the terrace near Harrison's body. It bothered him too that aside from Nampula, Potts, and the serving staff, Junius Harrison was the only black person on the premises at the moment Sergeant Paul Kubicek had begun shooting.

Lieutenant Zagreb re-entered his office just as Battle was poking the copious material back inside the file folder. With him were two men in suits; or rather one in charcoal tweed with a showy brown vest and one in a snappy rust-colored Kmart blazer with lapels as wide as Woodward Avenue and twill trousers that didn't match under the fluorescent lights at police headquarters. Some cops would put up with anything to avoid being fitted.

"Finished?" asked the lieutenant, and without waiting for an answer, "Great. Charlie Battle, this is Sergeant Walter Stilwell and Officer Aaron Bookfinger. They'll bring you up to speed on the Crownover case."

Stilwell had carroty-red hair brighter than

his blazer, teased forward from the temples into classical curls to make up for the recession in front. His face was flushed and mealy, and when Battle rose to accept his iron grip his gray-blue eyes twinkled, but it was more the glint of a pair of fresh nailheads than light from within. He smiled with his lower teeth only, which were the precise shade of an amber traffic light. Bookfinger, taller and less beefy — Mutt to Stilwell's Jeff — wore his black hair in an Elvis pompadour, lacquered to a high hard shine; but for that and his contrasty vest he had nothing whatever to mark him. Shaking his slender and decidedly limp hand, Battle thought the man's pale and ordinary features resembled ninety-nine out of a hundred sketches drawn by police artists from the vague descriptions of suspects provided by agitated victims.

"Buy you a cuppa?" Stilwell asked.

Battle agreed, handing the file to Zagreb, who riffled a broad thumb through the contents as if to make sure none of them had strayed. Then he shook hands with Battle. "Welcome to the Spec squad. Every now and then I make a choice I know I'll never question."

The lieutenant said nothing more and it was clear Battle had been dismissed. On that

58

ambiguous note, he turned his back on the Uniformed Division and went out for coffee.

"I'm worried about the guns," Battle said.

True to his offer, Walter Stilwell had tossed thirty cents into the cardboard Chock-Full-o'-Nuts box in the squad room and the three had gone to a vacant interrogation room with their steaming Styrofoam cups. The plastic woodgrain-printed veneer was peeling away from the particleboard table they were sitting around and the government green of the Bowles administration had begun to bleed through the beige-painted walls. Stilwell, apparently the department philosopher, had wondered aloud about the irrepressible quality of truly ugly colors: figure a different shade for each mayor and that lead-based dinge had found its way through seven coats of paint. Whoever said a thing of beauty is a joy forever, he remarked, had sure never been busted in Detroit.

Which seemed quite an assertion coming from a man in an orange suit.

"What about the guns?" Aaron Bookfinger, who held his cigarette between the third and fourth fingers of his left hand, had a way of covering the entire bottom half of his face when he inhaled that annoyed the newest member of the shooting team. It reminded

59

Battle of a girl he'd dated for a while in school who was self-conscious about her crooked teeth and put her hand over her mouth whenever she spoke. One reason they'd broken up was he couldn't understand what she was saying half the time.

Battle said, "Couple of things. To start with, Nampula's shotgun and Potts's thirty-eight were among the guns reported stolen from a collector on Grosse Ile last summer. Forensics lifted a partial from the burglary scene that matched Potts's prints."

"Makes sense," Bookfinger said. "Potts had a prior for B-and-E."

"Thing is, Harrison's piece wasn't on that list. It traces straight back to Bucharest without a stop, a virgin. What's that suggest?"

"Gee, you don't suppose the collector left something out of the burglary report?" The red-headed detective swallowed coffee, pulled a face. It did taste a little like stewed barbed wire. "Sergeant I play dominoes with in General Services recovered two Thompsons last year in the same lot with a Russian rifle and six revolvers. Rifle and handguns showed up in a B-and-E report in Highland Park in '71, but not the tommies. You need a dealer's license to own a machine gun, which the guy filing the report didn't have."

"A Saturday night special isn't a Thompson. Anyway the shotgun was an Ithaca and the thirty-eight was a Colt. Name brands. Harrison's thirty-two was chunked out by some company behind the Iron Curtain that also makes gas ranges and farm implements. What kind of collection is that?"

Stilwell showed his amber lower teeth. "How long you been in again?"

"Eighteen months."

"You ought to have met a gun nut or two. God knows we got our share. Belanger in Auto Theft's got a bazooka and a couple of Korean grenade launchers, but when his wife's birthday come along he bought her this little chrome-plated twenty-five with pearl grips that looks like a cigarette lighter, which is about all it's good for. If it makes noise on one end when you pull on the other, they want it. Somebody trading with this character in Grosse Ile throws in a junk piece to sweeten the deal, he don't figure it's worth listing when it comes up missing. That don't mean he throws it out with the empty toilet paper rolls. Harrison was new to the hard crap, a rookie. He got the last turn at the grab bag. Piece like that, I might've ran myself instead of shooting it out with Kubicek. Better odds."

"That's the other gun I'm worried about, Kubicek's forty-five auto. Department regs

61

prohibit automatic pistols."

Stilwell reached behind his back and clunked a blue-barreled Smith & Wesson nine-millimeter automatic onto the table. "Regs haven't been updated since Dillinger," he said. "What good's one of them Dick Tracy snubnose thirty-eights when every sixteen-year-old puke in the railroad yard packs a magnum?"

"The forty-five was Kubicek's personal piece." Bookfinger covered his nose and mouth, drew deep, and let the smoke trickle out of his nostrils. "What a cop carries when he's not on call is nobody's business."

This was news to Battle. "He wasn't on duty?"

Stilwell and Bookfinger exchanged glances. Stilwell said, "That don't leave this floor. The department line is he was working under cover for STRESS."

"You mean he was there as a guest?"

"Oh, yeah. Kubicek's old man worked in the block plant at Dodge Main seventeen years. Every Saturday night he climbed out of the coveralls and into a tux and went to the ballet with Abner Crownover. Paul and little Caryn played doctor behind the tennis courts at Fairlane. Shit. What do you think he was doing there? He was working."

"Private security?"

Bookfinger smiled primly at his partner. "We've got a born detective here. And you thought we'd have to take him to the toilet."

"If he was moonlighting against policy, why's 1300 standing behind him? This should be between Kubicek and his lawyer."

"It should, should it?" Stilwell swallowed coffee.

Battle pushed his away, rested his forearms on the table. "It doesn't take a detective to see what we've got here. Three suspects go down during a bad heist. Two have sheets as long as your arm. One has almost no record at all, a good job, and a legitimate reason to be at the party. He's found with the only weapon that can't be traced to a previous crime. What do you get from that?"

"Throwaway piece," Bookfinger said. "We thought about that. Cop gets caught up in the heat of the shoot, finds out he's put down an unarmed man, plants a clean weapon on the body. None of us knows a veteran who doesn't carry one around for just that purpose. It's a theory, no doubt about it."

"It's shit." Stilwell fixed his nailheads on Battle. "This is a nineteen-year officer with a shitload of commendations in his jacket and a certificate of valor. In sixty-eight he walked in on a heist at the Shell station downtown, took two in the chest, and still managed to

63

put down the perp when he was holding a gun to the head of the kid behind the counter. Eight weeks in the hospital, and he's still carrying around a forty-grain slug an inch from his spinal cord. How much lead you carrying around, rook? How many certificates of valor you got taped inside your locker next to Miss April's tits?"

Battle looked from one detective to the other. "That's the line, is it?"

"You're goddamn right it is. Question is, which side of it are you standing on?"

"Let the kid breathe, Wally." Bookfinger squashed out his cigarette in a tin Salem tray. "He doesn't know Kubicek. What say we fix that?"

Battle said, "He's in the building? I thought he was suspended with pay."

"Limited duty. He's keeping the dust off a chair in the Media Room."

"What's that?"

Stilwell stood, checked the magazine in the Smith & Wesson, and returned it to its clip. "File room back of STRESS. It's got a TV. Let's go ask him what's going on with *Days of Our Lives.*"

Chapter Six

For a man who loathed boredom and cold weather more or less equally, Joe Piper reflected that he spent a good deal of time freezing his ass off on some windswept spot waiting for someone.

On this particular flinty Sunday morning in January, that spot happened to be the old interior parade ground at historic Fort Wayne, where the wind from Canada blasted between the buildings containing the barracks and the powder magazine, flinging bushels of grainy snow and ice splinters from the river against his coat and into his face, where they stung like sparks. Around him, a denser shade of gray than the low sky and the bare earth and the jagged water, stood a number of humpbacked tanks and big guns mounted on swivels: products of the Arsenal of Democracy, borne there on flatbed trailers from the converted weapons plants of Ford, General Motors, and Chrysler and never used, rendered obsolete by the Japanese surrender while still warm from the foundries. They belonged emphatically to a redoubt constructed one hundred twenty-five years ago for the defense of a city that had never been threatened. He wondered what compelled people to visit vestal arms in a spinster fort.

He looked at his watch, tapped it, wound the stem, and held it to his ear on the leeward side. It was ticking. It seemed incredible he'd been there only five minutes. In that time his nose had begun to drip, his feet in their thin leather shoes had turned to flatirons. The only place on his body where he still had feeling was the tender flesh beneath his chin. He had given up shaving that area to avoid breaking open the scab, and the stubble kept the bandage so loose it chafed him whenever he moved.

He couldn't believe he'd stood there and let Wilson McCoy slice him open like a brisket. It wasn't as if he hadn't known the business had changed since he'd come into it. None of the old rules applied since the Sicilians had pulled out of Detroit. New to the rackets, the blacks had learned nothing from the last fifty years and duplicated all the dumb, violent mistakes their predecessors had made during Prohibition. They slaughtered one another in the street, shot it out with cops, and even butchered their own suppliers, obliging themselves to find replacements, often without checking their references. The undercover presence of STRESS made every white face a threat to be eliminated on the slightest suspicion. What for Joe Piper had been a relatively safe area of criminal enterprise had in a field of excitable amateurs become dangerous in the extreme. He'd known all that, and still had managed to place himself in hazard.

What was worse, here he was again.

At last a drumroll of pistons drew his attention to the Jefferson side, where a Jeep Cherokee was rolling through the main gate. It was painted a dull green and as it entered the parade ground he saw that it had been stripped of most of its options, including the wheel covers and radio antenna. The vanity plate on the front read USNO-1. Joe Piper took two steps backward as it squished to a stop on waffle-patterned tires.

Homer Angell uncramped his legs from under the dash and stepped down. At six feet seven he towered over the gun dealer in pleated khaki trousers, an insulated coat splotched with jungle camouflage, size fifteen combat boots, and a tight canvas cap whose bill rested on the bridge of his nose. His pale hair was cropped a quarter-inch from his scalp and he had blue eyes that were painful to look at, like a bright sky. He had a long slack jaw and ears that stuck out.

Joe Piper, who never knew quite how to speak to the man, opened with the weather. "Cold enough to freeze the balls off a brass monkey."

"It's summer in Nam. On the Mekong Delta the frogs are frying."

"I didn't know you were over there."

"I read up on it. My unit was about to be called up when Kissinger threw in the towel."

"Well, it was a shit war."

"It didn't have to be. When you've got guns and you're fighting pygmies, you don't go in with spears. I'm just glad my old man didn't live to see us tucking in our tail. He was on the *Enola Gay*."

"Mine was with the marines. He sent back a case of captured Schmeissers. My mother and my older brother traded them for meat stamps and made a bundle."

For reply, Angell fingered a crop of pimples on his jaw. The gun dealer was pretty sure he'd said something wrong. Homer Angell had first come to Detroit with the 82nd Airborne during the riots, apparently found the chaos there to his liking, and when his enlistment ran out moved to Highland Park and joined the Michigan National Guard. Implicated when a cache of automatic weapons came up missing from the downtown armory, he had been allowed to resign his lieutenant's commission in return for a promise not to prosecute. Since September he had been employed part-time as a caretaker at the Fort Wayne museum. His appetite for illegal gun money notwithstanding, he had an aversion to any calling that took him away from things military. It was his private opinion — not so private among those who knew him and had the patience to listen — that the army had lost another Omar Bradley when it refused to promote him above the rank of quartermaster sergeant.

Joe Piper changed the subject. "I may have a customer for those Ingrams."

"How much?"

"Thousand apiece."

"Two thousand's the price. I said that before."

"I'm not talking about a couple of guns here. This is a shipment. Twenty grand in a lump."

"I'm not sure I can deliver twenty."

"You told me just last month you had twice that many sitting around in cases under an Indian blanket."

"Iraqi. And that was last month. Come the new year, when they tot up those shooting statistics, Congress shakes loose appropriations. The ATF cracks down. I can promise maybe ten. If they haul me over with more than that I'm looking at three to fifteen in the federal house."

Joe Piper said shit. "I don't fucking believe this. You sort mail for a living, you might get a paper cut. Cops and the ATF are the reason we're talking thousands instead of hundreds. You got such a hard-on for safe you should've stayed in and kept on stacking undies till retirement."

"Not enough thousands. Two's the price if it's twenty you want."

"Twelve hundred then. Shit. My balls ain't exactly off the block either."

Angell walked away and laid a jersey-gloved palm against the fender of a tank. The milky vapor of his spent breath frothed and shredded in the wind. "Sherman Mark Five," he said. "Tiger eighty-eights punched holes in that eighty-five-millimeter skin like your finger through cheap toilet paper, but they couldn't punch holes in all of them. Not enough shells in Europe for that. Volume, that's what wins our wars. If we dumped one-third of the material we've got rusting on parade grounds and in museums on Vietnam, the whole damn peninsula would break off and sink. Only that's not how we do war now."

Joe Piper wiped his nose on his sleeve and waited. Christ, he was getting to hate the people he had to work with. Between the redneck hawks and niggers with razors, the wild-eyed Irish revolutionaries his Uncle Seamus used to bitch about sounded like bankers. The business was filling up with psychos. Just the kind of people you wanted to put behind a gun that fired 1,145 rounds per minute.

". . . hear of Billy Brock?"

Angell was looking at him now, ice-crystals glittering on his pale eyelashes. Jesus, it was cold. "Who?" Joe Piper had quit listening. He had heard the where-we-went-wrong-in-Nam speech before.

"General Sir Isaac Brock. You won't see the name next to Napoleon and Kutuzov, but he pulled off something no one could before or since: force a North American city to surrender itself to occupation by a foreign army. In August 1812 he lobbed a couple of four-pounders across the river from the Windsor side, hit a tree on East Jefferson, and the next thing you know the Union Jack was flapping over city hall. One shot from the seventy-five mounted on this Sherman would've made a hell of a difference."

"Not as much as an ICBM, but they didn't have them yet either."

"Not the point. Return fire from a couple

71

of dozen flintlocks would have at least made the Brits sweat a little. As it was the commander in charge of Fort Detroit didn't do so much as fire a musket in its defense. That's the kind of mentality we've got running the Pentagon now. Fifty thousand dead in twelve years and in went the towel. The Romans lost sixty-three thousand at Cannae and went on fighting for nine more years and wound up throwing Hannibal clean out of Europe."

"Shitty damn shame."

"Who's your customer?"

The question surprised the gun dealer. "Forget it, Homer. You don't have the temperament to peddle your own merch."

"If I did we wouldn't know each other. Are they commies? Because if they are the deal's smoke. It's bad enough they own the rice paddies in Saigon."

"Worse than commies. Black Panthers."

Angell nodded almost imperceptibly. "Great military organization. The discipline is admirable. You don't just put on that black beret and call yourself a Panther. Their boot camp stands up beside any in the world. Except the Dutch, of course."

"Of course." He wondered if the wooden shoes got in the way of the drills. "Twelve hundred's the offer."

"Eighteen. At that price you have to score

your own ammunition."

"Bullshit."

"It's a legitimate purchase. Just walk into any sporting goods store and lay your money down."

"You have to sign for it at the counter. I haven't written my name on a piece of paper in three years."

"What about IRS?"

"I retired from the cement business in sixty-nine. Signed everything over to my wife. She lists me as her dependent. Fifteen hundred apiece, ammo included. That's the last trip to the well. My ass fell off ten minutes ago."

"I hope for your sake the marriage is airtight." Angell stepped over and stuck out his hand. "How soon do you need delivery?"

"I'll let you know." Joe Piper grasped the hand, grateful for the moment that he had lost most of the feeling in his fingers. Later, when they thawed out, the aftermath of Angell's crushing grip would be agony. "The feds are too busy roasting Nixon's nuts to haul you over anyway."

"They should've let him finish what he started in Cambodia."

Chapter Seven

Paul Kubicek reminded Charlie Battle a little of his uncle; but only superficially.

Since his stroke in 1971, Anthony Battle, three-time professional wrestling Heavyweight Champion of the World, had spent most of his time in the eggshell vinyl Strat-O-Lounger in the extra bedroom in his nephew's apartment, watching television. Battle, who found it more and more difficult to drag any kind of response out of his uncle, had no idea if the old man was following what was happening on the screen or, if not, what pictures were playing inside his cast-iron skull. He seemed alert and far away at the same time. So the STRESS sergeant appeared in his threadbare padded swivel, staring at the dusty picture tube of the black-and-white Zenith on the same table that supported an electric percolator and an open box of powdered doughnuts in the file room behind the STRESS command center at 1300.

The program was *The Mod Squad*, one of Battle's personal picks for early cancellation, but now bumping along through its fourth season. Linc, the black and beautiful under-cover cop with a weakness for wraparound sunglasses, hula-hoop afros, and dashikis short enough to run in without having to hold up the hems like Scarlett O'Hara, was chasing a scuzzy white drug pusher through a maze of L.A. alleys, accompanied by a syn-thesized score that sounded like a truckload of skillets rolling over. A few minutes and several commercials later, having made his collar, he would receive a pat on his up-holstered head from his partners, the Hol-lywood hippie and the blonde tart in love beads, and the three of them would go out to a rib joint and celebrate. It was enough to make Battle nostalgic for *Amos 'n' Andy*.

The station broke and a bullet-headed man in an undershirt came on to intone that he couldn't believe he ate the whole thing. Kubicek, the trance shattered, sat back and hooked his thumbs inside his belt. Jesus, it was braided white, just the thing for his Stay-Pressed suit with flared trousers; if the ecol-ogy shrills were right and the world's petroleum supply was running out, the entire plainclothes division was going to wind up naked.

"Man, I love cop shows," Kubicek said. "Keeps my mind off work."

"*Kung Fu* does it for me." Officer Aaron Bookfinger, seated astraddle another swivel with a bumper sticker on the back reading HAVE A NICE DAY, covered the bottom half of his face as he pulled smoke into his lungs. "You can cut that guy Caine's balls off and feed them to him in the first half hour and he won't say shit, but you better not ask him directions in the last fifteen minutes."

Sergeant Stilwell rearranged the red curls covering his baldness. "That boy thinks he can kick. I dated an exotic dancer from the Pussycat that could fold both feet behind her neck."

"She any good?" Kubicek asked.

"Like fucking a mackerel."

They laughed, Battle too. Kubicek laced his fingers together and stretched his arms over his head. His knuckles went off like a string of firecrackers. "Ain't it the truth. Them broads save it for the runway."

Bookfinger said, "Charlie here wants to ask you a couple about the Crownover shoot."

The STRESS detective took in Battle's crisp uniform. His eyes were the dull gray of soft-nosed slugs. "What's this, Saint Patrick's Day?"

"He's on loan from City Hall," Stilwell said. "Zagreb's idea."

76

"Cap'n Crunch. Shit. He still floating plastic boats in his bathtub? Cuts a fart, hollers 'Torpedo'?"

Battle smiled. He was leaning back against the closed door. "I want to talk about Harrison's gun."

"Hunky piece of junk. I'd rather pick up a fresh turd."

"Did he have it in his hand when you spotted him?"

"He was going for it. His hand was in his pocket."

"Did you shoot Nampula first because you weren't sure Harrison was armed?"

Kubicek grinned lopsidedly at Stilwell, standing near the room's only window. Greektown glowed cheerfully through the steel mesh, Detroit's best-lit block. "You never hunt duck?"

"Duck? No." Battle was pretty sure the question was meant for him.

"You got two in formation, you shoot the farthest one first. Plenty of time to get the closest one after."

"Especially when the farthest one has a scattergun," Bookfinger offered.

"So you shot Harrison second."

"Hell no. Didn't you read my report?"

"What's the procedure with three ducks?"

"There ain't no procedure. The best

shooter that ever lived never got more than two at a pop."

"Let's forget the ducks," Battle said. "As close as you say Harrison was when you spotted him, he had to be a lot closer after you shot Nampula. But you shot Potts next. Wasn't that taking a risk?"

"Shit fire, I never thought of that. I wouldn't get mixed up in no shooting if I thought there was risks."

Stilwell chuckled. Bookfinger covered his mouth and blew a rattling jet of smoke at the ceiling, already tinged orange from generations of nicotine. Battle was beginning to feel like the freshman at a hazing.

"Help me out, Sergeant. I'm just trying to get a picture of what happened New Year's Eve."

"There was a lot of civilians running around. I lost track of Harrison. Meanwhile there was Potts pulling down on me with a fucking magnum. What would you do, rook?"

"The same thing, probably. And I'm not a rookie. I've been with the department a year and a half. Why do you suppose Harrison made a break for the terrace? He must have had a clear shot at you while you were dealing with Potts."

"Just because you got your dick in your

hand don't mean you can get it up. He seen his partners go down and he rabbited."

"Did you see his gun before you shot him?"

Kubicek looked at Bookfinger. "You boys in Special Investigations need to lay off me and sit in at the academy. They're leaving out some things. Or maybe Mr. Year-and-a-Half skipped class the day the rest of the fish learned you don't have to see a gun when a suspect fleeing an armed robbery forgets to stop when you tell him to."

"I was just asking if you saw it. It landed on the terrace next to him when he fell, and I'm curious to know why he took it out if he wasn't going to use it."

"Don't ask me. I don't know how them people think."

"What people? Black people?"

"You said that, not me." Kubicek leaned forward and snapped off the set in the middle of the opening credits for *Owen Marshall.* Instead of leaning back, he remained in a kind of crouch with his forearms resting on his knees. His stiff suitcoat pouched behind his neck in a way that reminded Battle of a snapping turtle. "Everything's race with you colored guys. I'd of shot them three just as quick if they was white. What do you think I am?"

"An experienced cop collecting dust in a

back room watching TV while the murder rate goes to Pluto. The quicker we get through this the quicker we can get you back on the street where you're needed. Is that okay with you, Sergeant?"

"Yeah. Okay." He sat back. "Excuse the nerves, son. I got a pension to think about and a daughter who wants to be F. Lee Bailey. That's spelled M-O-N-E-Y. If I knew this guy Springfield and his Ethiopian Congress was going to hang me out to dry over a scroat like Harrison, I wouldn't of taken the Crownover job and that's for damn sure."

"Let's talk about that. Did Crownover — no, not Crownover; what's the husband's name?" Battle looked at Stilwell, who was still playing with his curls next to the window.

"Ted Ogden. I guess that's the downside of marrying that old auto money, nobody remembers your name."

"I could live with it," Bookfinger said.

"Did Ogden say he was expecting trouble when he hired you for security?" Battle asked Kubicek.

"No, he wanted to keep his insurance company happy. There was jewels and shit there."

"What about the motorboat?"

"It was a motorboat."

"Do you think it was a coincidence it was

80

there by the dock and took off after the shooting?"

"Yeah, and it was running on Kentucky sipping whiskey. What do you think a boat was doing there New Year's Eve, fishing for confetti? Them boys wasn't going to walk across the lake after they shook down all the guests."

"You didn't see the pilot."

"No. Christ, how many times am I going to have to answer that one?"

"No registration numbers? Not even a partial?"

"It was dark. I was in the light. You ever try to catch a license number standing under a streetlamp at midnight?"

"Well, was it a four-cycle or a high-speed job? They sound different."

"No shit?" Kubicek lifted the end of his necktie, apparently searching for stains, then smoothed it down. Battle was pretty sure it clipped on. "It was a speedboat. One of the fiberglass jobs, probably. You don't see no wooden rowboats on Saint Clair."

"Think it was stolen?"

"I ran it through Records. Nothing reported since Labor Day. Nobody heists boats in December."

"Back to Harrison. Your report said you identified yourself and ordered him to halt.

What exactly did you say?"

The sergeant grinned with one side of his mouth. " 'Guess who, cocksucker.' "

"That was it?"

"What'd you expect, *Ironside*? Fucking 'Freeze'?"

Battle stood. "Thanks, Sergeant. Sorry to have to crank you through it again."

"Just so you get me back outside. I know that damn *Brady Bunch* song backwards and forwards."

Stilwell announced he had to pee. Battle, himself feeling the effects of the coffee he'd ingested earlier, accompanied him to the men's room. Bookfinger went along to be sociable. The room, all black-and-white 1920s Art Deco under half a century of cheap wax and grit, smelled of Lysol, industrial-strength lemons, and an officer defecating in the rear stall. The walls were a directory of penciled telephone numbers, belonging mostly to lawyers and bailbondsmen and somebody named Alice who was evidently a retired circus performer. Stilwell went on streaming against the back of his urinal a full minute after Battle had zipped up and washed his hands. Bookfinger flipped his cigarette butt into a vacant basin. No one said anything while the man in the stall flushed, pulled up his uniform pants, and went out after drying his hands on a sheet of coarse brown paper. He was a hulking black with gray in his hair and a thick bar of moustache.

"The man's a Neanderthal," Battle said as the door sighed shut.

Bookfinger tapped a Benson & Hedges out of his pack. "That's Jackson with General Service. He went to Michigan on a basketball scholarship, but he flunked out and got fat."

"I mean Kubicek. Is he always like that, or was he just rutting for my benefit?"

"He's an arrogant asshole. Twenty more like him and the riots never would've gotten beyond Twelfth and Clairmont. It's always a mistake to underestimate that old guard."

"The department *has* twenty more like him. That's why we had riots."

"How old were you then, sixteen?" Stilwell flushed and turned away from the urinal. "I'd of closed this out by now except for this Ethiopian thing. We got three criminal records, three guns, and a shitload of eyewitnesses that didn't see a thing wrong."

"They also didn't see Harrison's gun until the shooting was over. Or hear Kubicek say anything before he shot him."

Stilwell scowled at his hairline in the spotted mirror. "Well, hell, that's good enough for me. Let's string the fucker up."

83

"Not just yet. I want to talk to someone else first."

"Who?" Bookfinger lit the cigarette off a Cricket lighter.

"The guy in the boat."

Chapter Eight

Crownover Coaches had been serving America's transportation needs since 1848.

In March of that year, Abner Crownover, who had left a wife and three children in England when he emigrated to Detroit to take up cabinetmaking, built and sold the first of a fleet of covered wagons to a pioneering family bound for the Oregon Territory. Lighter than the more famous Conestoga and sturdier than the Dearborn, the Crownover caught on swiftly. Ten years later, with the antebellum westward migration at its height, A. Crownover & Company was the largest private employer in a city that challenged Philadelphia for the title of wagonmaker to a restless nation.

Politics killed the dream. In 1859, Abner, an ardent abolitionist, met with John Brown on the northern end of the Underground Railroad and agreed to finance Brown's mad plan to storm the federal armory at Harpers Ferry, Virginia, and procure weapons for armed insurrection against the United States. After the raid collapsed and Brown was hanged, Abner stood trial for treason. His acquittal for lack of evidence failed to save his reputation, and he was forced to sell his interest in the wagonmaking business to support himself and his second family. He died a broken man on the eve of the second Battle of Bull Run, his country aflame with civil war.

His son, also named Abner, went to work for the company at age eleven to feed his mother and three sisters. By virtue of hard work and intelligent suggestions, he rose from grease boy to regional vice president before his eighteenth birthday. Wagon trains had by this time begun to grow scarce, and as a result of his persuasion the firm turned its emphasis from cross-continental carriers to short-haul freight vehicles, passenger coaches, and finely crafted carriages for the landed gentry. Abner, Jr., himself was credited with the invention of an elaborate system of suspension that smoothed the ride to the theater and the opera and made Crownover's distinctive coronet emblem a symbol of position and excellence in places as distant as New York, Boston, and San Francisco. In 1874, having ascended to the board of directors, Abner Crownover II sold his house on the River Rouge and took advantage of depressed stock values created by the '73 Panic to acquire controlling interest in Crownover Coaches. He was twenty-three.

Abner's first wife having died childless of scarlet fever, he remarried in 1876 and fathered six children, two of whom died in infancy. The eldest of the three surviving boys, Abner III, assumed directorship of the Detroit office in 1898. Edward, the youngest, was placed in charge of the upholstery shop. Harlan, born second and pronounced feeble-brained at an early age, became a dock foreman. When Abner proved himself incapable of making a decision and seeing it through — he would sign a contract with a lumber firm on Friday for the hickory required to frame the company's popular Town and Country Phaeton, change his mind over the weekend, and dispatch a messenger to intercept the contract on Monday — his father discreetly reassigned him to the new position of Executive Director and appointed a more competent colleague in his place. Upon the colleague's retirement in 1902, Edward ascended to the regional post widely regarded as the final step before the company presidency. By this time there was pressure among the board of directors to retool the plants in Detroit and Dearborn to provide bodies for the burgeoning automobile industry. Abner II, past fifty now and beset with health problems, resisted, believing that the motorcar was merely a rich man's toy, beyond the means of even his wealthiest customers, and furthermore was too contrary in its mechanism for practical use. Edward, who had never gone on record in opposition to any of his father's views, concurred.

Harlan Crownover had been considered slow-witted throughout his first thirty years, his reluctance to join in family discussions interpreted as inability to understand. Six months after taking over the loading dock at the Detroit plant, he inaugurated a system that allowed workers to offload a freight wagon in half the time with less muscular strain, almost eliminating sick days among the crew. He used the extra hours in his working day to meet with automobile pioneers, including Ransom E. Olds and young Henry Ford; convinced by their enthusiasm for their invention, Harlan canvassed the directors for support should those convictions lead to a fight.

On October 15, 1903, old Abner, with Edward in tow, stormed onto Harlan's dock, shaking a bony fist and denouncing his second son's conspiracy to ruin the company Abner had rescued from bankruptcy. In later years Harlan would declare his life's brightest moment to be the time his father fired him, only to be confronted with a sheaf of letters assigning Harlan power of attorney to dispose of the largest single block of Crownover stock as he saw fit, signed by three members of the board and Edith Hampton Crownover — his mother, to whom Abner had presented ten thousand shares on the occasion of their wedding. Thus began the Harlan Crownover Era, and Crownover Coaches' period of greatest prosperity.

Abner died in 1918, having spent his final decade and a half in forced retirement, wandering the halls of the River Rouge house he had bought back out of his first year's dividend as board chairman and muttering to himself about family ingratitude. The sight of the belching chimneys of the Ford Rouge plant outside his windows must have seemed to him the final insult.

Harlan's wife, the debutante daughter of a failed New York banker who had blown out his brains with an English dueling pistol when his books were opened, was barren. To compensate her for this lack, her husband — in his only known act of human compassion — granted her request to construct a house that would reflect the status of one of Detroit's first families on Lake Shore Drive in Grosse Pointe. He could hardly have realized the size of the Pandora's Box he had opened. For months, materials arrived at the River Rouge docks by the shipload: slabs of marble from Italy, oak timbers from Germany, ceramic tiles from Mexico, carved mahogany panels from the Brazilian rain forest. From Spain came an entire eleventh-century chapel, dismantled stone by stone and packed in numbered crates for reassembly in the garden. A 1,600-piece chandelier landed from a villa in France, each crystal pendant individually wrapped in blue tissue and placed in boxes lined with shredded newspaper. Tapestries from Berne and rolls of carpet from Tehran and Cairo went directly from the hold of the *S.S. Mauritania* into a warehouse on East Jefferson to await installation. Behind the materials came the craftsmen: Greek stonemasons; Belgian cabinetmakers; Florentine sculptors; and an army of painters, carpenters, and bricklayers whose foreign chatter drowned out the general din of construction like the excited babble of immigrants at a train station. And above the peaks of the other houses in a community not known for the modesty of its dwellings rose the shining slate gables of Xanadu, sheltering thirty-six thousand square feet on a twelve-acre lot studded with stately oaks that had witnessed Chief Pontiac's siege in 1763.

No sooner was the manor house at The

Oaks completed, in 1922, than the Crown-overs set sail for Europe. While Harlan met with financiers and industrialists in London, Paris, Weimar, and Rome, wife Cornelia descended upon the museums and auction houses. Back home, servants worked far into the night opening and unpacking crates she had shipped. Into the foyer they carried a marble bust by Michelangelo of a prosperous Venetian merchant; over the arch in the Great Hall they hoisted an eleven-by-twenty-foot Tintoretto of Babylonian maids bathing in a spring, encased in a bronze frame weighing half a ton; along the walls in the parlor they arranged the only known complete set of Louis Quatorze chairs outside the palace at Versailles; and from the west wing to the east, starting at the rooftop observatory and ending in the vast flagged basement, maids in white aprons and footmen in breeches and leggings filled shelves with porcelain vases from Pompeii, jeweled masks from Constantinople, Athenian reliefs, Gothic shields, Viennese miniatures, Portuguese lace, and a curious jewelry box made of native Corsican woods, said to have been a gift to Josephine from Napoleon to commemorate their betrothal.

Following a party in celebration of the return of the master and mistress from abroad

— attended by the Henry and Edsel Fords, the Horace Dodges, the Walter P. Chryslers, the Pierre DuPonts, and deaf old Thomas Edison in his rumpled evening clothes with stubby yellow pencils poking out of the vest pocket — The Oaks featured prominently in *Harper's*, *The Literary Digest*, and newspaper rotogravure sections throughout the country. Like Hollywood's Pickfair and the Astor House in New York, the mansion with its seventeen bedrooms, two kitchens, and tiled ballroom became a set piece for the New Gilded Age and the place to stop for persons of note on their way between coasts. Charlie Chaplin stayed there while researching *Modern Times*. Herbert Hoover, resting during his whistle-stop campaign for the 1928 Republican presidential nomination, shot pool in the game room with Harlan and discussed the stock market. Johnny Weismuller swam in the Olympic-size pool. All through Prohibition the champagne gushed from the stock in the cellar while the grace and charm of Cornelia Crownover contributed to the inebriation of the guests and softened the regret of the morning after.

With Repeal came Depression. Retrenching after his 1929 losses on Wall Street, Harlan slashed wages and increased hours at his plants in Detroit, Dearborn, and along the river. When the fledgling American Federation of Labor and United Auto Workers hit the bricks, Crownover Coaches locked them out, replacing the strikers with non-union labor. Picketers assaulted the scabs on their way through the gates and punctured the radiators of trucks carrying coiled steel and hardwood planks to the loading docks. Pinkerton detectives waded into human seas with truncheons, splintering wrists and staving in skulls. Retired bootleggers struck back with brass knuckles and blackjacks. A Lewis gun mounted on a tripod fired orange tracers into a crowd blockading the assembly plant in Wyandotte. A Remington rifle resting on the hood of a Packard snatched a security officer out from under his cap at the foundry on East Jefferson.

In 1938, pressured by his directors and the threat of a federal investigation, Harlan Crownover signed a three-year contract with the union guaranteeing wages and overtime pay. Sixty-five now, embittered in spirit and his eyesight failing, he lapsed into semi-retirement, placing the company's day-to-day operation in the hands of his closest confederate, a former *Wunderkind* he had hired after his father's ouster to oversee the transition from carriages to convertibles.

His wife had other plans. Four years after

finishing The Oaks and crowding it with treasures, she had found the house strangely empty. What was needed, she had decided, was to fill its stately rooms with the laughter of children. In the fall of 1926 the Crownovers had adopted a nine-month-old boy whom they named Abner IV. Two years later an infant girl, Caryn, had joined the household. From an early age the daughter received lessons in ballet and the piano, while the son was drilled in the arts of responsibility and leadership. Only twelve and a half when his adopted father stepped down, young Abner was incapable of taking his place, but his mother was determined that when the time came he would not be overlooked.

Meanwhile the *Wunderkind* shone. A youthful and energetic fifty at the time of his promotion, Francis Brennan caught the scent of gunpowder from the east that summer before the invasion of Austria and went to bat lobbying for defense contracts in Washington. The news that Henry Ford had gotten there first didn't faze him. By Pearl Harbor he had completely overhauled the downriver plants and, subcontracting from Ford, set them to work around the clock, cranking out cockpits and bridges for the B-29 bombers and Liberty ships Henry was putting together at Willow Run and Rouge. On D-Day, thirty percent of the materiel pouring onto the beaches at Normandy contained parts manufactured by Crownover.

Postwar prosperity was especially kind to Detroit and those companies that had transformed it into the Arsenal of Democracy. Rolling fat on government allocations, the automobile industry re-geared its factories for a generation of returning veterans and their families. On the occasion of their son's twenty-first birthday in 1947, Cornelia petitioned Harlan to place Abner on the board of directors. The old man demurred. In his middle seventies, gaunt, blind, and absent-minded, Harlan held that a man like Brennan who had grown up with the industry was better qualified to direct the company than a son who lacked both experience and the Crownover blood. Further argument only strengthened his resolve. Since he had learned from Abner II's mistake, controlling interest — and the decision as to who would mind the store — remained with him. Months would pass, and a suit pressed by Cornelia to have Harlan declared mentally incompetent to direct his business affairs, before he relented. Henry Ford was dead. The patriarchal system of commerce Harlan's grandfather had created nearly a century earlier was defunct, its place taken by a corporate antheap with its swarms of faceless cyphers in gray suits. He had neither the strength nor the will to fight it any longer. In his spidery, old-fashioned hand he signed his name to a document releasing his proxy to Cornelia. Brennan resigned the next morning, and on the morning after that Abner Crownover IV, displaying the black armband he would wear to his father's funeral that afternoon, took his place behind the president's desk.

The irony was, the old man was right. Snapped up by General Motors, Frank Brennan took over the Buick Division, which quickly outsold the corporation's other four divisions combined. Abner, following a brief and desultory period of indoctrination, began to spend most of his time in his box at Briggs Stadium, cheering on the Tigers, of whom he became a part owner in 1961. Eager young executives soon learned that an investment of fifteen minutes with the box scores in the *Free Press* sports section each morning paid off better in encounters with their employer than two hours with Dow Jones. Older colleagues called him "L'il Abner" behind his back and updated their resumes.

This weakness at the top did not pass unnoticed outside the company. One who took note was Roger Gashawk. Preferring to be addressed as Sir Roger — despite the confiscation of the family baronetcy by the British monarchy — this sixty-year-old owner of a Chelsea perfumery came to the United States in 1952 with his two grown sons and a stupendous claim: He was the great-grandson of Abner Crownover I and Abner's English wife. At a press conference on the steps of Detroit City Hall, Gashawk announced that because his mother's grandfather had failed to obtain a divorce before taking a new mate, the American marriage had no basis in law, rendering all of Abner's U.S. descendants illegitimate; therefore, on behalf of himself and his sons, Sir Roger had filed suit in Probate Court to secure majority ownership of Crownover Coaches and all personal properties currently in the possession of the Crownover family.

This was a serious threat. When an army of genealogists retained by the Crownovers' private counsel were unable to discredit Gashawk's assertions, a distraught Abner IV turned for advice to his mother. But that old lady declined, wishing only to be left to her duties as caretaker of the mansion in Grosse Pointe. In that role she would approach her centenary, donning a powder-blue dress and frothy jabot to conduct the local television audience on a tour of the last stately home associated with Detroit's auto-pioneering past.

Rescue came from an unexpected source. Abner's sister Caryn, best known in area society for her patronage of the arts, arranged a meeting with Gashawk at the Book-Cadillac Hotel, where after some argument she persuaded the attorneys to leave the room and emerged ninety minutes later to announce a compromise: In return for abandoning a litigation guaranteed to run many years and exhaust the war chests of both camps, Sir Roger and his sons would sit on the board of directors and accept joint ownership of a block of shares in Crownover Coaches equal to Abner's. This kept control of the company in the American branch of the family while dividing the responsibility of operation between the indifferent U.S. heir and the more attentive Gashawks, who had bought a bankrupt English perfume distillery and made it a player in the cutthroat European market. Both sides benefited.

Caryn, wed recently to a successful young investment counselor named Ted Ogden, had as a child quickly mastered the rudiments of *Swan Lake* and the Steinway in the conservatory at The Oaks while eavesdropping on her brother's business management lessons in the library across the hall. What she learned, combined with a gift for strategy, had proven valuable to her husband during late-night conversations in the master bedroom of their large airy house on Lake St. Clair, and impressed shrewd old Sir Roger at the Book-Cadillac. Mutual acquaintances of Caryn and her brother thought it a cruel trick of gender that Abner should have inherited the orb and scepter while her talents were squandered on hundred-dollar-a-plate dinners to support the Detroit Symphony Orchestra.

She, however, was sanguine. When late in the 1960s her shrink — a pinch-faced woman several years Caryn's junior with the look of a bra-burner about her — suggested she drank heavily to compensate for being forced to stifle her natural abilities, she considered the explanation; but the truth was she had been adopted into a family of imbibers. Her father had fueled himself on boilermakers from his days on the loading dock until he died of a cerebral hemorrhage thirty minutes after signing over his proxy to her mother, and no small amount of the champagne that flowed so freely all through Prohibition at the huge white elephant of a house down the street had found its way into Cornelia's long-stemmed glass. No, Caryn's habit was strictly recreational. She had experienced no withdrawal symptoms during her pregnancy, when her obstetricians had placed the Fear of Deformity in her regarding the evils of alcohol in gestation. And she envied no man. Little Opal, a surprise gift at age thirty-nine to a woman whose husband's sperm count had been pronounced borderline hopeless, was compensation enough for anyone. Abner had his baseball team, Cornelia her mausoleum, Robin and Cedric Gashawk their late father's legacy. Caryn had her daughter. And she didn't have to worry about the Japanese.

It had been a comfort that Opal had missed the shootings New Year's Eve. Sobered instantly, her mother had flown to the child's bedroom as soon as things cleared and wept grateful tears to find her sleeping quietly with both arms wrapped around her big Snoopy doll. A new security system involving intercoms and invisible lasers had gone in the next day, and hang double time for the holiday labor. She'd hoped all that "Murder City" horror stopped at Eight Mile Road. Now she was contemplating taking Opal to the house in Palm Beach two weeks early. Ted could join them there after his January meetings were finished.

Caryn was seated in the bay window looking out on the frozen lake, nursing her first highball of the afternoon, when the governess came in holding Opal's hand. The six-year-old was wearing the emerald dress Caryn had chosen to go with her red hair. Her large eyes and small sharp face had come from Ted, but she owed that bright copper top to her mother. Caryn kissed her and trilled over how pretty she looked and checked her platinum watch and declared they were late for their visit with Grandmama — not that time meant anything to the ancient woman wandering among her lacquered chests and two-hundred-year-old stopped clocks — and helped the governess get her into her little white suede coat and fur hat and boots. Looking at the result, Caryn wondered why any woman would choose a lifetime of work over five minutes of motherhood. She finished her drink, called down for the Lincoln, and fixed another while she was waiting.

As the gunmetal stretch swept out of the cul-de-sac with the snowy-haired chauffeur at the wheel, Wolf swung down his sun visor, obscuring his face. He had parked the blue Duster behind a delivery van by the curb and slid into the passenger's seat, where anyone who saw him would assume he was waiting for the driver to return and waste no time on him. In a black felt coat with his long hair gathered inside a Giants cap he looked older, and more Italian than Indian.

He had gotten only a brief glimpse of the little girl before her mother bundled her into the limo's back seat and climbed in after, but he was pretty sure he would recognize the red-haired tyke when he saw her again.

Before starting the motor, he read his rubberized scuba diver's watch and noted the time in the pad beside him on the seat. When he flipped it shut, the Indian in full feathered headdress on the cover scowled at him. Big Chief tablet. Wilson's little joke.

PART TWO

The Empty Bag

Chapter Nine

Half asleep, Charlie Battle groped under his grandmother's silk counterpane, found one of Thea's breasts, and grazed the nipple with the ball of his thumb until it became as firm as a rubber eraser. She mewed and slid a hand down his stomach to his genitals, where her fingers seemed to wake up and apply themselves. Soon he was on top of her and sliding inside.

Suddenly she caught her breath. Battle opened his eyes and saw his wife's pupils glittering in the moonlight reflecting off the snow outside the window. He stopped moving. "Charlie, I think your uncle's up."

"So what? So am I." He resumed his rhythm.

She placed a palm against his chest. "You'd better check on him. I can hear him moving around."

He said shit, rolled off her and out from under the spread, found his robe and slippers, and put them on. In the living room he snapped on the overhead light and tapped on the door to his uncle's bedroom. "Anthony, you all right?"

There was no answer from inside, only the sound of a drawer closing and another one opening. He tapped again, then tried the knob. The door was unlocked. He opened it.

The bedside lamp was on. Anthony Battle, big and bulky and naked, the way he'd slept for as long as his nephew could remember, was on his knees in front of the chipped dresser Thea had found at a garage sale on Livernois, rummaging inside the bottom drawer with both hands. He needed a trip to the barber. Charlie noticed for the first time that his uncle's shaggy hair was almost all white. The skin of his buttocks hung like wrinkled bunting. Charlie asked him what he was looking for.

"Boy, you been playing with my lucky trunks? I'm gonna paddle your ass you done went and lost them. I gots a bout with Leaping Larry Shane today. That white motherfucker can stand right in front of you and kick you in the chin with both feet."

"Larry Shane's dead, Unc. He got killed in a car crash ten years ago. We went to his funeral, remember? Anyway, you're retired now. No more bouts for you. Why don't you go back to bed?"

"What you talking about, retired? When I retire I'm taking the game with me."

The room was chilly. Battle walked over and closed the window. The old man insisted on sleeping with it open. It was five degrees outside and the heat was always coming on. Their landlord had threatened to raise their rent, either that or make them pay utilities, which was just as bad. A police officer's pay, together with what Thea made working part-time for a company that provided temporary office help, barely covered their rent and groceries and automobile maintenance. You couldn't live in Detroit without a car: That was the whole *point* of the Motor City, for chrissake.

He found Anthony's robe in the closet and draped it over the old man's shoulders, helping him to his feet. "That's just what you did, Unc; took the game with you. When was the last time you were able to find professional wrestling on *any* channel, even those ghosty UHF jobs you have to twist the rabbit ears and hang tinfoil all over them to get? I think when Battling Anthony Battle hung up his trunks they just figured what's the use and said bring on the game shows. You know, like on *Bonanza* after Hoss died."

"Hoss ain't dead. I seen him just today."

"That was a rerun." All the time he spoke,

Battle was gently turning his uncle and guiding him toward the bed. The portable TV on the cart in front of the Strat-O-Lounger was on, with the sound turned down: George McGovern's beaten-sheep face wearing earphones, probably rebutting whatever Nixon had had to say about Watergate that evening.

No wonder the old man had decided to withdraw.

Once he had him in bed, Battle covered him to his chin with the top sheet, nylon thermal blanket, and quilted spread. When he leaned down to kiss his uncle good night, Anthony was already snoring. Battle had always admired that ability to drop off instantly; a requirement of the old wrestling circuit with its long rides in broken-down buses, more often than not conducted directly from one arena to the next with no time to stop at whatever fleatrap hotel the Guild had lined up for its precious natural resources that evening. The trick would have come in handy when Battle was studying for his twelfth-week exams at the academy.

When he reached out to turn off the TV set, McGovern was gone. In his place was the brutal chiseled face of Quincy Springfield, chairman of the American Ethiopian Congress. On the wall behind him hung the organization's colors, a conglomeration of someone's idea of the flag of Ethiopia and the ebony-fist emblem of the Black Power movement. Battle wondered wearily if America would ever move beyond the sixties.

He flipped off the knob, went out into the living room, and switched on the console set Thea's parents had given them at their wedding reception, keeping the sound low to avoid disturbing his uncle. The color tubes were unkind to the garish flag and Springfield's preference for electric-blue suits. The reformed numbers boss's tailoring had yet to catch up with his raised social conscience.

". . . no longer tip our hats and shuffle aside to give the white man the sidewalk," he was saying. "We *poured* the sidewalk. We *sweep* the sidewalk. Five and one-half years ago, we painted the sidewalk with our blood. We *own* the sidewalk!"

Acquiescent grunts, shouts of "Speak the truth, brother!" His listeners were into it now, with all the carefully choreographed responses of the faithful at a church revival. Only the room with its heavily shaded windows and bare ceiling bulbs didn't resemble a church so much as what it was, a blind pig above a chop joint on Erskine, where a brother or sister who didn't want to go home when the legitimate bars closed at two in the morning could go for a drink or a lid or a three-digit shot at Long Green Street scribbled on a square of flash paper. In Detroit, politics came mixed with pleasures of a more agreeable sort.

Springfield continued. "Black voters outnumber white voters in this city four to one. We pay sixty percent of the taxes and provide eighty percent of the labor force. The only two places where we are a minority in Detroit is in the government and the police department. Oh, and we got the jails covered too. Lots of representation in the Wayne County Jail and DeHoCo."

Hoots and laughter. Battle grinned. You had to hand it to the guy. Mayor Gribbs couldn't pry a smile out of his electorate if he dropped his pants and sprayed seltzer.

But the speaker wasn't smiling. "I don't have no statistics from the morgue, on account of dead folks don't answer the census. Take my word for it, though, we ain't no minority there neither." His voice rose. "And I don't need no numbers in a column to tell me we got one more vote there than we should. Junius Harrison's stretched out in a refrigerator tray with three holes in his back, and all because he crashed the white man's party New Year's Eve."

The tape stopped there, and newsman Jac

LeGoff's long weary countenance filled the space. Behind him on the blue background appeared a clean-cut-looking head shot of Harrison, a relaxed, smiling picture that Battle hadn't seen, while LeGoff read Police Chief John Nichols's statement that the shooting was under investigation and the department wouldn't comment pending the outcome.

Heating up, thought Battle as he turned off the set. When the media stopped using police mug shots, it meant their sympathy was swinging the dead man's way. But then they had been cranking up the burners under STRESS almost since its inception. In the locker room at 1300, he himself had heard the unit referred to as SANESS: Shoot A Nigger, Eliminate Stinking Shines. The Harrison thing showed signs of becoming just the glue required to bond the Springfields and the LeGoffs and the Coleman Youngs against the administration in an election year. Battle had no great love for either Roman Gribbs or John Nichols, but he had seen enough of revolution even in his young life to know that a lot of babies wound up floating in discarded bath water.

One day on the shooting team and he already felt wet.

"Everything okay?" asked Thea when he

slid into bed beside her.

"Just my ass on the line. Nothing new."

"What?"

He realized she was asking about Anthony. "He's asleep. He just got confused. Thought he was late for a match."

"He's getting worse."

"He just woke up foggy. We all do that."

"I think we ought to start thinking about a place for him."

"No."

When she propped herself up on one elbow, the sheet fell away from her left nipple. It was chocolate brown in contrast to her dusty-beige skin. Before they were married he used to call her his personal Hershey's kiss. It had embarrassed her, even though his listeners didn't know what he was talking about, and he had stopped. "Charlie, you work. *I* work. He's here alone all day. What if he wanders away and gets hurt?"

"Fat chance of that. Fifty-eight and he can still bench press a Chevy."

"Even worse. He might hurt someone else. He was in a violent line of work."

"No more violent than the ballet. When I was just a kid he showed me how he could Atomic-Drop the Beast of Borodino, set him down on the canvas as gentle as an egg and make it look to the suckers like he busted every bone in his body. He was the best there was."

"*Was.*"

He pretended she hadn't spoken. "Last year when I was pulling double shifts I sat on the edge of the bed one morning with one sock on for ten minutes, trying to figure out if I was getting dressed to go to work or getting undressed to go to bed. You going to put me in a home?"

"It's not the same thing. Charlie, I know it's hard. You're like father and son."

"Not like." He scrunched himself into a sitting position and wedged his pillow behind his back. The moonlight in the room glowed like hoarfrost and he could see their reflections in the glass of his framed group cadet photo on the wall opposite the bed. He'd attended the funerals of two whose faces shared the frame, dress blues and a rifle salute; if anything was getting worse, if anything had a violent past, present, and future, it was Detroit. The whole city belonged in a home. "I was a year old when my old man went to Jackson for life. Anthony could've let me go to a state house, but he took me to his apartment the day the cops came and I never left till I signed up downtown. I don't give a shit what it says on my birth certificate, The'. He's my father. I'm not about to do to him what he wouldn't do to me."

"What about you and me? We want to start a family, but we can't if every time we try to do something about it he interrupts us."

He craned his neck suddenly, cocking one ear in the direction of his uncle's room. She stopped talking and listened with him.

"What? Do you hear something?"

"Snoring." He slid down and hooked a bare leg over her hip. "He ain't interrupting nobody just now."

"I hate it when you talk like that," she said.

"Like what?"

"Like Anthony. He can't help it. He dropped out in the ninth grade to go to work when his father was killed on the picket line. You graduated in the top third of your class and had twelve weeks' police training to boot. We're never going to get anywhere as a people as long as we insist on sounding like Uncle Remus."

"Yes'm."

"Charlie, I'm serious."

"So am I." He ran a palm up the inside of her thigh. When she opened her mouth to say something, he closed his over it. She whimpered a little and turned into him.

On the other side of the living room, Battling Anthony Battle awoke to the noise of a headboard thumping against a wall.

Fucking Larry Shane, he thought. *When he ain't got nobody to kick he jumps all over the fucking canvas like a fucking rabbit.* He wondered what that little shit Charlie had done with his lucky trunks.

Chapter Ten

Kubicek wore his blue suit to the Detroit Club. He had wanted to wear his heavy-duty gray, mostly because it was tolerant of his physical shortcomings and provided protection against the Michigan winter, allowing him to leave his topcoat at home; but his wife had insisted upon the more businesslike serge. Snug across the chest and too light for the razor winds of January, it was stiff with the newness of clothing that was worn only when absolutely necessary. The inspector's tag was intact in the right saddle pocket of the coat, and a sheaf of old funeral programs occupied the left inside breast pocket. One bore the name of his Aunt Milka, gone to compost these seventeen years. In that time he'd worn out three cars and the chest of drawers she'd left him. But not that fucking suit. If Audrey buried him in it he swore he'd haunt her until the insurance ran out.

He was in uniform the only time he'd been inside the Romanesque brownstone at Cass and Fort, when a waiter went apeshit over a mixed-up order and stabbed an assistant chef with a grapefruit knife. The chef had recovered, the waiter did two hundred hours of community service for assault with intent to commit great bodily harm other than murder, and the incident never made the press. Eleven mayors and two governors had been elected from inside the club's walnut-paneled walls. Kubicek supposed the waiter forfeited references.

He traded his topcoat for a green plastic check and followed a bald geezer in a red jacket past the moosehead into the dining room. This was a square candy box, wood-walled and carpeted and hung with burgundy velour, as quiet as a fart at a formal wedding. Utensils clicked, crystal pinged, conversations conducted in normal voices drifted toward the high ceiling and dissipated like tobacco smoke. The wing collars were gone, also the ruby stickpins and tall hats worn indoors, but aside from that nothing had changed from pictures of the place he had seen in a calendar of Old Detroit on the wall of an inspector's office at 1300. The same basic faces had gone on slurping soup while outside the brown stink of horseshit gave way to the blue-gray stench of auto exhaust and five wars came and went. The must in the air reminded him of the Collector's Corner at the Historical Museum, a building he'd visited twice, both times to have his picture taken as Policeman of the Month.

Nothing about which was conducive to his appetite. When it came to eating, he'd take the heat and the noise and warm, still-quivering meat at the Butcher's Inn over this place any day. But he wasn't here for the eating.

Two men in business suits rose from a corner table as the geezer approached, towing Kubicek. As they did so, several faces turned the sergeant's way, clearly wondering what this man in ill-fitting serge had to talk about with the mayor and police commissioner of the City of Detroit. Roman Gribbs, shorter and thicker than he appeared on television, took his hand in an iron politician's grip and uncovered bonded teeth in the same professional smile he had displayed while presenting him with his framed certificate at the museum. That had been three years ago, when his administration was new. The mayor had aged considerably in the time between, sparky council meetings and hot TV lights and the spiraling homicide rate having slackened the pugnacious jowls and carved deep lines in the executive forehead and whitened the distinguished gray at his temples. The practiced twinkle in his eyes had frozen into the kind of desperate glint the sergeant had seen in the eyes of fugitives crouched in the dark corners of freight cars down by the river, their owners torn between making a stand and running for it. And he thought, *Shit, and all I'm worried about is my pension.*

Everything about John Nichols was steel gray: suit, tie, wiry hair bent into a pompadour and clipped close above the ears, metal-rimmed glasses tinted gray. Like Gribbs, who had stepped into the shoes of a broken man when Jerome Cavanagh left office two years after the riots, Nichols had inherited his authority from a punch-drunk predecessor: Ray Girardin, longtime *News* police reporter and believer in the basic decency of his city, stunned into paralysis by the events on Twelfth Street in July 1967. First as a district inspector and later as deputy superintendent, Nichols had stressed the importance of a strong police presence in times of civil disturbance, only to see his precepts ignored when they were most needed. Of all the high-placed officials involved in that affair, beginning with Girardin and ending with Lyndon Johnson, he alone had come out with his reputation enhanced. He was Gribbs's only choice for top cop, and it was a foregone conclusion that when November came around he would be running for mayor. Certainly there was something of the office-seeker in the way he shook Kubicek's hand, squeezing just before he let it go. In the past, on podiums and in the receiving lines of police pageantry, he had seemed to want to get rid of it as soon as possible. Or maybe that was too much to try to get out of a simple pressing of flesh. Since New Year's Eve the sergeant had found himself turning over every gesture and studying it from both sides to learn whether the department was going to stand with him or throw him to the ravening pack.

"Have you dined here before, Sergeant?" Gribbs asked when the three were seated.

"Yeah — yes. Kind of. A Big Mac in a TMU out front when I was waiting for back-up."

"TMU?"

"Tactical Mobile Unit," said Nichols.

"Oh. Of course. You forget codes and jargon when you talk to the press all the time. They appeal to the fifth-grade mind. Well, you're in for a pleasant experience. I particularly recommend the abalone."

"I don't know what that is, sir."

"It's a Pacific shellfish. They pry it open and butterfly it and just generally pound hell out of it until it's tender enough to chew." He grinned self-consciously, and Kubicek understood the profanity tasted unnatural in the mayoral mouth. Gribbs was making an effort to acclimate himself to his company. "I think you'd like it. They serve it in a delicate horse-radish sauce."

A waiter assembled himself suddenly out of the molecules at the sergeant's elbow and handed him a menu bound in burgundy leather. He was nearly as old as the ancient who had escorted Kubicek into the room. Kubicek wondered if there was anyone to take their place when they finished dying out, or if the club would perish with them. But then there wasn't a dark or a blond hair in the place and maybe nobody under fifty would even notice.

By nature and environment he was a red meat man. There was a Black Angus New York Strip that called to him from among the half-dozen items printed on the menu; but the mayor had mentioned the abalone and that was what he requested. At least there were no prices included to embarrass him. Nichols, to whom nothing had been recommended, ordered the Strip. Gribbs wrote the dishes on a sheet provided by the waiter — something new to the sergeant, who had always stated his preferences orally even when dining at the toney London Chop House for his twentieth anniversary — and added merely a bowl of mushroom soup for himself, explaining that he anticipated a heavy bill of fare at a fund raiser in Greektown that evening. Kubicek was the only one who had opted for the shellfish.

While the mayor was present, most of the conversation centered around the Tigers' last season and what Billy Martin had in mind for them in 1973. Nichols said he didn't hold out much hope for the club as long as Abner Crownover insisted on running it as if it were his own electric train. At the mention of Crownover's name his voice faltered, and he hurried up and finished the sentence. After a short awkward silence, Gribbs touched his lips with his linen napkin, pushed away his soup half finished, announcing that he was hosting the Commission on Community Relations in his office in ten minutes. He uncased his politician's teeth and clamped the sergeant's hand a second time. "How's the abalone?"

"You were right, your honor. They sure pounded the living shit out of it."

The smile turned stiff, as if held too long for a tardy shutter button, and Kubicek was sure he'd committed a social blunder. But the mayor gave his upper arm a pat, shook hands with Nichols, and strode out of the room, pausing briefly at a table to exchange beaming words with *News* columnist Doc

Greene. Remembering the easy Irish charm with which Gribbs's predecessor, Jerry Cavanagh, handled the press — at least until the riots came along — Kubicek thought this mayor looked stilted and mechanical. Somehow it reminded him of the differences between the combat veterans of his own generation and those who had served in Vietnam; far from the conquering hero, Gribbs appeared to be interested chiefly in keeping his head down and getting out of office with his ass in one piece.

Nichols appeared to share the sergeant's thoughts. "Poor dumb son of a bitch. I thought when I talked him into withholding the homicide stats he'd take the hint. Don't even give those newspaper bastards the time of day. I'll never forgive them for what they did to Ray Girardin. As a cop he was piss-poor, but he was one of their own for thirty years and they turned on him. They're worse than fucking lawyers."

Kubicek, who had had his share lately of dealings with newspapers and lawyers, said nothing. He wondered if the commissioner was testing him. Certainly the air had changed with the departure of the third party.

"How you getting on with the shooting team?" Nichols dissected the fat from a square of steak the size of his thumb and forked the lean into his mouth.

"Okay. I'm not too sure about the colored guy."

"Good. Better you get the hard questions from your friends in the department than the assholes in the media. Getting antsy indoors?"

"Well, I'm a working cop." He decided to lighten the conversation. "Don't them soap opera people ever get a chance to relax? I seen more suicides and pregnancies in the last two weeks than my first ten years on the job."

"Gribbs wanted me to suspend you without pay. I guess you can put up with the fucking organ music for a little longer."

His face stung. "I'm not complaining, sir. I know the department's backing me up."

"If it were just you I'm not sure I wouldn't hang you out like a rug the dog pissed on. The STRESS program is taking a lot of flak. It's my horse and if I don't ride it into the mayor's office it's going to throw me off. I'd have bounced you on New Year's Day — I had due cause on the moonlighting rule — only that would've put the DPOA on my ass and I need the cop vote because I'm sure as hell not going to get it from the inner city. Do me a favor and explain to me why you're worth all this bullshit."

The DPOA was the Detroit Police Officers'

Association, and this was the sergeant's first indication that the union he'd been paying into for years was doing anything for him besides sitting on its hands.

"You seen my jacket," he said.

"Citations and commendations don't mean yellow shit to civilians. In this town a police officer's only as good as his last headline. I guess I don't need to tell you the headlines lately haven't been anything to issue a citation over."

"If somebody told me the pissant reporters ran this department maybe I'd of paid more attention to them."

The commissioner crossed his knife and fork on his plate and pushed it away. Behind the glasses his eyes were pewter-colored. "If that means you'd have thought twice before you tossed a hideout piece beside Junius Harrison's body, you can put your shield and gun on this table and walk out right now. Is that what you're saying, Sergeant?"

Kubicek shored himself up. "No."

"Because if I had a speck of evidence to support it, I'd throw you in a hole and roll the sod over on top of you. That's the difference between me and a politician. A politician would've tipped you in the first time a finger pointed your way. Cops stand by cops. STRESS is better than the couple of rotten apples rolling around in it and I mean for it to survive. If it comes down to STRESS or you, and Forensics finds so much as one of your cock hairs on that gun, I'll hang you with my own belt. I don't know how I can make that any clearer."

"Yes sir."

Nichols watched him for a beat, then sat back, wiping his hands with his napkin. "I've got a detail for you that should keep you busy and out of sight. What do you think of cop movies?"

The sergeant felt himself smiling crookedly. "You mean like *Dirty Harry*, blow down ten perps an hour and no paperwork?"

"Well, nothing so big as Clint Eastwood. An independent production company has applied for permits to shoot a crime picture on location in Detroit. The mayor's hot on the project, wants Hollywood to get into the habit of coming here and spending money. The company needs a technical advisor. I suggested you."

"What's that?"

"Theoretically it's to keep the director from arming the actors with revolvers with safeties and worse. Since they keep making the same mistakes I figure they just want somebody to blame. Are you interested? The pay's good and you'll get to see your name in the credits."

"Ain't that moonlighting?"

"Say I'm assigning you to public relations. Who knows? Maybe you'll get Richard Roundtree's autograph."

He wondered who the fuck Richard Roundtree was. "Well, if it gets me out of the back room."

"Fine. They start shooting next week. Wear thermals. It's exterior at first and I'm told they take all day to film five minutes."

"Thanks, Commissioner."

"Just don't kill any movie stars." Nichols stood.

Chapter Eleven

Russell Littlejohn loved his Bronco.

It was the only thing his parents had given him that he truly valued. White over green and six years old, it had been rolled on Long Lake Road by some little puke from Birmingham High School before Russell's father bought it for $1,500 and then let it sit in the garage for two years until he tracked down a top and a windshield in his price range. In return for helping with the repairs Russell had been allowed to drive it until he finished school, whereupon Dwight Littlejohn had presented him with the title as a reward for not flunking out. Russell had invested his first two weeks' wages from the marina in an eight-track tape player and four Panasonic speakers, and as he tooled down East Jefferson with the piss-poor vacuum wipers twitching at the granulated snow that collected on the windshield, he bobbed his afroed head to the throb and thrum of "All Along the Watchtower": Saint Jimi riding the music out as far as it would take him, only it wasn't far enough, not by half, and so he went the rest of the way on Horse, away out there beyond the Big Dipper where the Man couldn't follow. He was a constellation now, a halo of stars with a Mongol beard, comets in his eyes.

The lake was chalk-colored, less so in the middle where the river current prevented the surface from freezing in all but the most severe winters, and the wind skinned away crystals of ice and serpentined them across the asphalt ahead, where they made dusty white S's in the doldrums. From time to time a brawny gust took the top-heavy Ford in its teeth and shook it, once nearly twisting the wheel out of Russell's hands. He enjoyed the fight for control. He pretended he was the captain of an ore carrier, or better yet the master of a square-rigged schooner, piloting his fragile craft through the storms of January, defying Nature to pop her stays. Memorizing *The Diary of Che Guevara*, *The Autobiography of Malcolm X*, and Mao's little red book had not entirely lifted the young man away from the boy who had nursed on the thirteen-inch image of Errol Flynn sticking it to the King's pigs on *Bill Kennedy's Million-Dollar Movie*, so many Sunday afternoons ago.

At length, Captain Peter Blood steered his six-cylindered man-of-war into the parking lot in front of Pinky's Marina and Snowmobile

Rental, where Pinky was waiting for him when he got inside.

A large, florid man of sixty, with a bald head dented all over and anchors tattooed on his forearms — exposed by the white T-shirt he wore in all seasons — Stan Pinicus was trying to clear the nozzle of a spraygun with a tenpenny nail. He had served with the navy through two wars and had owned marinas in Santa Monica and Corpus Christi before moving to Michigan to be near his daughter and grandchildren. Some of Russell's fellow employees referred to him as the Commodore, not entirely behind his back nor, Russell suspected, without his approval. Today he wore the expression of a chief petty officer who had discovered a poorly tied bosun's knot in a net containing valuable cargo.

"You're almost late," he said.

"I call that on time." Russell shed his Pistons warm-up jacket and hung it on the broken trident in Neptune's hand, part of an antique carved wooden figurehead that went with the room's runaway nautical theme. He bet Pinky wore Popeye pajamas and sang his grandchildren to sleep with bawdy sea chanteys.

"There's propane tanks need filling out on the dock and them boxes in the storeroom ain't going to sprout legs and walk out to the dumpster. Don't put your coat back on yet. That big window's so dirty I can't tell if I'm looking out at the lake or the Mojave Desert. It's all on this side."

Russell stretched himself over the service counter and scooped a sea sponge and a bottle of Lestoil off the underside shelf. "Wish to hell we had us a squeegee."

"Use newspapers. We got stacks of them in the back too, going back to Custer I think. Cops was here," Pinky added without pausing.

Russell looked at him. His employer was testing the spraygun, squirting jets of paint-tinted air into a stained rag in his other hand. "What kind of cops, coasties?"

"Detroit. Just one, a black guy. Plain-clothes."

"When?"

"A little while ago. He said he'd be back."

"He ask about me?"

"Not at first."

Jesus. Like pulling teeth with his toes. "Well, what did he want?"

"Wanted to know was I missing any boats New Year's Eve."

"We were closed New Year's Eve."

"That's what I told him. Only a damn fool'd be out on the lake after Christmas.

Hit a chunk of ice and play *Titanic*."

"What'd he say?"

"Wanted to know about my employees. I said, ask away, I ain't got but three. He asked about you most." He wiped off the nozzle with the rag.

"I guess you told him I'm your best worker."

"I don't lie to cops. I said you got in trouble once but you was up front about it when you put in for the job. Been clean ever since so far as I know. He asked what kind of trouble. I said I think assault, some kid rap. He said he'd be back after he checked it out."

"Fucking cops. They got no imagination. Every time something goes down they go to the fucking books."

Pinky's scowl reminded him of Neptune's. "He comes back, you answer his questions. And watch your fucking language. In Grosse Pointe only the customers swear."

"Why'd you have to tell him about my juvie?"

"He asked."

"Shit." He lifted a bucket and tossed the sponge inside.

"Maybe you ought to be grateful he didn't ask about the gas."

"What gas?"

Pinky set down the rag and spraygun and

mopped his palms on his denimed thighs. Although he was shorter than Russell his hands were nearly as big, with knuckles the size of ship's bells. "I drained the tank on every boat Christmas week. January second Everett and I pulled them up on the dock and carried them to storage. One of 'em sloshed when we lifted it. The *Maybelline*. Tank was damn near half full."

"So you missed one."

"No, I drained it all right. Everett didn't know nothing about it and neither did Pete when I asked him yesterday. Did you gas up that boat and take it out?"

"*Hell,* no. New Year's Eve I was home sucking on a reefer and listening to Wolfman Jack."

"I didn't say New Year's Eve. Cop said that. It could've been any time between Christmas and the second."

"I don't even like the water."

Pinky rose from the low stool, listing slightly when at his full height. One leg was shorter than the other due to some bone that had been removed from his knee along with several ounces of shrapnel, a souvenir of his tour aboard the *Hancock*. "Well, be ready to tell that to the cop." He steadied himself against the counter as he worked his way behind it. Although he took a rubber-tipped cane to work every day he seldom used it.

Russell scrubbed the big lakeside window, put on his jacket, and went out to dump the bucket into the lake. When that was done he carried the first of a row of propane tanks from the dock to the side of the building and filled it from the big tank. He forced himself to put his brain on suspension while he performed these menial chores. He had topped off the last of the portable tanks and was on his way to the storeroom to dispose of the empty boxes there when he spotted the gray Plymouth parked at the edge of the lot in front of the building. Looking at the twin whip antennae mounted on the rear fenders, Russell wondered why they didn't just go ahead and paint PIG on all four sides. He wondered too how they managed to make their vehicles materialize in select locations without anyone noticing them approaching. He swore the spot had been empty five seconds earlier.

The pig was standing inside the storeroom when Russell entered through the door from the dock. The man was black — which threw Russell, although he knew there were black officers with Detroit — coarse-featured, and obviously well built beneath his charcoal suit and tan topcoat. Russell might have taken him for some kind of athlete if he hadn't spoken to Pinky or seen the unmarked police unit outside. He looked to be in his early twenties and wore his hair in the understated natural that had begun to spread through the black middle class after the shock of the sixties wore off. When it got so you couldn't tell the pigs from the regular brothers, maybe it was time to start looking in some new directions.

"Russell Littlejohn?"

That nailed it. Only a pig called you by both names.

"Who's asking?"

This one carried his shield in his bare palm, no hot-shit leather folder. It wasn't gold either, but the plain silver of the uniformed cop on the beat. Russell felt a little more sure of himself then. This was no full-time detective. "See they let you wear long pants today."

The pig didn't look offended. He even smiled a little. "My name's Charlie Battle, Russell. You can call me Officer Battle."

"You can call me busy. Pinky don't like us talking on shop time." He lifted an empty carton off the top of a stack and carried it out to the dumpster. He half expected the pig to follow him, but when he went back inside, Battle was standing on the same spot. When Russell reached past him to pick up

135

another carton, Battle swept out a hand and closed it on Russell's wrist tightly.

"I talked it over with your boss. He said it was okay." There was no strain in the detective's tone.

Russell, who had tensed his biceps when his wrist was seized, relaxed them. Battle turned the young man's hand palm up and squeezed the tendon at the base of his thumb, spreading Russell's fingers. Then he let go. Russell could still feel the pressure afterward. The detective's fingers were like articulated iron.

"I'm looking for a speedboat," Battle said.

"We got lots. Don't look for no low rates just because the lake's froze over, though. Pinky don't give discounts."

"Actually I'm looking for the pilot of a speedboat. Someone took this one out late New Year's Eve."

"It wasn't nobody here. We was closed from Thanksgiving till the day after New Year's."

"So was every other marina on the lake, or the half of them I've been to, anyway. None of them reported a boat stolen, so I'm assuming somebody borrowed one. Pinicus says you have a key to the back door. Did you use it that night?"

"You don't need to get in to take a boat.

136

They was all tied up at the dock."

"All the ignition keys are hanging inside, behind the counter."

"Anybody can hot-wire a boat."

"Russell, I'm getting a lot of answers from you and none of them fits the question. Did you take a boat out New Year's Eve?"

"No. I stayed home that night and read *Motorcycle World*."

"It took you all night to read one magazine?"

"Who'm I, Evelyn Wood? I got up a couple times to take a leak."

"That's not a very exciting evening for a young guy like you."

"I guess you don't know what kind of young guy I am."

"Is there someone who can confirm you were home between nine and ten-thirty?"

"My parents, maybe, but I didn't see them. I got an apartment with its own entrance. What if they can't? You going to arrest me?"

Battle put his hands in the pockets of his topcoat. "I found your record at Juvenile Division. You were busted when you were seventeen for sticking up a movie theater. The crime I'm investigating is armed robbery."

"You need a gun to stick up a place. They didn't find no gun on me when they picked me up. I pleaded guilty to assault. Anyway

I got no record as an adult. This that Crownover thing, right? I heard about it from the TV. Seems to me this pig that blowed away every brother at the party's the one in trouble."

"That's what I'm investigating. Whoever drove that speedboat away from the party when the shooting started is the only one who can tell us whether Junius Harrison was in on the heist or just happened to be standing in the wrong place at the wrong time. Everyone else involved is dead. I'm not saying that boatman is going to walk, but if he comes forward and tells the truth, some judge will consider that when he hands down his sentence. The robbery itself isn't important."

"Bullshit. When you're in on a stick-up and somebody gets iced, don't matter if it's one of the stick-up guys, whoever's left gets nailed for felony murder. I know that much."

"That's the theory, only it almost never works out that way in court." Battle took his hands out of his pockets. There was something in one of them. "I could arrest you right now, Russell. Those needle tracks between your fingers are fresh. That's probable cause for a warrant to search your apartment. A gram of heroine is enough to send you to Jackson for a couple of years."

"Go ahead and toss it. You won't find nothing." Russell wondered what was in the pig's hand. It was too small for a piece.

"I don't like that," Battle said. "Everybody has something he doesn't want found. Unless he's got a good reason to get rid of it."

Russell said nothing.

In the silence a heavy truck whined past on Jefferson, chuckling over a break in the pavement. Battle stuck out the hand. Russell jumped, but there was nothing but a card between the fingers.

"That's Special Investigations. Ask for me, Charlie Battle. If I come back here uninvited, there won't be a thing I can do for you."

Russell took the card. Without removing his gaze from the detective he tore it in half, then tore the halves into quarters, and let the pieces flutter to the floor. Battle's eyes, soft and sad for a pig's, followed the last piece until it came to rest. He shook his head.

"Dumb."

He went out through the office.

Alone in the cluttered room, Russell stretched out his arms and spread his hands. He'd learned the trick from one of those little hot-blooded lizards in a *National Geographic* special; something to do with getting oxygen into its system in the desert. He stood like that for a full minute. Then he carried the rest of the boxes out to the dumpster. The wind came off the lake, hurling icepicks into his face. Detroit sure was a long way from the Kalahari.

Chapter Twelve

Caryn Crownover Ogden's Tuesdays belonged to the Charlotte Gryphon Foundation.

Named for a quasi-mythical young Frenchwoman who had warned the commander of Fort Detroit of Chief Pontiac's plan to invade the garrison in 1763 — a distant ancestor of the Crownovers — the foundation had been established by Caryn in the wake of the 1967 riots to identify and reward deserving minority students with college scholarships. Although Ted Ogden, an investment counselor by trade, served as the group's treasurer, it was Caryn's grasp of business organization that prevented it from dissipating its energies in directions other than those stated in the charter, and to keep the various community leaders who served on its board from bludgeoning one another with their chairs.

This Tuesday had been one of those days. Henry Ford II, already well in his cups at 9:30 A.M., had pounded the conference table with a pudgy fist when Caryn reminded him that the foundation did not exist to help underwrite his plans to build a glittery office complex and shopping center in the warehouse district, but rather to educate the architects and engineers who would design and construct its successors. Studying him through her platinum-framed glasses, she saw a deteriorating giant much like her grandfather, his flabby cheeks a map of purple blood vessels burst by drink, the famed Ford eyes out of focus and a little afraid. Of what, she wondered? Of the younger, talented men on his own board of directors, with their cargo load of revolutionary ideas, ideas of the dangerous sort that when he possessed them had blasted aside his own grandfather and his ring of cronies like loose metal shavings on an unpainted chassis? Of Christina, his second wife, whose patience with his infidelities could only be expected to carry so far? Of Caryn? Or — and this was most likely — of Henry Ford II, and the myriad weaknesses of his own poor clay?

Poor Hank the Deuce. She wished she'd known him better in the days before the Edsel. It was plain he had never quite recovered from that personal Little Big Horn.

The meeting, convened to decide whether to expand the scholarship's horizons beyond the sciences so beloved of industry to encompass the liberal arts, had adjourned with a motion to table the measure until tempers had cooled. In this manner the happy problem of what to do with a surplus that threatened Gryphon's non-profit status had become a crisis that might require an army of tax attorneys to lay to rest. Their fees would eliminate the surplus, with no advantage gained for the promising minority members the foundation existed to encourage. It was no wonder so many of them turned to the street.

As if to confirm the suspicion, the radio in her Corvette as she drove away from Gryphon's headquarters in the Penobscot Building reported an astonishing assortment of fresh horrors that had taken place the previous night: County workers had rolled four members of a family out of their house on Sherman that morning under sheets, punched full of bullet holes by persons unknown in an incident believed to be connected to the family's heroin business; a police officer was in critical condition at Receiving Hospital with a bullet in his chest, delivered at close range during a routine traffic stop on Outer Drive at 3:00 A.M.; the unidentified corpse of a young woman with her hands cut off and her teeth knocked out had been gaffed in the River Rouge around midnight by police on Zug Island; and a newborn infant, found blue and comatose in a dumpster by a restaurant worker on the east side shortly after dawn, had expired thirty minutes ago at St. John's Hospital. A teenage girl thought to be the child's mother was in custody.

Caryn wondered if Henry Ford ever listened to the news, and if he was truly convinced his proposed glass-and-steel headstone for a culture that had gone West with his horsecollar-grilled Dream Car would make a difference. At the national level, Walter Cronkite and David Brinkley had dubbed Detroit the Murder City, a place where the violent crime rate had tripled in five years, three out of five citizens owned unlicensed firearms, and homicide was the fourth leading cause of death. Network pundits analyzed a recent joint directive issued by Mayor Gribbs and Police Chief Nichols advising Detroiters to avoid arguments with strangers. The concept of politeness as a weapon of self-defense kept things lively between commercials for ring-around-the-collar.

From Eight Mile Road to the foot of Woodward Avenue, from the self-consuming chimneys of the coke ovens and glass plants downriver to the black iron jockeys of Grosse Pointe, established order in the City of Detroit had broken down. Street gangs named for dead movie stars took in wandering youths in lieu of a stable family environment. Even the police had fallen into vigilantism, stripping the uniforms from its officers and the insignia from its cars and turning them loose in alleys and railyards on hunting expeditions for suspicious persons. The place was any civic architect's picture of hell.

As the daughter of a man who had shipped Negro laborers north to break the strikes of the 1930s, Caryn was sensitive to issues of race, and did not share the opinion of some of her colleagues at Gryphon that the community's black majority was somehow responsible for the decline. Rather, it was the almost criminally nearsighted refusal of its white governing class to recognize that majority. But she did agree with the assessment of department store magnate Joseph L. Hudson, Jr., when on the fifth anniversary of the riots he announced: "The black man has the feeling he is about to take power in the city, but he is going to be left with an empty bag."

Until the incident in her own living room at the close of the old year, Caryn had comforted herself that the anarchy was confined to the Inner City, that alien place where her father had continued to recruit the labor to build automobiles to carry his customers north and west from the squalor downtown;

but the cancer had spread.

Not for the first time since the killings at the party, she considered sending Opal to an eastern school when she came of age. But that would mean moving, as Caryn couldn't bear to be separated from her daughter, and that was unfair to Ted, all of whose clients were in Michigan and Ohio. They had never discussed, *would* never discuss the fact that her income through Crownover Coaches would support all three of them for several lifetimes even if he never put together another portfolio for another prosperous client. There would always be people without imagination who clung to the obvious conclusion about their marriage. Although they were easily ignored, they exerted a kind of reverse influence on the way Ted and Caryn conducted their lives. Always the Ogdens would go to the opposite extreme to prevent those people from crowing that their impressions were right.

The only alternative was to make the city safe for Opal.

Cadillac Square and her best route to Jefferson and home was sealed off. Police barricades and a city blue-and-white with its roof light flashing compelled her to take Woodward north to Grand River. As she maneuvered around an obviously cold and miserable patrolman directing traffic in fur hat, collar, and black leather gauntlets, she rolled down her window and asked if there had been an accident.

"No, ma'am. They're shooting a movie."

"A movie? What kind?"

"Crime picture. What else?"

Maybe it was a good sign, she thought as she followed a grumbling caravan of slow-moving vehicles through the detour. If Hollywood was tiring at last of New York City and southern California, had in fact begun to discover the great interior part of the country that provided the bulk of its audience, it meant more money in the city treasury. Money enough, perhaps, to tear down the black and twisted remains of Twelfth Street, erect decent housing on the site, and maybe even help fund Hank's glitter palace. She thought it a fine irony that the bad reputation that inspired a motion-picture company to shoot its bloody scenes on location in Detroit should help to eradicate the conditions that had attracted it.

She was meeting Abner for lunch at Sinbad's on the river. The sight of his bottle-green Mercedes in the parking lot, with its vanity plate reading DUGOUT, made her mouth pull lines in her face. She had discussed with him the questionable form of driving a foreign car when the family income was tied so firmly to Detroit, but his interest in the company their adoptive ancestor had carved out of the wilderness extended only so far as the walls of his office and their usefulness as a place to hang Tigers pennants and uniforms. No one disliked the Gashawks more than Caryn — Robin and Cedric epitomized the predatory nature of their late father while possessing nothing of Sir Roger's rough-hewn candor — and yet she shuddered to think what would happen to Crownover if her brother were truly running it instead of their capable and acquisitive British cousins.

The lunch was a waste of time. Abner, brooding over a portfolio of sketches for a new Tigers logo, barely touched his salmon mousse and grunted in response when Caryn recounted the details of the Gryphon meeting. His tiny eyes, set close above a nose that had been broken the one time he had actually tried to play baseball, showed a flicker of interest only when she mentioned the movie being shot downtown.

"Casting anybody local?"

"I don't know. Why? Are you considering a career in show business?"

"Maybe there's a cameo in it for Kaline. It might be good for attendance."

"I'm sure someone in Dallas is going to hop a plane east and buy a season ticket because Al Kaline ordered a cup of coffee in a movie."

"It worked with Alex Karras, and the damn Lions haven't won anything since 1957. What do you think of this one?" He held up a sixteen-by-twenty sketch in pastels of a cartoon tiger in a baseball cap winding up to pitch.

"It looks like Snagglepuss. Abner, give it a rest. Spring training doesn't start for two months."

"Six weeks. Anyway the season's just the tip of the iceberg. A big win in September starts in January. How's my niece?"

"Coming down with a cold. I almost canceled the meeting so I could stay home with her."

"That's great. She's a cute kid." He was looking at Snagglepuss.

Caryn sat back and ordered another highball.

Driving home, floating a little, she decided that if it weren't for Cornelia she would never see her brother except at family events. The old lady sitting in her big empty mansion placed a lot of store in blood relationships, possibly because she could never bear children of her own. Caryn hadn't discussed with

Abner what they would do with the house once their mother passed on. She didn't care to live there herself, and she didn't think even Abner could fill it with trophies and autographed baseballs. The paintings, tapestries, and statuary that decorated it would bring a fortune at auction even by Crownover standards, but she doubted the house itself would attract a private buyer. When it was built, the enormous staff required to maintain it had cost only pennies a day, but in recent years adequate help for a reasonable wage had become scarce — *good* help, as perceived by the vanishing members of Cornelia's class and generation, was close to nonexistent — and brass went unpolished and cobwebs laced the crystals of Catherine the Great's chandelier in the front hall. It was simply too much house even for a billionaire, and billionaires no longer even changed planes in Detroit on their way between coasts. Probably the family would donate the building and its six acres to the City of Grosse Pointe to beat the taxes, and probably the city would tear down the building and sell the lot to a developer. The materials and fixtures alone would fund another war memorial.

Ted's Eldorado was parked in the garage when she pulled in and cut the Corvette's motor. When she got out he was leaning through the connecting doorway to the kitchen. He was in his shirtsleeves, but his necktie was done up, which meant he hadn't been there long. His curly hair needed combing. It usually did. It was a weave, and he thought if he left it a little disheveled, no one would notice. It was one of several areas where his and Caryn's opinions differed. He looked anxious.

"I expected you home earlier," he said.

"I didn't expect you at all. Is Opal all right?" A fist in an ice glove closed on her heart.

"She's running a fever. Netta called me at the office when she couldn't reach you. I called Doctor Farhat. He doesn't think it's serious, but he's sending an ambulance."

She was sure she'd given the governess the number at Sinbad's, but she didn't stand there arguing. At the mention of *fever* she pushed through the doorway, nearly colliding with her husband. He followed her into the living room and up the stairs to Opal's bedroom, saying something reassuring. But she heard the concern in his tone. Whether it was over their daughter or because Caryn hadn't been on hand when the situation changed, she couldn't tell.

Opal's voice was small — "I'm hot, Mommy" — and her forehead was burning up. Caryn stretched out next to her on the bed, holding her, and got off only when the paramedics came and strapped her daughter to a board. They were kind, warmer and more genuine-sounding in their reassurances than Dr. Farhat, Opal's pediatrician, whose bed-side manner Caryn had always thought oily. She kept her hand on her daughter's as they carried the stretcher down the stairs and out the front door to where the ambulance was parked with its doors open and its lights twin-kling. They didn't even wait for Caryn to ask if she could ride along. One of them stood aside and held the door for her to climb in. When the doors were secured and his partner in back, the driver strapped himself in and swung the boxlike vehicle out of the drive and into the private road, expertly avoiding the blue Duster parked on the other side, which pulled out behind and stayed there all the way to the hospital.

Chapter Thirteen

Hollywood people were pussies.

Kubicek had suspected as much for some time — a couple of Christmases ago his wife had dragged him into a theater for the first time in fifteen years to see *A Clockwork Orange*, whose faggy British accents and phoney liberal worldview had almost made him puke up a twelve-dollar prime rib dinner — but his first exposure to the talent behind *Detroit P.D.*, an independent production starring somebody Kubicek vaguely remembered as one of the mobsters wiped out in the climax of *The Godfather*, confirmed the suspicion.

The director, whose name was Corky, came up to about Kubicek's sternum in platform boots with a beaded Indian band around his forehead, black hair to his shoulders, and an untrimmed beard spilling down the front of his tie-dyed sweatshirt. It had taken the sergeant the better part of the morning to sort the honcho from the rest of the crew, none of whom looked to be a minute past thirty. Most of them were clearly freezing despite their heavy quilted coats, big fuzzy earmuffs, and mittens. Mittens, for chrissake; he kept looking to see if they were tied to their sleeves. He himself was comfortable on this moderate day in mid-January in a belted top-coat with a zip-out pile lining and black Cossack hat. An old-fashioned Alberta Clipper of the kind that closed schools and brought out the county plows would probably send these California feebs squealing back to their topless beaches and hot tubs. There wasn't a Pappy Ford or a John Huston in the bunch.

They all appeared to know what they were doing, he gave them that. While the actors and extras stood around pounding their shoulders and gulping steaming coffee and tea from Styrofoam cups provided by a catering truck, young men and women in baseball caps with film titles stenciled on the fronts unwound miles of cable from portable reels, pulled out the telescoping legs of tripods, erected big silver umbrella reflectors, swung booms, plugged cords into the backs of control panels, trundled cameras, switch-started a gas-powered generator the size of a city bus, laid out hand props on a folding table, and just generally screwed tight, spread out, clamped down, snapped shut, winched up, rolled, pounded, dug, tested, taped, chalked, wired, strapped, wheeled, pushed, tugged, slapped, cursed, replaced, and shouldered equipment both familiar and alien to the sergeant from 7:00 A.M. until noon, at which point everything shut down for lunch.

This was beef Wellington and baked potatoes served in the Motor Bar at the old Book-Cadillac Hotel, closed to the public that day. Shamefacedly, Kubicek asked the production's leading lady, recruited from one of his wife's favorite soap operas, for her autograph, which she gracefully granted on a paper napkin over her vegetarian plate. While he was waiting, an assistant director even smaller than Corky shoved him aside to deliver a message to the actress, then manhandled him again on his way out. Kubicek resisted the urge to break the little turd in half.

With an hour to go before they lost the light, the company was ready to shoot its first scene, a shrieking, arm-flinging argument between the soap girl and the *Godfather* guy in front of the statue of the Spirit of Detroit outside the entrance to the City-County Building. Of the three, Kubicek thought the great sculpture, a muscular giant holding a man, woman, and child in one hand and a sunburst symbolizing Industrial Progress in the other, was the best actor; but he supposed they did something back at the studio to improve the scene. After two takes, Corky stopped the cameras and asked three of the uniformed city officers working Crowd Control if they would mind being in the background.

"Doing what?" This from Horace Hyde, a Traffic Bureau cop Kubicek knew slightly. He had silver temples and a horseshoe moustache just this side of regulation.

"Just walking through. The scene needs a note of realism."

"Well, we're on duty."

"It'll just take a few minutes. Your commissioner offered us the complete cooperation of the police department. I'm sure he won't mind."

"I don't know."

"I'll see you get tickets to the premiere. Think how proud your wife will be to see you up on the screen."

"I'm divorced."

"Your girlfriend, then. Don't tell me a big strapping hunk like you doesn't have to beat them off with your baton."

"I guess it's okay."

"Great. This is Grace, our wardrobe supervisor. She'll put you in a nice suit."

"What's wrong with my uniform?"

"You've got plainclothesman all over you. Surely your boss sees that. A forty-four long,

I think, Grace. Make sure there's room for a shoulder holster."

This was Kubicek's job. "Corky, the department doesn't much use shoulder holsters any more. They're uncomfortable as hell and it's a bitch to get your gun out in a hurry when you have to. This is standard." He unclipped the belt rig from behind his right kidney and showed the director his standard issue .38 in its shiny black sheath. (Imitation alligator, $29.95 from the *Police Times* catalogue plus $1.95 postage and handling.)

Corky laid a hand on Kubicek's upper arm. "Thanks, Paul. It is Paul?" The sergeant nodded. "Paul, I've got the same hard-on for realism as you. I'm shooting for mean and gritty. I mean, this ain't *Adam 12*: 'Take the license out of your wallet, please, lady. By the way, Jim, how's your hemorrhoids?' But the studio's competing with double-oh-seven. Art?"

The assistant director, always close, moved in tighter, and Corky rested his free arm across the little man's shoulders, creating a huddle with Kubicek in the center. "Fetch me one of those shoulder harnesses from Props, okay? And a gun. That's the ticket." Art bustled off with a pat on the butt. "I see what I'm doing here as a kind of *Satyricon* of crime pictures: Real backgrounds, genuine cops and crooks in the cast — hey, my second lead did seven months at Q for uttering and publishing — none of that glitzy Hollywood shit. But the studio doesn't see it that way. Burt fucking Reynolds takes on a team of hit men with flamethrowers and the next thing you know fifty percent of the budget on every film in production is set aside for firesuits for the stunt crew.

"I could piss and moan," he went on. "I could throw up my hands and say if it's shit they want, I'll give 'em shit. Only I've been around a long time. Did you know I directed an episode of *Leave It to Beaver*? Got an Emmy nomination. Point is I know the game: Give 'em something small so they think you're playing by the rules, then while they're busy congratulating themselves and kissing each other's asses, kick 'em in the nuts. Ah."

He took the shoulder holster Art had brought, brown suede with a torso strap, the kind of rig Kubicek hadn't seen since he was a rookie. "Sure, it's old-fashioned, but it's got romance. That thing you use looks like a bicycle clip."

"It's got me this far alive. The underarm setup I wear when I'm off duty is a speed release. If I'd been wearing this thing New Year's Eve I wouldn't be standing here talking to you now. Also we got a regulation against magnums. That hogleg could get a cop busted."

"You got to admit it's photogenic." Corky worked the big .44 out of the holster, nickel-plated with a mother-of-pearl grip, as big as a T-square. "The boys in Special Effects goose up the charge for night scenes. Powder flare's brighter. We've got a firefight on page twenty-three that's going to make you forget every fireworks show you ever saw." He socked the revolver back into its sheath and thrust the tangle of straps into Art's hands. "Thanks for the information, Paul. Just keep on calling 'em as you see 'em. Okay, let's try to get one decent take in before Mr. Sun goes down."

The actors stood on their marks and began the scene for the cameras. *The Godfather* guy tripped over his lines halfway through and they went back to the beginning. On the next try the soap queen started giggling and they took it again from the last cue. Technical problems spoiled the next two takes. By then tension was high and Corky called a five-minute break while a woman from makeup fixed the actress's eye shadow and the sound crew checked their equipment. A lighting technician with a walrus moustache peered at the lowering sun, shook his head, and spat a wad of pink gum at the base of a street-lamp.

Kubicek wondered when the glamor kicked in.

Everything went well right up to the end of Take Seven. The actors were wrapping up the scene when an ear-splitting screech turned every head on the street in the direction of the police barricades. A gold Chevy Nova pitted with rust slammed through the brightly painted sawhorses, scattering uniformed officers and spectators from its path. Kubicek's .38 was in his hand before the car came to a grinding halt just short of the curb where the two actors were standing transfixed. The pale, confused face of a girl not much older than sixteen showed behind the windshield.

In the silence that slammed down after the smoking tires stopped rolling, the clatter of something metallic striking the pavement swung heads back the other way, where Officer Horace Hyde had dropped his service piece trying to claw it out of his prop shoulder holster. One of the other cops-turned-extras, younger and childish looking in a suit from Wardrobe that hung on him like an awning, had snagged the hammer of his own .38 in the lining of the coat and he was still struggling to extricate it.

Holstering his gun, Kubicek caught Corky's

eye as he was getting out of his canvas chair.
"See, that's why," he told the director.

When he got home he found a note from his wife in the kitchen, informing him there was a pot of homemade chop suey in the refrigerator that only needed to be micro-waved. He was famished, but chose instead to warm it up the slow way on top of the gas stove. The Amana Radarange, a square silver box the size of a chopping block, had scared the living shit out of him ever since a pound of butter his wife was melting inside had exploded, setting the neighbor's dog to barking and lathering the inside of the oven with grease. The device had been an anni-versary present from his father-in-law.

While the chop suey was warming, he went through the living room into the bedroom without turning on a light, put his revolver and belt clip into the strongbox, and locked it out of long habit, even though his daughter was grown and out of the house. He peeled off his suit coat and hung it on the back of the wooden chair and on top of it his necktie, whose knot he merely pulled loose so he could slip it off over his head. His shirt clung to his back like wet cellophane.

"Paul?" Jean Kubicek's voice was sleepy, muffled by the bedcovers.

"Go back to sleep," he said. "I'm coming to bed right after I eat."

"No, you're not. You'll go to the toilet first and read the paper for an hour. What time is it? I thought you'd be home early."

"Corky wanted to shoot the shift changing at Thirteen Hundred. The eight o'clock came and went while he was still setting up, so we had to wait till midnight. That picture shit ain't such a soft spot after all."

"Umm-hmmm. Oh, someone called from Special Investigations."

"Shit. That pest Battle?"

"No, Stilwell, I think his name was. He wants you to call him back. It's on the pad by the phone."

"Okay, go to sleep."

In the living room he switched on a lamp. On the ruled tablet next to the black telephone on the walnut stand, Jean had written Stilwell's name and home telephone number. He dialed it and sank into his old green recliner. Stilwell answered on the second ring, a surprise. He was sure he'd catch him asleep.

"Wally, it's Paul."

"Yeah, I been waiting for your call. Saw you on Channel Seven at eleven o'clock, back there in the crowd. What happened out there?"

"Not a lot. Some little cunt got confused and drove through a barricade. She got a ticket. What's the rumpus?"

"Just keeping you posted. Looks like Battle's got a line on your speedboat pilot."

"Yeah?"

"The black son of a bitch is playing it close to the vest, but I got it out of his notebook tonight when he went to the can. Got a pencil?"

He picked up the pen Jean had used and swiveled the pad. Listening, he wrote. "Common spelling Russell? Okay. Littlejohn two words or one? Got it. Pinky's Marina, shit, I know that place. Thanks, Wally. I owe."

After hanging up, he sat chewing on the end of the pen and reading what he'd written until his nose told him the chop suey was burning. He tore off the sheet and folded it into his shirt pocket on the way to the kitchen.

Chapter Fourteen

Junius Harrison's mother lived in one half of a duplex in East Detroit on the Stephens Highway, a steep-pitched frame house that had started out Georgian sometime in the twenties, lost its distinctive colonnaded front porch in either the Depression when lumber was negotiable tender for groceries or the postwar period when the stripped-down ranch home became the ideal to emulate, and acquired Victorian gingerbread probably during the nostalgia binge of the sixties. Charlie Battle, who had flirted with a career in architecture, thought it construction's answer to the geological timetable: Slice into it, examine the substrata, and it would tell you everything you needed to know about the peripatetic nature of American culture in the twentieth century. It had been painted recently, gray with red trim, and there was a strip of lawn in front and flower boxes in the windows, heaped with fresh snow like scoops of ice cream. An almost desperately well-kept place in a community constantly striving to avoid being sucked down the same hole as its much larger namesake to the south.

Battle stamped the snow off his Totes on the freshly swept concrete stoop and used the brass door-knocker. After half a minute the isinglass curtain on the other side of the stained-glass pane stirred. He made his face look innocent in the few seconds it took for the person inside to determine whether to unlock the door. Finally a latch snapped and it swung inward.

"Mrs. Harrison?"

It came out sounding more uncertain than intended. This tall woman in a knitted ivory dress caught at the waist with a wide black leather belt didn't fit his picture of a grieving mother, although her expression was serious enough. Her hair, grayed only slightly, was pinned up in patrician waves and the powder on her face, matched perfectly to her nutmeg coloring, was skillfully applied. It was a long face without creases, wide in the mouth and mahogany-eyed.

"My name is Randolph," she said. "Mr. Harrison was my first husband."

"I'm sorry. I'm Charles Battle. I'm investigating Junius Harrison's death." He showed her his shield.

"My son was no criminal."

"I wouldn't be here if I were sure he was."

"The department you work for is. The day after it happened a dozen police officers came here with a search warrant. They said they were looking for stolen merchandise. I made them wait outside while I called my brother-in-law. He's a paralegal. He came over and followed them through every room, just in case they tried to plant something. The sergeant in charge was angry he was here. He threatened to arrest him for obstruction. I really think if he wasn't here they'd have 'found' something. But they went away empty-handed."

This was news to Battle, who had seen nothing about a search in the file. "Do you remember the sergeant's name?"

"I'm sure my brother-in-law has it. I can call him."

"Thank you. I can come back later if this is a bad time. I tried to call, but your line was busy."

"I took the phone off the hook. The newspapers and TV have been calling ever since it happened." She stepped aside to let him in.

The living room looked as if it had been done over in the recent past, not in keeping with any of the house's stages of evolution. A pale orange shag carpet hugged the walls and there was a lot of heavy dark wood furniture rounded at the edges to look like aged oak. Pictures of someone he assumed to be Junius taken at various ages crowded an octagonal table with a shelf for magazines: *Ebony*, *Argosy*, *Better Homes and Gardens*, *TV Guide*.

Another feature of the room looked as solid and rough-hewn as the furniture, but unlike the furniture gave no impression that it was merely veneer. As Battle entered, this fixture stirred and rose from a wood-framed sofa upholstered in red velour.

"Mr. Battle, this is Quincy Springfield."

The chairman of the American Ethiopian Congress was even bigger than he looked on television — a first for Battle, who usually found the opposite to be true — bull-shouldered and heavy-boned, with a head the size of a medicine ball, a fact which may have influenced his decision to forego the ubiquitous afro in favor of a skinhead cut reminiscent of Malcolm X's. His features were even coarser than the policeman's, and frozen in a brutal scowl, the kind of expression that made even white liberals cross the street when it came into view.

"*Detective* Battle, I think." His voice, light for his size, still had resonance, a byproduct of public speaking. "I couldn't help overhearing."

167

"Just officer. When the investigation's over I go back in uniform."

"Maybe not. If Kubicek walks for murdering Junius."

There was no anger in his tone, only deep conviction. Springfield didn't shake hands. His hands were enormous. The delicate rose-patterned cup and saucer he was holding looked like part of a child's tea set pinched between his thick fingers. Without thinking he could have crushed them to powder, and had probably done a good deal worse in his past life as a mover in the Detroit numbers racket. His flamboyantly tailored bright blue sharkskin suit, another holdover, was a startling incongruity encasing so much personal gravity.

"Murder's an emotional word," Battle said. "When an officer's involved we call it 'deadly force.' I'm here to find out whether it was necessary in this case."

"I believe you, brother."

"Well, thanks for that."

"Don't thank me till you learn something. I believe you when you say you're here to find out what you're here to find out. You're a tame bird dog. You shuffle here and shuffle there and sniff around and bring back what you dug up like a good yard nigger before anybody else can dig it up and your lily-white boss rubs your head and says, 'That's fine, boy, now you go put on a clean pair of overalls and drive the commissioner's wife down to Hudson's.' And what you brought goes into a locked file if they don't just haul off and throw it out and Paul Kubicek goes right on back to what he does best, which is what John Nichols calls keeping the peace and what the history books call genocide, and when the black brothers and sisters howl, Massah John he say, 'We put a darky on the case, what more you people want?' " He threw an internal switch and shut off the redneck honk. "They still lynching us, boy. Only now they got one of us fetching along the rope."

"I'd have more faith in that if you stumbled over some of the words," Battle said. "I get the feeling I'm just a guinea pig for something you've got planned for a bigger audience."

"I'm no public speaker. All I got on my side is a great big mad. I don't guess you're old enough to remember a fellow who called himself Mahomet. That was a speaker."

"I remember hearing about him. I never heard him speak. I was in junior high when he was shot."

"They gunned him down like an animal on Kercheval in sixty-six. You know what he done wrong? He tried to stop a riot. He stopped three bullets instead. We laid him

169

out in one of his white suits. Mayor Cavanagh and Governor Romney came to the funeral. See, they knowed how much us people like all them flowers and big cars and hymn-singing and carrying on. It didn't take, though. Well, you know what happened in sixty-seven."

"You're the first person I've met who thought the riots accomplished anything. Forty-three families might give you an argument."

"Saints, the lot of 'em. Martyrs to the cause. Like Junius. He's dead, and he looks better than you. Not every Jew followed Jesus, but none of them put on Roman armor neither."

Despite everything Battle found himself liking Springfield. It was clear the activist had some education, which he hid behind his studied street talk, and that made the officer wary; still, he believed in what he said. Battle had heard mayors, city council members, and the police department brass speak and it had always sounded like something that had been put up in jars and labeled and taken down and opened for this or that particular occasion. He remembered the solemn dignity with which his Uncle Anthony would outfit himself, inside and out, for the travesty of the professional wrestling ring, the way he would channel all the anger and frustration of a circumscribed life into a ceremony whose major moves and outcome were preordained according to the receipts at the gate, and he respected the pride if not its application. Certainly Battle felt a stronger bond with this hoodlum-turned-rabble-rouser than he did with the other members of the shooting team at 1300.

Mrs. Randolph's voice startled him. He'd forgotten she was in the room. "Please sit down. I never saw a fistfight start between two men who were sitting."

Springfield lowered himself back onto the sofa. He actually looked shamefaced. Battle chose a rocker with the marks of a chisel manufactured into its frame. Mrs. Randolph offered coffee. He seldom drank coffee after breakfast, but he accepted. He remembered his first partner telling him that saying yes cut through a lot of bullshit. His hostess filled another dainty cup from a china carafe on a matching tray on the coffee table. He said yes again to cream and sugar and sat back balancing the cup and saucer. Junius hadn't come from the sort of household that usually bred armed robbers.

His mother perched on the edge of a straight chair and rested her hands in her lap. They were calloused at the fingertips, not from handling porcelain dinnerware. Battle had noticed, too, that her face was scarred at the corner of one eye and to the right of the center of her lower lip. She had covered the marks expertly with makeup, but they were raised slightly and showed when the light struck her at certain angles.

"Mr. Springfield is here at my invitation," she said. "I've asked him to speak at the memorial service for Junius and he's accepted."

"I hadn't heard a service was planned."

Springfield said, "You weren't meant to. The police aren't invited."

"My boy was cut up by the coroner. His brain was taken out and weighed and put back. Three funeral directors told me they could cover the stitches so no one would know they were there. But I would. I had the body cremated as soon as it was released to me. The urn will be present at the service." Her face was tight. The hands in her lap were balled into fists, and Battle had the impression she was holding herself together from inside with invisible cords wrapped around them.

"I'd like to ask you about your son's juvenile record."

"Now, how do you suppose I knowed that's the first thing you'd ask about?" Springfield said.

"The question was for Mrs. Randolph."
He waited.

"He was nineteen, attending classes at Wayne State," she said. "A policeman stopped him on Washington — failure to yield — and searched him. The prosecutor said he was carrying too much marijuana for his own use. He went to Jackson for three years and served every day."

"Busted for selling grass. There's a profile of your hard-line criminal."

Battle said, "Jackson's been known to turn out a few. What was your son like when he came out?"

Her lips formed words that found no voice. "Changed," she said finally. She looked down at her hands.

"Was he bitter?"

"Now, why should he be?" Springfield said. "He only done more time than Billy the Kid for passing out reefers to his classmates. I imagine he was happy they didn't give him the chair."

"You'll get your chance to talk at the service, Springfield. Right now I'm talking with Mrs. Randolph."

"Not bitter. Just — changed. You'd have to have known him before he went to prison and after he came out to understand what I mean. He used to sing around the house

173

all the time — Lord, but that boy would sing! His father had this old seventy-eight of Tennessee Ernie Ford singing 'Sixteen Tons.' Junius asked us to play it over and over when he was little. You never knew when he'd bust out with that song."

Battle smiled. "Did he have a good voice?"

"Lord, no! Owen — that was Junius's father — he always said that boy couldn't string two notes together if he drilled holes in them. In high school, when everyone was starting bands, he taught himself to play the guitar, put a down payment on an electric one with what he made cutting grass, and got some boys together in the garage. It being our garage, he made himself lead singer. Well, they rehearsed a few times, and then one Saturday nobody showed up. Junius went out to find out why. He never said what they told him, but he returned that guitar to the store two days later. Owen went back to parking the car in the garage Saturdays." She blinked. "I guess you think that was the end of his recording career."

"It doesn't sound like the Stevie Wonder Story," Battle said.

"Wait." She got up and went through an open doorway into a hall lined with pictures.

After an awkward moment Battle broke the silence between him and Springfield. "I

174

caught you on the news the other day."

"Which channel?"

"Seven."

"They cut out some of my best stuff. Channel Two ran the whole thing."

"Guess they got tired of Nixon."

"Everybody's tired of Nixon."

Battle glanced down the hall, then turned his head to look at the staircase to the second story of the duplex. When he turned back, Springfield was watching him.

"Don't waste your time looking for Randolph," the activist said. "Land mine blowed his legs off in some ratshit place called Phu Loc in sixty-eight. He died in a tent hospital while the medics was busy wrapping up some white colonel's gouty big toe."

"Was that before or after Junius got busted?"

"Before." He moved a shoulder. "Yeah, I asked. I conducted my own investigation. Couldn't afford to have Junius Harrison blow up in my face. You got to pick your symbols carefully."

"So you admit you're using him."

"How long you been black? We been getting used ever since we put down our spears and picked up a hoe. Difference here is I'm using one of us to make things better for the rest of us, not to make sure the cotton gets to market and Miz Scarlett gets her new buggy."

" 'Consider the end.' That it?"

"Brother, there ain't no end."

"Randolph's pension pays for all this?"

"Just part. Mrs. Randolph fronts for MichCon with a clipboard, going from door to door asking don't they want to ditch that ugly oil tank in the back yard and hook up to the line. Junius picked up the rest with his pay from the law office. Guess she'll have to move soon. I bet Sergeant Kubicek has his own place."

"You're right. Let's hang the son of a bitch."

Springfield didn't smile.

Mrs. Randolph returned carrying an eight-by-ten manila envelope. She flipped up the lid of a large console stereo, another item of rustic veneer over particle board, and transferred a flat black plastic disk with a big hole in the center from the envelope to the turntable. After a moment a light baritone issued from the fabric-covered speakers, wavering on the low notes and cracking on the high notes of "Mama Didn't Lie." It appeared James Brown had nothing to worry about from the Detroit quarter.

Mrs. Randolph remained standing next to the machine until the song ended, then wiped both eyes with the heels of her hands and lifted the 45-rpm record from the fat spindle. She walked over to the rocker and showed it to Battle. The typewritten legend on the yellow label read:

JUNIUS HARRISON
TO MARIAN HARRISON RANDOLPH
HAPPY MOTHER'S DAY 1972

"Boy loved his mama," Springfield said. "There's your profile of a big-time stick-up artist."

Battle looked up into the woman's face. "Mrs. Randolph, would you mind telling me where you got those facial scars?"

Chapter Fifteen

There were no pure races.

Wolf, whose real name was Andrew Porterman, was three quarters Ottawa on his mother's side and God only knew what on his father's, although he suspected German-Irish. The chromosomal lottery had determined that the Indian side take precedence in his features and coloring, and so after eighteen years of cursing that particular piece of luck he had chosen to embrace his maternal heritage, growing his hair to his shoulders and attending classes in his native language and ceremonial dances at St. Ignace, twelve miles from his birthplace in Michigan's Upper Peninsula. He was thoroughly steeped in the tribal way of life by the time he hitchhiked to San Francisco in the fall of 1969 and boarded one of three boats that November for the unlawful occupation of Alcatraz by militant members of the American Indian Movement.

He never was clear on just why the island was chosen, other than that it had been left derelict ever since the prison closed down in 1963 and no one was there to stop them. Certainly neither the pile of rock anchored like a petrified turd in the busy harbor nor the decaying structure that stood upon it held any cultural or historical significance to native Americans, whose ancestors had been the first to abandon the archipelago as soon as it became apparent it would support neither crops nor game. A far better choice — and a more convenient one to Wolf — would have been Mackinac Island, site of the capture of Fort Michillimackinac and the most conspicuous victory in Chief Pontiac's seven-tribe conspiracy to drive the British from the Northwest Territory in 1763. But November was a bleak and bitter month on Lake Huron, and unlike the warriors who followed the great Ottawa leader, the braves of the late twentieth century preferred to dance around their campfires off the coast of California.

Wolf, who had settled upon his lupine name somewhere on the road between Peoria and Des Moines, had enjoyed himself tremendously during the first days of the occupation. He had always found the Indians of northern Michigan a dour lot, many of them alcoholics who found no pleasure in drinking, only obliteration, professional fishermen who denigrated the white man's wasteful ways while emptying the lakes of fish with the great gill nets that they alone were allowed to use because of the old treaties; miserable creatures mostly, ashamed of their ancestry, taking out their black moods on their women and dying with enlarged livers before age forty. By contrast, the Bay Area tribes were fierce, proud, and fun-loving. Their moccasins sprouted wings as they whirled around campfires of brush and driftwood. They shared Black Jack and Thunderbird bottles and peyote buttons, and under the mellow influence of these substances they told the ancient stories handed down by their great-great-grandfathers of old wars and dead gods and hunting the buffalo. Wolf, who from his researches knew that Utopian society to be as straightlaced as any Victorian village, was gratified to learn that the flower children of San Francisco had had their influence, and spent one particularly memorable night in Al Capone's cell with three women ranging in age from seventeen to thirty-two.

But the Brave New World could not sustain itself. During the second week, old tribal enmities erupted into fistfights, a gang of button-heads vandalized the office of the warden for no other reason than that the defunct post represented authority, smashing windows, ripping out light fixtures, and shitting on the floor, and Wolf acquired a severe case of crabs. When he caught a Seneca picking his pocket for cash to score a lid off a Cheyenne with connections to Jimmy Lanza, he felt he'd had his share of the native life. The morning fog rolled in and he shipped out aboard a stolen launch. As soon as his feet hit pavement his thumb went out for any transportation pointed east.

He didn't go all the way back home. The Upper Peninsula was as rocky as Alcatraz and just as incapable of supporting life, or what he thought of as life. The copper and iron deposits and virgin pines that had fueled the mining and lumber industries of the last century were gone. Tourism shut down during the seven long months of winter, and was never all that good in summer in a place that was largely unknown outside Michigan. Fishing was backbreaking work and he loathed the stench. Detroit, coming off the ropes at last from the one-two punch of the Edsel disaster and the massive effort to re-gear to meet the safety consciousness of the late sixties, was hiring, and Wolf went to work assembling the great lumbering barge that the T-bird had become at the Ford plant in Rawsonville.

A wildcat strike ended that. The cost of living, goosed up by phases one through three of Nixon's surefire plan to end inflation, soared to Pluto while wages stalled on the launching pad. The United Auto Workers brass post-Walter Reuther, grown fat on their seats on the boards of the Big Three, declined to authorize a strike, and so Wolf and a couple of hundred of his fellow employees hit the bricks on their own. Scab labor stepped in, the cars kept on getting made. Wolf and another striker procured awls and divided the employee parking lot between them, singling out tires on cars belonging to temporary workers. The other striker was nowhere around when the sheriff's deputies came in. Wolf drew 180 days in the Washtenaw County Jail for malicious destruction of property.

There he became friendly with Dexter Flood, who was coasting through his last month on a ninety for exposing himself to a policewoman masquerading as a school bus driver. Flood confessed that he had plummeted from his pinnacle as an armorer with the Black Panthers when he fried his brains on a combination of acid and Preparation H, self-administered anally, and attempted to hold up the downtown office of the National Bank of Detroit with a staple gun. He did three years in Jackson for that, at the end of which he wasn't good for much beyond running the occasional errand for the Panthers, an organization disintegrating just as rapidly after taking heavy hits from FBI commandos in face shields and flak jackets. In the lunchroom one day toward the end of his sentence, Dexter asked Wolf if he wanted to meet Wilson McCoy.

The name was vaguely familiar to the Indian, who associated it with the civil unrest of the time just past. "Isn't he in prison or something?"

"No. *Hell,* no! Oh, they done busted him once, but you don't pen up a brother like Wilson for long. He's one of the ten."

"Ten what? He part of the Crest test?"

"No. *Shit,* no!" — nothing was just *no* with Dexter — "Most Wanted, *that* ten! Three months on the feds' hit parade come September."

"Well, how do I meet him if the FBI can't find him?"

"Oh, they know where he is. They just too chickenshit to go in after him. Not yours truly, though. I got the bona fides."

"I don't see you using them to get out that door." The door in question, leading from the lunchroom to the main corridor, stood open, but with a guard the size of Saginaw Harbor standing in front of it.

"I go through it next week. After that I

183

don't come back till I pick you up. That's when I take you to see Wilson."

"Why do I want to see Wilson? He got a job for me? What's it pay?"

"Nothing. To start."

Those were the last words on the subject until the day he found Dexter waiting for him outside the jail door. Wolf didn't recognize him at first out of coveralls. In their place he wore a black windbreaker and beret to match over a navy turtleneck, unpressed khakis, and black high-top combat boots polished to a mirror finish. He shook Wolf's hand, escorted him to a green Chevy Nova gone lacy with rust around the wheel wells, and drove nonstop from Ann Arbor to Detroit, talking the whole way.

"Man, I fell into soft warm shit when I took up with Wilson. That indecent exposure thing was an old rap. That's what I was down to when he pulled me in and put me to work. See, he can't leave the neighborhood on account of the feds is waiting for him, so somebody gots to go out and round up shit. You know: eats, clothes, toilet paper. That shit."

"Girls?"

"Sometimes, only not so much now. Now old J. Edgar's got bitches on the payroll Wilson's scared he'll see a badge when he pulls off their panties. So I expect he uses his hand. I don't spend a whole hell of a lot of time thinking about that part."

"What's in it for me?"

"Room and board, for one. Where you staying?"

"I had a furnished room. I guess I don't now. I haven't paid rent in six months."

"I gots me a cot off Wilson's room. Good stereo in there and a color TV and fridge. Pop the top off a Stroh's, watch *Columbo*, and groove out to Aretha."

"Sounds like a good gig. Why share?"

"Man needs a day off now and then. I can't take a bitch to the room — freaks Wilson out on account of what I said before — and I ain't like him, whacking off's like chink food, I'm horny again a hour later. Also I miss the blind pigs. Wilson stopped going when he thought one of the brothers tending bar at the Center for Community Action tailed him home one night. I figure you and I could trade off."

"If he likes me."

"He already likes you."

"I must have more charisma than I thought. We haven't met yet."

"I done told him you was injun. Injuns got more reason to hate feds than the brothers, to his way of thinking. You know, losing America, that shit. You're as good as in."

"You said there was room and board in it for one. What's two?"

Dexter grinned at the windshield. "Well, hell, the honor! Wilson's the Man. He Jesse James, Billy the Kid, Johnny Dillinger, and Geronimo all rolled into one. Shit, who wouldn't jump at the chance to be a chunk of history?"

At first, Wolf's brush with history promised to be short. Although, as Dexter explained, an extension cord had been run into the living quarters on the top floor from the next building, the room where Wilson McCoy received them on the floor below was lit only by a Coleman lantern standing on the Formica table behind which the black revolutionary sat. McCoy looked far older than his twenty-two years that summer of 1970, hollow-cheeked, vague-eyed, and — the newcomer suspected — balding beneath his Panthers beret. As the interview went on, McCoy lit reefers off one another from a row of them on the table without offering any to his visitors. When Dexter piped up to answer one of the questions put to the applicant, McCoy barked at him to leave the room. Alone with Wolf, the man behind the table asked him if he was queer.

"Are you?"

"That's none of your fucking business!"

McCoy snapped.

"Same answer."

"I got nothing against Indians, but you can't trust a fag. You know Hoover's a fag."

"I didn't know."

"Well, he is. He only hires fags because he's afraid his agents will spill confidential information to their wives."

"But a lot of agents are married."

"That's just for looks. You don't look queer, but jail's been known to turn a man around."

"Not in six months."

"You still haven't answered my question."

Wolf unzipped his fly and pulled out his cock.

He still treasured the look on Wilson McCoy's face, the only time he had seen him look truly surprised. His eyes flicked down, lingered, then back up to Wolf's face when he realized they were lingering. And the Indian learned then that black people can indeed blush. His mouth worked, he glanced toward the door through which Dexter had left. Wolf really thought the longest-lasting fugitive on the FBI's Most Wanted list was afraid he was going to be raped.

The Indian looked down at his limp phallus. "It isn't very hard, is it? Now tell me, could any self-respecting fag show off his prick to a stud like Wilson McCoy and avoid getting a boner?"

For the first and last time in their association, McCoy laughed.

"Put it back," he said. "You made your point. When can you move in?"

"Right now. I left some clothes in my old room, but I bet they sold them to a secondhand store by now for back rent."

McCoy rolled over on his right hip, pried a thick fold of bills from a back pocket, and flipped it onto the table. "Buy what you need out of that. Your first job's waiting for you when you get back."

"What's that?"

"Throw Dexter out. I'm sick of looking at the perverted son of a bitch."

That was more than two years ago, and Wolf had almost walked out himself more times than he could count. He had never known anyone to be more caught up in his own orbit than Wilson McCoy. The former Panther — he could only be spoken of as former, because he had had no contact with the rest of that decaying society in all the time Wolf had been with him, or with almost anyone else, for that matter — seemed convinced that every member of every law-enforcement organization in the country was spending every conscious moment on the effort to bring Wilson McCoy to justice. He pored over each issue of the *News*, *Free Press*, and the national news magazines Wolf brought him, and when there was no mention of him — which was usually the case — he was certain that a blackout had been declared to cover an all-out campaign to pry him loose from his safe house. At first Wolf thought him paranoid. In time he realized Wilson was far less afraid of being caught than he was of being forgotten, and that he had constructed the fantasy of *The United States v. Wilson McCoy* out of his own superinflated, easily torn ego. And as Wolf watched this sworn enemy of the white conservative establishment assembling his meager press clippings like some half-remembered starlet, he knew, ahead of all the pundits, that the sixties were over.

Why he had remained loyal to a pile of quivering self-delusion was harder to understand. He supposed it had to do with his lost heritage. Try as he might, the twentieth century had destroyed his ability to believe in the old gods; his exposure to others of his kind, desperately denying the gulf of decades that separated them from the ancient ways, had made him feel alone in a way he had never felt before he went in search of his origins. He had no tribe, no village of his own to look after and to look after him. What he had was Wilson McCoy. It was a poor enough totem, but unlike the legends this one had substance. It didn't die down with the coals when the sun came up, and it could be depended upon to remain, which was more than could be said about union solidarity. Wilson was there. It didn't matter that he had no choice. Better to worship the twig caught in the snag than the limb speeding by in the current.

No, there were no pure races.

All this fluttered through Wolf's mind as he waited for the public telephone to ring outside the emergency room at Harper Grace Hospital. Standing guard by the instrument, he had fended off two people who wanted to use it. One, an old woman leaning on a cane who had come in a few minutes earlier with an old man whom Wolf took to be her husband, called the Indian a name in a language that might have been Hungarian and hobbled back to her seat. The other, a man about Wolf's age and weight but three inches taller, a heavy lifter by the look of him, had stormed up demanding he surrender the receiver, then shut his mouth when Wolf reached conspicuously into his jeans pocket for the buck knife he carried whenever he left his magnum in the car, and joined the line behind the teenage girl who was using the only other telephone. That was the thing about Detroit: Go for any place where you might be keeping a weapon and the gesture was understood.

Calling Wilson was a chore the Indian tried to avoid. No lines ran to the condemned building where the wanted man lived and worked, so Wolf had to dial the number of the rib place around the corner and wait more often than not for one of the restaurant's two full-time employees to free himself up long enough to go fetch Wilson. Ten minutes was the record. While he was waiting, the Indian slid a sample vial of Brut from the inside pocket of his quilted vest and slapped a third of its contents onto his neck and cheeks. Any time he went too long between applications he smelled fish.

After eighteen minutes the telephone rang. "I hope to hell this is good," Wilson said without greeting. "I froze my favorite testicle off getting down here."

As if you ever used the son of a bitch, Wolf thought. Aloud he said, "Opal Ogden's at Harper Grace. Her mother came with her by ambulance an hour ago."

"What's she got, honky's disease?"

"Pneumonia, they think. Anyway that's

what I overheard. I didn't want to draw attention to myself by asking. If they hold her it'll probably be at Hutzel. That's the children's facility here."

"She going to croak?"

"I doubt it." Actually pneumonia scared the shit out of him. He had seen it carry off relatives and acquaintances in epidemic numbers. The Upper was a severe place, and especially hard on the constitutions of a people given to alcoholism. But the Crownover-Ogden thing was the first real action Wolf had persuaded Wilson to take part in as long as they'd been together. He wasn't about to discourage him. "I'm thinking this could be a break for us."

Wilson said nothing, but Wolf could hear him breathing. He went ahead.

"By now the Ogden place is screwed down tighter than Fort Knox. Casing the house all over again to see what they've done will take another six weeks."

"Time enough for 'em to get lazy. We talked about that."

"*You* talked about it. I said at the start we had to do this fast or forget it."

"I ain't in no hurry."

"You should be. We don't know that Piper will hold the merchandise six weeks."

"Oh, he'll hold it. After what happened

here a couple weeks back he'll hold it between his knees."

"That razor of yours won't reach to Pontiac."

"You got wheels. There ain't no FBI paper out on you."

"I didn't hire on for that shit," Wolf said. "Listen. The stuff's burning a hole in his supplier's pocket. Once Piper takes possession of the merch he's going to move it as fast as he can. The longer he sits on it the better his chances of going to Marion on a federal firearms rap."

"He won't stand trial."

The Hungarian woman was coming his way, clutching the arm of a hospital security officer. The guard was close to sixty, white-haired, with thick glasses and a belly that hung down over his belt buckle. Wolf turned his back on them, shielding the receiver with his body.

"You're not listening," he said. "I'm saying maybe we won't have to wait."

Wilson sucked air, which meant he'd lit a joint.

"I got ears."

Chapter Sixteen

Friday night was Russell's night.

The rest of the brothers and sisters could have Saturday night: Buy a number at Benny's Flamingo Barber Shop on Twelfth, pick up a bottle of Ripple at one of the markets with plywood in the windows since '67, hook a pair of big tits and legs all the way up to her ass on Euclid, groove out to some tenth carbon of Aretha or Little Stevie at the Chit-Chat Lounge, show off that new yellow suit from Didney's Bottom of the Barrel on Burlingame. Sleep it off all day Sunday and back into the coveralls Monday morning. Live one Saturday to the next till you were too old or too full of clap to work, then sit on your welfare checks at the Shrine of the Black Madonna and bitch about your landlord.

Not for Russell. He hated crowds, drinking took too long, and sex never went right for him somehow, he always wound up disappointed or disappointing his partner. Fridays were quieter and less congested. He stopped off at home after work, changed from his marina clothes into a new pair of striped jeans with flared legs — no fucking bellbottoms — and a sunset-colored shirt with long collar tabs and four buttons on each cuff. On Twelfth he bought a *Chronicle*, read it on a bench in Virginia Park until his connection showed, bought five capsules, and with the prospect of a mellow evening warming his insides, went on to Greenleaf's and finished the newspaper while waiting to be served his ham hocks and rice. The urge was just beginning to claw at his stomach — a pleasant flutter, actually, this early and with the capsules safe in his pocket — when he left the restaurant and stopped to play a little air ball at his favorite basketball court on Clairmount. *Kareem, you better watch your ass.*

The streetlamps plinked on as he was leaving. He was starting to get serious cramps. He'd waited a little too long. He stretched out his arms, spread his fingers. Picked up the pace.

He'd left the Bronco at a vacant service station on Chicago, by a rusting pump frozen at twenty-two cents per gallon. It was his favorite street in the area his parents still referred to as the Black Bottom, with its median of well-kept grass and trees on both sides. As he turned the corner, the door of a big

Plymouth parked against the curb popped open in front of him. He stopped short, then started around it.

The man behind the wheel came out fast for his bulk. A vise closed on his wrist and drew it across his middle, pivoting him. His back hit the side of the car hard enough to empty his lungs. Before he could fill them, a thick hard forearm pressed against his throat, shutting off his windpipe. Instantly he was strangling.

The burst of breath in his face was hot and sour with beer and bad digestion. "Russell, Russell. You shouldn't run when there's ice on the street. You could break your fucking neck."

He was trying to identify the voice when the hand holding his wrist let go. Before he could react, something blunt drove deep into his belly. The street went red and white. His bladder let go. His knees liquefied and he grasped at the arm across his throat. In his last conscious moment he thought it was the shits what a man would reach out for to keep himself from slipping beneath the surface of his own urine.

PART THREE

The Taking of Opal Ogden

Chapter Seventeen

After six years, Joe Piper wondered when he would come to think that his house was worth the crap he had gone through to build it.

For two years after the death of his first wife Maureen, the gun dealer had effectively gone on living in one room of the little house they had shared on Trumbull. Unable to sleep in their old bedroom, he had camped out on the sofa, fully intending to move back in after he had sold or given away their five-piece Joshua Doore bedroom set and donated Maureen's clothes to the K of C. Only he never got around to it. A chill gripped him every time he passed the uninhabited room on the second floor. When he could no longer bear to climb the stairs, he bought new clothes to replace the ones in their closet. Finally he sold the house and every stick of furniture in it to a well-dressed black real estate agent from Redford. He knew the man was only looking to bring down the housing values in the predominantly Irish neighborhood by renting the place to a black family, after which he would acquire the adjoining properties for a fraction of their former value and sell the lots to the city for parking for nearby Tiger Stadium, but he didn't care; although he had to stop going to the Shamrock Bar for a while after one of his old neighbors offered to throw a bowl of peanuts into the face of "the nigger-loving bastard" if he attempted to take a seat in the establishment.

The next year found him relatively contented, renting an apartment in one of the newer complexes on the northwest side and dealing guns and explosives out of a barn he leased in Washtenaw County from one stupid son of a bitch of a German farmer who believed him when he said he sold bottled salsa to Mexican restaurants. Then he met Dolly, nearly half his age and twice as pretty on her worst day as Maureen was on her best, God rest her immortal soul, and almost before he knew it he was getting married again and throwing himself into hock for thirty years on a 2,800-square-foot pile of redwood and fieldstone in a glorified trailer park of a walled subdivision in Pontiac. Or rather the promise of one, because when he laid down his $23,900 deposit there wasn't but one house in the tract, a model unit complete with Palladian windows, a slate-gray kitchen, and underground sprinklers in the front *and* back yards.

By the time the house was finished, four months later than the projected completion date, Joe and Dolly Piper were barely speaking to each other. He had sold most of his school and hospital bonds, a portfolio he'd fondly expected to see him through a comfortable old age, to cover the closing costs at the bank, and having been overcharged, duplicate-billed, double-talked, piggybacked, raked off, skimmed, scalped, skewered, shilled, and taken to the cleaners on every item from the staircase in the front hall to the porcelain knobs on the closet in the laundry, the lord of the manor decided he had too much conscience ever to go into legitimate enterprise.

The first jolt was small but irritating. Ceremoniously putting away their first two sacks of groceries in the new house, the Pipers found that none of the cupboard shelves in the kitchen was tall enough to contain a cereal box standing up. By the end of that day, faced with windows that either wouldn't open or refused to stay up, a door that swung the wrong way so that the person entering the room had to walk around it to operate the wall switch, and an almost studied lack of straight lines and level surfaces anywhere on the premises, the prospect of having to lay their Post Toasties horizontal for the rest of their lives hardly seemed worth mentioning. It was as if a construction firm that had been in business since 1936, and whose reception room walls were papered over with awards and citations, had suddenly and with breathtaking thoroughness come down with advanced senility.

Flushed, however, with the fever of ownership and a little high on turpentine fumes and the odor of fresh sawdust, the couple had shrugged off each unpleasant discovery. They agreed that in time none of the things would matter.

They mattered.

Six years later, as he sat drinking Cutty-and-water in front of some dumbass cop show in the room he called the living room and Dolly insisted on referring to after the brochures as the lounging area, he had only to turn his head a quarter to the left to see the fireplace whose sunken hearth he had specifically requested be raised to create an extra seat, while a full turn to the right would confirm that the blue Mexican tiles Dolly had ordered for the foyer had during the process of installation magically transformed themselves into wall-to-wall carpeting over plywood; and he saw again the curl on the kid contractor's fuzzy upper lip and heard his bullshit Boston accent as he pointed out that since neither of these details was on the work order, Mr. Piper must have mistaken his *intention* to discuss them with the act of doing so. The changes would of course be made, but Mr. Piper must understand that he will be charged for the extra labor and material. Mr. Piper was too gentle-mannered, with his new wife at his side, to tell the little prick to invest some of his own labor and shove the material up his pimply Harvard ass. He often thought his sanity, during those next two years of working evenings and weekends to increase business and cover the mortgage payments, depended upon the belief that some of the people who wound up standing in front of the guns he sold were bound to be in construction.

For all that, the house was a showplace. Joe Piper had to employ all his Irish charm to keep the woman who organized the local home tour from adding the house to the itinerary, and once *House & Garden* had called. Dolly was disappointed, but she understood the necessity of avoiding attention. Photos and floor plans of houses where the IRS and burglars of the community imagined valuable guns were kept made their jobs a little too easy for the homeowner's comfort. It was a handsome place to begin with, and Dolly Piper had worked miracles with the interior details. Her husband had never lived in a house to compare with it; but more and more his thoughts went back to that little brick saltbox on Trumbull, with its faded wallpaper and pervading scents of corned beef and cabbage, and the gone past struck him in the chest like a blow from a baseball bat. That house had been one of a group built and owned by Big Jim Dolan, an old-time political boss who believed in keeping his family around him for their protection and his. From its cramped attic to the dugout basement Joe Piper had felt the old fixer's presence: big-bellied, red-whiskered, stinking of whiskey and cigars, secure in an environment that had remained fundamentally unchanged between County Cork and Detroit, and safer in the three steps that separated him from the street than Joe Piper felt inside his ring of burglar alarms and closed-circuit cameras. It was a world that had vanished with the onset of Prohibition, buried as deeply beneath the rubble of three wars as Troy. Now the house itself was a memory, even its basement filled in and covered with asphalt.

Change. It seemed to him the world kept on turning, and every time it turned it leaned on him.

Immersed in this sour reflection, he jumped when the telephone rang. On TV, the cop in the fedora with a nose that looked like a baboon's ass was boondocking a big black Bonneville over one of those ball-busting hills in Frisco while Kirk Douglas's kid chased a dope dealer down an alley filled with dumpsters and the cleanest garbage this side of Beverly Hills. Joe Piper got up and turned off the set, then went over and lifted the receiver.

"Piper, this is Scott."

"I don't know any Scotts. You got the wrong Piper." He started to hang up.

"*Scott,* you bricklaying son of a mick bitch. *Winfield* Scott."

Joe Piper's eyes went to the big glossy picture book of the Civil War lying on his glass coffee table, a gift from Homer Angell. Angell, it had turned out, modeled himself after General Winfield Scott, distinguished veteran of every American war from 1812 through Lee's surrender at Appomattox. Like many of Joe Piper's business contacts, the former militiaman was wary of wiretaps and used the name as a code when identifying himself over the telephone. The gun dealer, who employed a Jap to sweep his house monthly for electronic devices, and who didn't know General Sherman from General Foods, thought it was a dipshit affectation on the part of a man who he was convinced played with toy soldiers in his bedroom.

"Okay, Scott. What's the rumpus?"

"That salsa I picked up for you is giving me heartburn. When can you come get it?"

Puzzled, he turned that one over. He was getting old, having to drag himself out of his reverie to remember the shipment of Ingrams he was arranging for Wilson McCoy. Instinctively he stroked his neck. The bandage had come off finally, but a long thin crusty line remained, tracing the path of the former Black Panther's razor. He wondered what Big Jim would have made of that.

"You'll have to hang on to it for a while," he said. "I don't have the price yet."

"Ordinarily I might, but I've got a bleeding ulcer." Which Joe Piper took to mean Angell was under some kind of surveillance. He hated this cloak-and-dagger shit, everyone talking around corners. If James Bond were genuine he'd be jabbering to himself in the Old Spies' Home by now. "I've got a customer in Argentina willing to meet the market and take delivery next week."

Perón. He'd heard the Fascist asshole was planning a comeback. "We got a deal, Homer."

"Scott. I don't know any Homers. Did I

say this ulcer's about to rupture? Surgery's expensive."

"Who pays for most of your operations, you little shitpot Napoleon?"

Angell made a noise in his nose. "Napoleon. That squirt thought strategy meant outnumbering the enemy twenty-five to one. If Murat hadn't saved his Corsican ass with a suicide charge at Marengo, Waterloo would have come fifteen years early."

"Scotty boy, I don't give a rat's ass. Your market's in Detroit. There's a revolution going on here every night. If you can beat that in South America, my advice is to go ahead and brush up on your fucking *español*." He slammed the receiver into its cradle.

The bell rang again. He walked over to his chair and drained his glass, then came back and answered.

"Josephine speaking."

Angell said, "I might be able to hold things off ten days. That's the absolute limit. After that it's *buenas dias*, Buenos Aires."

Joe Piper glanced at the incredibly tasteful calendar Dolly had hung on the wall next to the kitchen, Tahquamenon Falls rendered in watercolors by an Ann Arbor artist. Suddenly he missed Maureen's pot roast-and-potatoes taste, big clunky crucifixes and fake jade lumps with fringed shades, her high color when she brought home a Day-Glo St. Sebastian on black velvet from a garage sale in Taylor. Grief swept over him in a wave. She had shot herself with a .38 Colt he had held out of a sale lot for their personal protection. From that day to this no firearm had come through his house.

"Give me to the first and I'll see what I can do," he told Angell.

"Two *weeks?*"

"Well, fifteen days. 'All the rest have thirty-one,' remember?"

"That's a long time to live with a bellyache."

"Take Pepto."

After the conversation he went out on the glassed-in porch looking out on the rest of the subdivision and the peaks of the buildings in Pontiac's crumbling downtown beyond. February, Michigan's bleakest and least predictable month, was on its way, casting its steelpoint shadow over the snow-heaped rooftops. Two more months of shoveling and snow tires, not counting the annual St. Patrick's Day blizzard. Big Jim would have embraced St. Patrick's Day with the fervor of a transplanted Dubliner. Joe Piper had never met Dolan, dead some forty years, but he'd seen the old man's photograph in the Shamrock Bar, his big mutton-chopped face above a cruel collar and stickpin, and he could picture him leading the parade on foot in a pressed-paper hat with a shillelagh in his bricklayer's fist. Behind him, perched atop the back seat of an open touring car, would ride the mayor and the chief of police, possibly the governor. Why not? All three owed him their jobs.

In those times, according to Joe Piper's father, the fixers danced jigs in their shirtsleeves and garters with red-headed women to the old music performed by live bands, then met in back rooms. They played cards, larded the air with blue smoke, and propped their feet in big square brogans and pearl-gray spats on the tables, doling out money and favors to their constituents and arguing over who would run their city. Their speech, laced heavily with the Gaelic, throbbed with the bass tremble of a tuba band. Whiskey ran like water. St. Paddy's was Christmas, Easter, and the Fourth of July rolled into one sodden orgy. Now it was just an excuse to swill beer tinted with green vegetable dye and listen to the Rovers. Half the people who dressed up as leprechauns weren't even Irish. Some of them were black. The atmosphere in the Shamrock on that most glorious of days belonged to a Presbyterian wake.

Again Joe Piper's fingers traced the scar

at his throat. More and more now he saw himself as Sebastian in Maureen's bargain painting, his hide pierced at every angle with barbed shafts that glowed in the dark. At those times the wounds felt as tangible as the one he bore in reality. They let in the chill even through the windows of the porch.

He bet that on February second nobody in California gave a shit whether the groundhog saw its shadow or not.

Chapter Eighteen

Weeds made Charlie Battle claustrophobic.

The officer, who had spent hours last autumn drilling holes and installing cedar panels in his four-by-four apartment closet, had once crawled headfirst down a broken sewer pipe in ninety-degree weather to rescue a four-year-old boy who had fallen in and broken his leg, all without breaking a sweat. Yet he found himself laboring for breath less than a minute after climbing down a bank covered with thistles and timothy off Schoolcraft Road. The growth, flattened somewhat by an earlier snowfall and winterkilled yellow, was thick, and he had to stand on tiptoe and fill his lungs with cold air before he could steel himself to go on.

He blamed the condition on fishing vacations with his Uncle Anthony, a lifelong urbanite who equated the wilderness with emancipation. Come the doldrums between wrestling's busy spring season and the fall start-up, he would bundle nephew and tackle into the car at 4:00 A.M. and take off for some northern lake or river that could only be reached by a long trek down a tangled bank. By the time they got to the water, young Charlie would be bleeding from a dozen thorn-scratches, bumpy with insect bites, and itching from poison ivy. In the heat of day the atmosphere became tropical. When the pair started home at sunset, battling their way back through the undergrowth, the air would be as thick as meringue. Invariably fears of suffocation forced the boy to claw through the last few yards of weeds in a panic, gasping for the oxygen and monoxide of the highway.

But he was unwilling to disappoint his uncle, and in twenty years he never missed a fishing vacation. In time he grew to dread the approach of summer. And so he had not been as regretful as he felt he should have when Anthony's deteriorating health caused them to give up the annual trip.

Now here he was again, and the absence of heat, mosquitoes, and noxious plants did little to lift that old sense of oppression. If anything, the knowledge of what awaited him at the base of the shallow slope contributed to it.

The January morning was all hard edges and pewter gray. The culvert, installed thirty years previously to prevent swamp runoff from covering the road, was chalky to the touch, the trickle that came through it frozen solid in a glinty braid. The usual detritus of cigarette filters, spent condoms, and Styrofoam Big Mac coffins was stuck fast to the ground. Even the vapor issuing from the throats of the five men standing near the mouth of the culvert seemed sluggish in the frost, curling spastically in a kind of stop-motion effect. Four of them were in uniform, but only two of the uniforms belonged to the city.

"Charlie, I almost didn't recognize you out of the blue bag." The officer who came partway up the bank to shake his gloved hand was black, and even bulkier-looking than usual in winter issue with a pile-trimmed collar and earflaps on his cap. Matt Kellog of the Public Vehicle Bureau was always fighting to keep his weight below the department maximum.

"I don't expect to be out of it for long, Matt. Thanks for the squeal."

"I broke chain of command there, but what the hell, I'm too young to make commissioner this year. I was reading this boy's name off his driver's license over my walkity-talk when it clicked where I heard it. Hell, it was on this morning's turnout sheet. Gene Grundy told me you was on the shoot team, so I asked for you. What the hell, I never seen none of them 1300 guys' wangs in the shower."

"Nor anywhere else, I hope." Battle had already lost interest in his former academy classmate. He was watching the two men in the uniform of the Wayne County Morgue using fishermen's gestures to argue the best way of getting the seventh man on the scene into the body bag they'd brought.

It would take some doing. Obviously far more limber when placed in the culvert, the corpse had gone into rigor and congealed in a fetal position with its chin tucked into its chest and its arms and legs crossed. Hoarfrost had glazed flesh and fabric a consistent white, making it difficult to determine just where the man left off and his clothing began. Battle could not even be sure the man was black until he was standing over him. Ice crystals glittered in his afro, which the officer was convinced would shatter like a glass lampshade if kicked. He had never before seen a human body frozen solid. The effect was like sculpture, and not at all connected with the mortal condition.

He had to sit on his heels and twist his head to see the crystallized features. At first he thought the identification was a mistake, that this was someone many years older than

Russell Littlejohn, perhaps his father; but it was only the illusion of age created by stalactites of white ice hanging from his eyebrows and the suggestion of a moustache. He recognized the face well enough. And he felt his own face growing haggard.

"OD's my guess. He's got tracks between his fingers. They crawl in any old place once they start feeling all warm and fuzzy."

This was a new voice. Battle rose to face the only other man there wearing plainclothes, a tall lean pale Nordic in a long black Chesterfield and black fur felt snapbrim hat who looked like a Swedish ski instructor. The only thing about him with any color was the end of his narrow nose, which was as red as a Christmas tree bulb. He dabbed at it from time to time with a handkerchief wadded in his gloved palm. In between dabs it dripped freely.

Battle showed his badge and introduced himself. "I'm investigating the shootings at the Ogden mansion New Year's Eve. Littlejohn was wanted for questioning. The BOL went out when he didn't show up at work Monday and hadn't been home."

"I saw the sheet. I put in a call to Lieutenant Zagreb, but I guess you've got more friends on road patrol. Daniel Iniskilling, lieutenant Homicide." He didn't offer his hand.

"We're all in the same boat. Who found him?"

"Couple of kids looking for a place to smoke, though they said they were ice skating. Kellog and Anderson here cruised past and they flagged them down. That was about eight-thirty."

"I don't guess we have time of death."

"The M.E. spent about five minutes. He said to call him when the stiff thaws. That'll be about this time Thursday. The microwave downtown isn't quite big enough."

"Any evidence on the scene of drug use?"

Iniskilling's face screwed up into what might have been an expression of contempt, but he sneezed into the handkerchief. Wiping up: "You can't walk two feet in any direction down here without tripping over a syringe. When Forensics gets through sweeping, this shithole will be clean enough to set aside as a national park. Just in time for the 1980 tourist season."

"If they find a needle with Littlejohn's prints on it I'll eat it."

"Meaning?"

"Meaning what it means. Material witnesses don't just overdose on cue."

"I guess that would be your long experience talking." Iniskilling blew his nose energetically.

"I'm not after your job, Lieutenant. This kid has probably been shooting up for years. It's damn convenient for someone that he'd pick now to lose count. I was getting set to pull him in for questioning."

"Jesus, Officer, I'm glad as hell you're not after my job. I spend most of my time worrying I'll come back from the toilet and find some shitbritches in his first pair of long pants with his feet up on my desk."

"That isn't what I meant."

"I know what you meant. You should try getting ahead of your rent with some old-fashioned overtime instead of sitting home watching *Get Smart*. I've pried a hundred of these pukes out of culverts and doorways and stripped cars, all just as dead, and it wasn't any of their first times. They don't buy the stuff at Cunningham's. They never know if what they just scored is one hundred percent pure Asian or D-Con." He swung his head toward the top of the bank. "Okay, you got to play Sherlock all morning. Run along now and let the grownups get to work."

Officer Aaron Bookfinger and Sergeant Walter Stilwell were making their way down from the street, grasping fistfuls of weeds here and there to slow the descent. Bookfinger had on a black trench coat and Russian-style fur hat. Stilwell looked like Elmer Fudd in a plaid wool cap with earflaps and a Mackinaw. At the bottom he strode forward to grasp Iniskilling's outstretched hand.

"Dan, you scandihoovian bastard. I heard you went back home and got your sex changed."

"That's Denmark, schmuck. My parents came from Norway. Who's the Jew, your lawyer?" The lieutenant shook hands with Bookfinger. It was clear all three were old acquaintances.

Matt Kellog touched shoulders with Battle. "Ain't no talking to that crew, man. They can't call us niggers no more and they run clean out of conversation."

Walking past, Bookfinger caught Battle's eye and nodded quickly. Stilwell, trailing him by half a step, didn't look in the black officer's direction. Battle understood with no words having been spoken that there had been a shift in his relationship with the other two investigators.

Stilwell nudged the clenched corpse with the black shiny toe of an unbuckled galosh. "Stiffer'n Gerald fucking Ford. You boys better not drop him on your way up," he told the morgue attendants. "Ain't enough Superglue in the metro area to piece the little prick back together."

"OD?" Bookfinger asked Iniskilling.

"What else? Charlie Chan there thinks he was poisoned and airlifted here by helicopter."

Stilwell said shit. "We could've phoned in on this one. Heater's piss-poor in the unit we drew. My balls fell off and rolled down the sewer clear back on Beaubien."

"Well, I thought you might want to take a look."

"Can't think why. One dead junkie looks pretty much like all the rest." Stilwell spun around and started back toward the bank. Bookfinger shook Iniskilling's hand again and followed. This time neither of them glanced at Battle.

Battle said, "That's it? That's your on-site?"

At the base of the incline Stilwell paused and looked back over his shoulder. "We're Special Investigations, sonny. We leave sticking fingers up dead assholes to the white coats at County. They went to college."

"Are we going to question Kubicek?"

Bookfinger had begun climbing. Stilwell touched his arm. The pair faced Battle. The icy wind was making their eyes water.

"Ask him what, if he's bringing a date to the funeral?" Stilwell said.

"I was thinking something more along the lines of where he was and what he was doing between Friday night when Littlejohn left work at the marina and this morning when the body turned up."

The sergeant's face, already flushed from the cold, went as red as his hair. He took a step toward Battle. Bookfinger caught his sleeve.

"We're all cops, Charlie," said the officer. "We don't go around accusing each other of homicide without evidence."

"I'm just saying we should ask him the same questions we'd ask anyone else."

"Paul Kubicek ain't everyone else," Stilwell said. "He was running into empty buildings after armed robbers when you were eating strained collards. He's what every cop ought to be. You tell me how tearing off a hunk of toilet paper and handing it to the mayor every time he takes a crap down at City Hall set you up to judge a cop like Paul Kubicek."

Bookfinger placed a hand on Stilwell's shoulder. "Cut the kid some slack, Wally. He's just trying to make an impression."

"I'll make an impression in his ass with one of my size nines." But the storm had passed. Stilwell swung around and started up the bank. His partner hung back.

"Just because I'm not coming out swinging doesn't mean I think any different from Wally," he told Battle. "The department isn't

America. Nobody's created equal down at 1300."

No one in the ditch said anything or moved until the two investigators were almost out of sight. Then Kellog's partner, a young black with sideburns shaped like scimitars, pursed his lips and sent a fleck of white spittle at the ground where they'd been standing.

"I got to apologize for Merlin," Kellog said to Battle. "He ain't much of a conversation-alist."

"I think he's eloquent as hell." Battle said his good-byes and left.

Chapter Nineteen

Caryn Crownover Ogden's first significant confrontation was with a day nurse on Opal's floor. It was also her last.

Diagnosed with pneumonia, the six-year-old was placed in a private room for observation in the Hutzel children's facility at Harper Grace Hospital. Caryn told the nurse, a pale undersize brunette whom she had at first mistaken for a teenage aide, that she wanted a cot set up in the room so she could spend the night with her daughter. The nurse frowned prettily.

"I'm not sure we can do that, Mrs. Ogden. The child needs rest."

"If rest were that important she'd be better off in a train station. Anyway, I don't snore and I'm not planning to throw a party. I'd appreciate it if you could dig up one of those egg-crate mattress pads. I have a bad back."

"The child is in the best possible hands. The personnel and equipment at Hutzel are —"

"After visiting hours, the personnel is one

222

nurse per floor, and the equipment is a monitor to tell her when something goes wrong with a patient's heart or respiration. I intend to be here when Opal's condition changes."

"Mrs. Ogden —"

"I'll discuss this with Mr. Dobrinski. Please do me the favor of calling him."

"The administrator is very busy."

"I hope so. His salary is sixty thousand."

Casimir Dobrinski was young for his position and, Caryn thought, far too good-looking to spend most of his time locked away in meetings. He was one of those tall blond curly-headed Poles more readily associated with white chargers and golden armor than with coarse jokes about the stupidity of the race. Although not a doctor, he affected tailored white sport coats for their subliminal suggestion, and striped ties in memory of the one semester he had audited at Cambridge following his army discharge. There was a time, earlier in Caryn's marriage to an ambitious man who lived at the office, when she might have gone after this prize with all the single-tracked determination of a Crown-over upbringing; but motherhood had changed all that.

But the young nurse was no one's mother, and as the hospital administrator approached the floor station twirling the tortoise-shell eyeglasses he never wore, Caryn could feel the vibrations emanating from the young woman at her side. It was a mystery to her how women who spent all day looking at naked men with nothing but professional interest — or men looking at naked women, for that matter — managed to melt into a puddle of hormones at the first sight of a pleasant-looking member of the opposite sex in full dress. She supposed it had something to do with the resemblance of a hospital corridor to a high school hallway.

"Mrs. Ogden, it's been much too long. I only hope your next —"

She sliced through the greeting. "I know this young lady has explained the situation, so I won't waste your time. You've enough on your mind as it is. I wouldn't be surprised, given your preoccupation with your responsibilities, if I had to remind you that I'm the director of the Charlotte Gryphon Foundation, which pumped two point four million dollars into the construction of this facility after the city bailed out."

Dobrinski folded his glasses with a click and socked them into the alligator case in his breast pocket. "Nurse, please see that Mrs. Ogden is comfortable." To Caryn: "I'm afraid we can't offer room service. This isn't the Book-Cadillac."

"I don't expect it. If it weren't for this back of mine I wouldn't even ask for a bed."

A rollaway was brought to the room that evening. Caryn, who had seen Crownover Coaches evolve from a patriarchal company owned and run entirely by her father to a sprawling corporation operated by committee, was scarcely surprised to learn that in a hospital complex dedicated to the eradication of human suffering, not one orthopedic mattress pad could be found in time to make her first night more bearable.

Not that it mattered. Her sleep was so light, with all her senses tuned to her daughter's faintest whimper and slightest restless movement, that she might as well have spent the time sitting up in a chair. Washed in liquid luminescence from the lights in the hall, her hair tied back, a tube in her nose and wires trailing from under her white gown to the bank of equipment beside the bed, Opal looked small and diaphanous, her fair skin barely discernible from the pillowcase and sheets. She seemed — transient; and Caryn did not dare to let go of her damp flexing hand lest she float away.

She was holding on to herself as well, so desperately that it was difficult to refrain from squeezing the blood out of the child's hand. For she knew that that brief life was all that sustained her from the abyss of an alcoholic middle age. And to her Opal's illness was so very much her fault that the thought of living with the knowledge constricted her lungs. Oh, she would not lack for concerned voices to assure her that her presence at home would have made no difference, that the girl would have gotten sick whether her mother were by her side or at Sinbad's ordering her third highball. She would be awash in soothing reassurances, when in fact blame and recriminations would be less cruel.

And thinking of it made her want a drink more than ever.

Strongly enough anyhow that she had to force herself to stay in the room, actually grip the angle irons of the bedframe so tightly they left creases in her palms, rather than desert her daughter yet again to go looking for a bar or a drugstore that would sell her a drink after hours.

Until Opal, her thirst had not seemed out of the ordinary. Her childhood had been one glittering string of parties at the mansion in Grosse Pointe, pink champagne sparkling in bowl-shaped glasses held by attenuated women in fringed dresses, ice cubes colliding in brown bourbon in thick squat containers clutched in the fists of thick squat former machinists whose two hundred-dollar suits bagged at the knees like two-dollar overalls. For them the great drafty drawing room was merely an extension of the Detroit Athletic Club, and before that the Pontchartrain Bar, where whiskey came two glasses to the quarter and a nickel beer was a nickel beer, and if the coin that paid for it smelled slightly of crankcase oil, it just slid faster down the bar top. Yet there was gold, or what passed for it, among this base metal. Caryn's mother still spoke of the time Charles Lindbergh knelt before her little girl to converse with her on her level, but Caryn's only memory of the incident was of the aviator's pale face and bottomless black eyes, like finger-holes in white flour. The year was 1932, after the kidnapping, and when she learned that, it helped to explain the fear she had felt at the time that those twin empty wells were enticing her to dive in, there to stay forever swaddled in moist warm darkness, safe from abductors and experience.

Her coming out, observed against red-white-and-blue bunting and orange-and-yellow Rosie the Riveter posters, had ended in a geyser of gin and vodka at someone else's house and the disturbing but mildly thrilling suspicion, while inspecting the ruins of her frothy green Dior gown the next morning, that somewhere in the alcoholic night she had sacrificed some part of her virginity. Liquor made it all right, absolving her of responsibility and fogging the details just enough to make the experience seem a deliciously wicked dream.

Then came peacetime, available men, and a return to business as usual, factories redirecting their military aggression toward the war against thrift: Make this year's model longer and lower, add fins and chrome, make last year's must-have look as far out of step as sleeve garters. The auto shows got bigger and shinier, the spokesmodels' swimsuits got smaller, the hospitality rooms became suites, and the service elevators in the Penobscot Building groaned beneath cases of Old Grand-Dad and Hiram's. Caryn decorated the arms of out-of-town dealers undecided whether to commit showroom space to Chevy's dependable Bel-Air or the sexy Buick Riviera. The West Coasters drank gimlets and daiquiries, the Texans bourbon and branch. Martinis and Manhattans, naturally, for the New Yorkers. Scotch and soda for our friends from D.C. — any brand, as long as it was Glen-something, and came accompanied by a complimentary two-year lease on an Eldorado to ensure all government cars continued to bear the company emblem. Caryn, photographed in Carl's Chop House with

Palm Beach Cadillac merchants and John Foster Dulles, quickly became multilingual in the study of mixology. Her own preferred choice in those days was a Brandy Alexander. When this was reported in the *Ford Times*, single women and housewives throughout Detroit abandoned their Carling Black Labels for the chocolated drink, guaranteed to knock them on their fannies while their brains were still convinced they were sipping Ovaltine.

She met Ted Ogden at a Monte Carlo Night held at the Fox Theater to raise money for the Detroit Symphony Orchestra, where he cut a simple figure in a perfectly tailored blue suit against all the formal gowns and cummerbunds. He impressed her even more when she ran into him again a few weeks later at the Caucus Club. She was sober then, and pleasantly surprised to learn he looked just as good to her as he had through a haze of Dom Perignon. Soon afterward he took her to see *My Fair Lady* when it played the Fisher, and escorted her backstage to meet Rex Harrison and Julie Andrews. "I Could Have Danced All Night" was the first number performed at their wedding reception the following June.

Europe for the honeymoon, and an audience with the young queen and a blessing from the Pope — events that would have brought apoplexy to Caryn's adoptive great-great-grandfather Abner I, anti-royalist and staunch Freemason that he was. Back home, an embarrassment averted when Ted, a success in his own business, chose to accept graciously Crownover Coaches' offer of a board seat rather than assert his independence by refusing. Three mornings a week he dutifully studied the documents placed before him on the long walnut table in Papa Harlan's old office, serving as the boardroom pending completion of the company's new building in Southfield, voted on each measure or abstained, then excused himself to see to the administration of his investment firm. Wary at first, the other directors, even the aggressive Gashawks, eventually came to respect the newcomer for the soundness of his decisions, and in particular for the charm with which he handled the odd irate attendee at stockholders' meetings. As years passed and Abner IV continued to demonstrate his indifference toward the affairs of the business whose profits had enabled him to acquire part ownership of his beloved Detroit Tigers, there were whispers in corner offices that Ted Ogden might succeed him in the chairmanship; but Caryn, who knew better than anyone how swiftly and savagely her brother could act whenever he sensed a serious threat to his security, downplayed the rumors wherever possible, maintaining quite truthfully that her husband was far more interested in the company he had founded on nothing but a bachelor's degree in business and a five-thousand-dollar savings bond than in assuming the inherited directorship of an institution.

But the pressure of such diplomatic chores took their toll on a debutante who had scarcely been brought up to deal with the demands of a corporation in flux. Frothy drinks photographed well for the Sunday supplements, but when it came to winding down from industrial and family politics, whiskey sours worked better in practice. Still, the escalation didn't alarm her. Liquor was recreation, as useful in its way as golf and the opera for working out the kinks of the week past and replenishing the stores of energy for the one upcoming. She had never thought to question this philosophy. Of those few mornings when old Harlan had not risen with the dawn and left for the office, his daughter couldn't remember one that didn't begin with a servant carrying a glass of beer up to his bedroom — a habit which, minus the domestic help, went back to his youth on the loading dock — and it was a rare sunset that didn't find an extra gleam in Mama Cornelia's eye courtesy of the voluminous wine cellars beneath the Grosse Pointe mansion. Hang-overs dominated the household schedule in the forenoon.

Caryn marveled at Ted's self-control the first time he declined a second glass of wine at dinner, but did not interpret his abstinence as a reflection on her own bibulous habits. He claimed a low capacity, which drew her sympathy, and it was certainly true that the mathematical nature of his work and the financial welfare of his clients required an early day and a clear head. When it developed that his temperance was customary, she began to feel self-conscious. For a time she drank only moderately. However, her intake remained greater than his. Soon she had drifted back to her old level.

It occurred to her now that she had never seen Ted intoxicated. No doubt she had been aware of this phenomenon all along without acknowledging it. Certainly the awareness had made her shrewish when her own drinking reached a particular intensity. A gay inebriate in youth, she faced the fact now that she had in middle age become a belligerent drunk, taunting her husband in public for the will-power she herself lacked. It shamed her, for Ted had never once lectured her.

Twice she had quit cold. The first time was on the severe advice of her obstetrician.

Visited so late in life with the miracle of approaching maternity, she had been so deathly afraid it would be snatched from her that whatever symptoms of withdrawal she experienced seemed minimal.

The second time lasted just a month. That had been two years ago, when in an alcoholic fog she had stepped into the stairwell on the second story of her own house thinking she was entering her bathroom and cracked a vertebra when she fell. Three weeks in traction followed by a visit on crutches to the basement of the Elks Lodge and her first AA meeting.

She hadn't gone back. She felt she could put up with the harsh fluorescent lighting and the supremely bad coffee served in Styrofoam cups — really, if they were serious about substituting group dependency for chemical craving, they could at least *try* to compete with the rosy atmosphere of a corner bar — but when the first speaker got up to announce how successful his life had become in the six years he'd been on the wagon, and went on to extoll the virtues of his appliance chain over those of his nearest competitor, Caryn drew the conclusion that when you finally managed to sober some people up, they proved to have been assholes to begin with. She took a cab home and put away her first glassful while the front door was still closing.

She thought now she would give it another try. Opal would recover (she refused to contemplate otherwise), she was coming into a time of life when the example of her parents was the matrix for how she would conduct herself in adulthood, and anyway the appliance salesman *must* have finished speaking by now. She would bring her own Thermos of coffee if that was what it took.

As if to confirm this fresh determination, the little girl in the hospital bed sighed in her sleep, a contented sound. She appeared to be breathing more evenly. Letting go of her daughter's hand for the first time since she'd entered the room, Caryn plucked a Kleenex out of a box on the nightstand and used it to sponge a fleck of spittle that had appeared in the corner of Opal's slightly open mouth. As she did so, she caught sight of her watch. 2:03. She realized she hadn't called Cornelia to tell her what had happened. Her mother would be awake, reading one of the paperback romances she devoured like chocolates; addictions of one kind or another ran in the family, and the old lady seemed to have outlived the need for sleep.

"Mommy will be right back, baby." She kissed Opal's forehead — it felt cooler; or was that wishful thinking? — and went out to ask the nurse at the station for directions to the nearest telephone.

When she returned, nine minutes later, the station was deserted. The nurse was running toward the little girl's room.

Chapter Twenty

"Day-for-night's a crock of shit," Corky said. "Don't you agree, Paul?"

Kubicek, who found himself falling into the director's habit of addressing people by name every time he spoke to them, said, "Corky, I don't know what the fuck you're talking about."

They were relaxing in the back of Corky's motor home, which the sergeant calculated had cost more to furnish than his own house. It contained an eight-foot sofa upholstered in lavender suede, rose-colored carpeting wall to wall, a burgundy leather Eames chair and ottoman, a bar *and* a soda fountain, and brushed aluminum paneling with framed original posters advertising *Touch of Evil*, *Torn Curtain*, *Gun Crazy*, and something Italian. The director had spent the entire afternoon stretched out on the sofa in yellow Tweety Bird socks with his ankles crossed, balancing a tall glass of carrot juice or somesuch shit on his stomach, talking about movies Kubicek hadn't seen whose titles he couldn't pronounce and telling stories that demonstrated what a straight-arrow the actor who played Eddie Haskell on *Leave It to Beaver* really was when the cameras weren't turning — waiting, apparently, for night to fall. Meanwhile the cast and crew were sitting around outside and in motor homes jerking off, and nobody was getting rich as fast as the Teamsters, who started collecting triple time at five o'clock.

Kubicek, who couldn't figure out why Corky had chosen him to kill the time with, spent most of it crossing from the Eames to the refrigerator behind the bar where the imported beer was kept and back, with the occasional trip to the chemical toilet behind a folding screen decorated with full-size cutouts of James Dean, Marilyn Monroe, and some frog actor with a wide-brimmed hat and a cigarette drooling out of the corner of his mouth. The beer tasted like swamp water and sitting in the backward-tilting chair made him queasy, as if he were waiting for a fucking Apollo launch. The conversation bored him shitless. He'd had more fun staking out a much-robbed Sinclair station with "Chili" Carbone, whose favorite dish, in addition to giving him his nickname, had seen to it that he'd changed partners three times in one year, each time following a period of enforced proximity in close quarters.

It didn't help that his muscles burned when he got up, and cramped painfully when he sat still longer than ten minutes. The time was past when he could close a day of intense physical activity with an all-night session in some noisy bar, sleep for two hours, and report for roll call the next morning clear-eyed, bathed, shaved, and ready for another day of the same. Now, days after a little workout, he felt as if an army of angry niggers had marched all over him with cleats. He opened a bottle with a lion and something in Swedish on the label, poured some of its contents down his throat, and waited for the numbness to crawl into his muscles. Rolling the aftertaste around his mouth, he wondered how those Swedes got the lion to piss into such a narrow neck.

"Day-for-night," Corky repeated, obviously impatient with the sergeant's ignorance. "You know, blue lights and filters. Dean Martin, for chrissake, in *Rough Night in* fucking *Jericho* and isn't it amazing how we can read 'It Pays to Increase Your Word Power' inside a stable at midnight? Phony as hell."

"I like Dean Martin westerns. You don't miss anything trying to figure out what you just saw. You see *Doc*? I couldn't tell Wyatt Earp from Doc Holliday, and that Dunaway broad's a skag."

The director ran a finger with grunge under the nail around the inside of his glass and sucked carrot juice off the end. Kubicek, who had heard Corky referred to as a genius around the set, decided he himself bathed too often to be a genius. He'd learned a lot this year about the other half: Rich people had to listen to bad music played live and loud, and great artists suffered from serious b.o. So why didn't he feel more contented? He took another swig and pretended to listen.

"Fellini almost never uses a filter. He goes with what's there. Truffaut too; he shoots by natural light even when there isn't any. You know you've got your audience by the nuts when they're willing to squint to see what's going on. Anyway, film is reality. That's why the Impressionists went the other way as soon as the camera was invented. They couldn't compete. You want to look out and see where the sun is now?"

"Romulus, I think." Kubicek let the Venetian blind drop. "Almost gone."

"Give it another ten minutes. Did you see the *Satyricon*?"

"I'm pretty sure I didn't."

"Brilliant fucking film. Do you go out to see movies often?"

"We used to, when our girl was little. You

could take a kid to the pictures then, without checking first to make sure some joker didn't pull out his schlong halfway through. I think the last one I went to see was *The Cowboys*. Say what you like about the Duke, he keeps it in his pants."

"Pretty soon you won't have to go out at all. Every movie ever made will come in a cartridge that you poke in a machine and watch on an ordinary TV set. That'll be the end of guys like me."

Kubicek waited. If he knew anything about the little twerp by now it was that he didn't need to be prompted to make a speech. It had something to do with being a genius.

"All the movies ever had going for them, the one thing that separated them from all the other arts — not counting live drama, which to hell with that, it's like going to the Louvre and not being sure if Mona Lisa's smiling this time or picking her nose — was you had to stay in one spot for a fixed amount of time to get the full benefit. The theaters cooperated by closing the doors and turning off the lights and hiring monkeys in uniform to tell the rowdies to shut up. TV doesn't give you that; the viewer has all the control. People talk when the set's on. They jump up in the middle of a scene to make a sand- wich or go to the can. They try to make sense of what they see and when they can't they say it's cool, it's just television. When this videotape thing is perfected they'll watch movies the same way. If they do go occasionally to the theater, they'll go on talking and getting up and moving around just like at home, and no army of ushers is going to get them to pipe down and sit still. So to beat that the movies will get louder. There'll be all kinds of explosions and blaring music and goosed-up stereogizmos to drown out the filibusters in the mezzanine. No dialogue. You can't expect a customer to pay attention to what the actors are saying when Aunt Effie's in the next seat giving him the lowdown on Cousin Phil's prostate. The next generation of movie stars will be retired bodybuilders and former fashion models, just like in the silents. It'll be as if the fifty years since *The Jazz Singer* never happened."

"It's the shits, all right."

"Well, hell." Corky drained his glass and swung his feet to the floor. "Let's go make some art."

Another forty-five minutes or so went by while the director checked with all the technicians, ordered some lights and big sheet reflectors moved, and rode the camera boom surveying the scene through a hand-held lens, looking like Sabu the Elephant Boy. Meanwhile the final rays of sunlight went down beyond Belleville, the streetlights poinged on, and the late-January cold came down straight from outer space without so much as a thread of cloud for insulation. The location was the warehouse district, specifically the foot of Riopelle where the rum-running boats used to dock during Prohibition, bearing cargoloads of illegal spirits from the Canadian side of the river. Brick warehouses with blank panes in their windows and inspired signs reading NO. 3 and DO NOT BLOCK LOADING RAMP made square shadows against the dusting of lights from Windsor. It took a native to identify the piles of broken asphalt that had been there since the First World War from the fresh debris at the other end of the alley where clearing had begun for the construction of a new building already being lauded by the city administration as a symbol of Detroit's coming renaissance: A shopping center. Kubicek wondered if he was alone in the knowledge that the only authentic Detroiters with money to spend on new clothes and sets of china were pimps and drug dealers.

While Corky was still aloft, a white stretch limo pulled onto the set and a trio of local celebrities stepped out: Councilman Kelly, red of hair and pocked face, a throwback to the city's Irish past; Judge Del Rio, a black rookie jurist in a sharp suit and camel's-hair coat that made him look every bit the two-bit procurer that Kubicek and most of his police colleagues thought him; and Doris Biscoe, WXYZ Channel 7 newscaster, a trim handsome black woman in a fawn trench coat with the station logo stitched on the shoulder flap. In a spirit of cooperation with Hollywood, the Chamber of Commerce had prevailed upon the administration and the halls of journalism to supply the production with bit players recognizable to the regional audience. According to the copy of the script Kubicek had seen, Kelly and Del Rio had a line apiece, while Biscoe was supposed to read a passage of invented news copy for a fictional TV camera crew. Also on hand was an engine company from the Detroit Fire Department. The city had given Corky permission to set fire to an empty warehouse, and the firefighters were there to make sure the rest of the river-front didn't burn down for the sake of art.

While the special effects team busied themselves planting incendiaries inside the designated building, the director shot the dialogue scenes involving the guest actors. Biscoe, experienced at delivering on cue, made her contribution in one take and went to the catering truck for a cup of coffee to warm her hands around while she watched the others. Kelly blew his single line six times in six tries, finally supplying adequacy on the seventh. Del Rio, notorious for packing a revolver beneath his judicial robes, out-shouting objecting attorneys into numbed silence, and convening court wherever he happened to be — a restaurant, the ground floor of police headquarters — and finding everyone present in contempt, kept trying to pad his part with hammy elaborations and was escorted from the set with effusive thanks for his performance, after which the director told his half-pint assistant to replace him with anyone in the area who happened to belong to Equity.

Even Kubicek, whose tolerance for cold weather went far back in his family, was stamping his feet and flicking icicles from his nose by the time the fireworks were set to begin. By this time the conversation among the actors and extras had all but dwindled away as they sought to keep their chins from freezing by tucking them inside their collars. A gray pall of breathed air hung overhead like nitre from the ceiling of a cavern so deep it had never known a temperature above zero. The snow creaked loudly when they shifted their weight.

The moment arrived. All the personnel who

had been in the building were present and accounted for. Corky's assistant socked down the telescoping antenna of his walky-talky with the heel of his hand, reporting that all cameras and sound equipment were in position. The director, at ground level now but still straddling the boom, peeled off both jersey gloves, blew on his fingers, tugged the gloves back on, jammed down the leather visor of his baseball cap, and jerked his head once. His teeth shone white in the thicket of his beard. The assistant director unraveled a white lawn handkerchief as big as a tablecloth from his jacket pocket and snapped it at the ground.

The head gaffer, a man built along Kubicek's lines — thick through the chest and abdomen but short in the limbs, with brown hair spilling to his shoulders from under a black knitted watch cap — had been watching for this gesture from his perch on the platform of a freight car parked on one of the sidings that networked the area. Now he pointed a device the size and shape of a garage door opener in the direction of the warehouse and mashed one of the buttons with his big thumb. In the instant before detonation, the police sergeant noticed that the man wore a black eye patch behind his glasses and that he was missing two fingers from his right hand.

It started slowly, with a dull rose glow behind the empty windows of the ground floor. The sound came behind it, a wheezy kind of a thud, as of a heavy weight striking the floor of a lake. It was followed by a sustained sucking noise as the glow turned yellow and the flames leapt to the sills. To the right of the loading dock, a bank of windows, all its panes miraculously intact, shuddered, then exploded, spraying glittering splinters in front of a fist of fire that opened when it hit the outside air, drenching the block in bronze light. Kubicek felt the heat on his face at a distance of sixty feet.

He saw the assistant director touch Corky's sleeve and point skyward. Shielding his eyes from the firelight with both hands, the director tilted his head back, peered, and nodded energetically. At first Kubicek saw nothing in that direction. He felt rather than heard the beating of blades, and then a constellation of orange and green lights, shaped just like a dragonfly, soared into view above the black smudge of smoke; a helicopter filming the conflagration from above.

The sergeant wondered at which point in the two minutes since the cameras had begun turning that the cost of the scene had exceeded his pension.

A heap of dirty snow piled against the base of the building by plows crumbled in on itself with a sigh, bleeding rusty water in a spreading pool from which steam rose. By now the windows on the top floor were aglow. Thick brown smoke, heavier at first than air, rolled out of holes and fissures and boiled around the foundation like the lower tract of an atomic blast. It clung stubbornly to the earth like ground fog. The cinders tickled Kubicek's ankles.

Through the haze poked a pair of headlights that caught the corner of his eye and made him turn in their direction. They winked off, the door opened on the driver's side, and a figure in a leather coat started walking toward him through the swirling smoke, looking exactly like something Corky might have filmed, although all the lenses were pointed the other way. Just then the door on the passenger's side popped open and two men dressed in the winter uniform of the Detroit Police Department climbed out.

Kubicek's eyes were smarting from the smoke. He slid his hand toward his automatic, recognized the man in the leather coat, and got out his handkerchief instead to mop away the tears. Officer Charlie Battle waited for him to finish, then drew his Miranda card from an inside pocket and began reading the sergeant his rights.

Chapter Twenty-One

Focus was the thing.

When she was still very young, Caryn had sensed that she could not count on her father, usually away at some plant, or her mother, constantly preoccupied with the search for the perfect caterer, to provide strength when Caryn needed it. Early on she learned that tears only complicated a bad situation, blurring her vision and closing her throat; and so at age six she had ceased to cry. To order her emotions she would select some singular object — the rosettes at the corners of the doorframe in her nursery were endlessly fascinating, and appealingly out of reach — a thing of substance and interest to focus on until her world stopped rocking. So completely had alcohol taken its place in the years between that she had nearly forgotten the device. Determined not to take that first drink, she now found her object in the person of one Special Agent Francis Riordan, Jr.

He was hardly as singular as the rosettes. At first glance, Riordan was just one more of that Hoover stamp she had seen so often at her father's side during the war: Pink-chinned, temples shaved, that subliminal American flag of red tie on white shirt with blue suit, black mirror wingtips with thin soles and shallow heels lest the wearer tower too obviously over the Director on a visit. Ten years earlier she wouldn't have noticed him at all. But the look of the world had changed. In a society whose CPAs, dentists, and even politicians had laid aside their white button-down oxfords for sunset polyester, sprouted muttonchops and granny glasses, and swaddled their throats in neckties the size of lobster bibs, quiet was loud, ordinary odd. The man was so purposefully in keeping with the bland wallpaper in the little hospital waiting room that had become Command Central for the Crownover-Ogden investigation that she couldn't keep her eyes off him, even when a semi-hysterical nurse kept wailing that it wasn't her fault that a sick little girl had been spirited away from her charge as easily as shoplifting a Snickers.

"Please try to concentrate, Mrs. Crownover," Riordan was saying, ignoring the nurse. "Are you sure you've received no threats over the telephone or in the mail?

Sometimes they come disguised as pleas for money."

"That doesn't narrow it down. I'm the president of a charitable foundation. Listening to pleas for money is in the job description. And please don't call me Mrs. Crownover. Crownover was my maiden name."

"Caryn, he's just trying to help." Ted, standing beside her chair, squeezed her shoulder gently.

She reached up and patted his hand, concealing her irritation. Ever since the call to the police, everyone had been treating her as the mother maddened by fear. Which she was, although not to the point of helplessness. She was the one who had asked that the local office of the FBI be notified. She was in no condition to repeat the details all over again when that inevitability occurred. Perhaps a little mania would have been more palatable. People were so much less concerned for a woman when she behaved as the pathetic idiot they expected.

"May I have your permission to order a tap on your telephone, Mr. Ogden? We'll have to work quickly. In cases like this the first ransom demand comes within hours."

"Certainly not. My clients call me at the house all the time. Our conversations are confidential."

"I shouldn't have to assure you of the Bureau's discretion."

"A U.S. Census taker used those exact same words. I happened to mention that I subscribe to *The American Rifleman* so my sportsmen clients will have something to read in my waiting room. Inside six months my mailbox was jammed with applications to join the NRA, the John Birch Society, and the Ku Klux Klan."

"With respect, sir, your child's life —"

"Oh, let him have what he wants, Ted. They've been listening in ever since Papa told H. R. Kaltenborn the Zero was a better fighter than the Corsair."

Riordan's mouth opened, but it was Casimir Dobrinski who filled the silence. The hospital administrator had on the same white sport coat and striped shirt he'd worn the previous afternoon, without the necktie; obviously he'd simply shaved and thrown on whatever was handy as soon as he got the call. "We're getting ahead of ourselves with all this talk of ransom," he said. "We don't know for sure this is a kidnapping."

"I'm sure you'd rather treat this as some sort of clerical error." Ted had gone pale, always a danger sign. "You can't keep this in house. Somebody waltzed in here and took my daughter. If you think we're not going to hold the hospital responsible —"

During the ensuing squabble, Caryn got up and walked down the hall to Opal's room. There the oxygen and i.v. tubes and monitor wire from which the little girl had been torn like a melon from its vines still dangled beside the empty bed whose sheets bore the child's imprint. Her big stuffed Snoopy sat in one of the visitors' chairs gazing expectantly toward the door as if awaiting her momentary return. Something inside Caryn that was only barely holding on slipped another sickening inch, but when she put her hands to her cheeks they were dry. That was abnormal. A mother who couldn't cry for her lost child fell outside the definition of the term. And the urge to partake was upon her stronger than ever, burning in every nerve and capillary like a million tiny white-hot buzz saws. She left the room abruptly, in search of a water fountain. Perhaps simple rehydration was all that was needed to put her tear ducts into working order.

In the hallway she almost ran into Riordan. The agent in charge was absorbed in a sheet of stiff paper held by a somewhat less successful carbon of himself in a gray suit and glasses with heavy black frames.

"The nurse has confirmed her description of the man she saw loitering outside your daughter's room earlier from the Identi-Kit," said Riordan, when he became aware of Caryn's presence. "Do you recognize him?"

The sketch reminded her of the art lessons of her childhood, only half attended to as she eavesdropped on her brother's executive exercises in the room next door: She could almost see the intersecting dotted lines through the center of the face oval, indicating that the nose and ears were to be found half-way between the top of the head and the point of the chin and that the eyebrows were level with the tops of the ears. But this face was fleshier than that anonymous model, strong-jowled, with a scowl tugging down the corners of the wide mouth and a squint in the eyes that brought to mind a lone figure in feathers and buckskin scanning a horizon for covered wagons. She had a hunch the baseball cap that had been added to the Identi-Kit prototype concealed a wealth of long black hair. Something fluttered in her memory and was gone. A face behind glass. She tried to bring it back, couldn't.

"It looks like some kind of Indian."

"That's what the nurse thought. Is the face familiar?"

A face behind glass. Not enough. "No." She handed back the sheet.

Riordan made a noise of smothered exasperation. Caryn had already pegged him as one of those civil servants who tried to make you feel guilty for forcing them to earn their government salaries. He returned the sketch to the agent in glasses. "Wire it to Quantico, then circulate it. Black on black, thirty to thirty-five, American Indian, five-five and a hundred and sixty. Go heavy on the reservations up North. Don't forget the island."

"Mackinac?"

"Did it sound like I meant New Zealand? Use a local informant. Those people have trouble opening up to anyone who looks like he's from the G."

"Can't think why."

Alone with Caryn, Riordan said, "You sure you didn't see the man? The nurse spotted him two or three times. Smelled him, too. She said his cologne would stop a runaway horse."

"I only left the room once. There was no one in the hall."

"He must've ducked into a vacant room at the end of visiting hours. Great security you have here," he said as Dobrinski joined them from the waiting room.

"This hospital covers nearly a million square feet. We haven't the personnel to watch every corner. It isn't a prison. People come and go: residents, consultants, visitors, full-time staff, temporary help, maintenance, outside delivery people. Every day I see a hundred faces I never saw before. In any case —"

"Windshield."

Dobrinski and Riordan looked at Caryn. An arm snaked around her shoulders and squeezed; Ted. "A face behind glass," she said. "It was a windshield. In a car, watching."

"Where?" demanded the agent. "What kind of car?"

"Thass him. Like Tonto, only short and squatty-like." Dwight Littlejohn handed the sheet back to Battle.

The officer was seated with the middle-aged couple among the plastic schooners in Lieutenant Zagreb's office at 1300. Zagreb had left early on a personal errand, his night-watch replacement didn't come on for another hour, and Battle didn't trust any of the interrogation rooms, whose walls literally had ears. He'd wanted Russell's parents alone in the first lucid moment after identifying their son at the Wayne County Morgue around the corner. Bookfinger and Stilwell were out, ostensibly interviewing yet another witness who had been present at the Crownover-Ogden mansion at the time of the shootings

New Year's Eve. More likely they were stretching a ten-minute routiner into two hours of saganaki and brews at the Grecian Gardens.

Littlejohn *père* bore no resemblance to his male offspring. Shorter and thick through the shoulders, running to fat and beginning to stoop, he cropped his graying hair almost to a stubble as if in some kind of reverse rebellion against Russell's afro. His face was big, soft, and sad — its perennial expression, Battle suspected — and his hands, relatively small for the maintenance work he did for a living, were broken-nailed and shone with calluses. Wife Elizabeth was four years younger but looked ten years older than her actual age of forty-four, with her hair up and pinned and white-framed eyeglasses attached to a gold chain around her neck, which she'd used to study the drawing of the man her husband had described, the man he had seen climbing the outside stairs to his son's room over the garage recently, he didn't know just when.

"Could it have been New Year's Day?" Battle asked.

Littlejohn looked at his wife, who said, "You saw him. I didn't."

"Coulda been," he said. "Coulda been a Sunday after. Anyway I was home. I only just seen him through the window. Russell's friends they come — came and went." His adam's apple worked. "I only remember this one on accounta he some kinda injun. You see *Two Rode Together*?"

Battle hesitated. "Uh, no."

"Woody Strode, he played a injun in that. Only he black. Well, this one didn't look like him. This one he all injun. Woop-woop, you know?" He patted one cupped hand to his mouth, holding two fingers of the other behind the crown of his head like feathers.

"Dwight," Mrs. Littlejohn said.

He looked at her, eyes bright as a child's leaving a movie theater. A dark shade slid down behind his face when their eyes made contact. The big soft sadness came rushing back in. "Oh." He lowered his hands to his lap.

Battle gave the charcoal sketch back to the artist, a blonde officer in the regulation cheap white shirt and pleated pants with a .38 in a holster strapped to his belt. Reedy and pale, he would have looked more natural in a paint-streaked sweatshirt and sandals. Battle had to wonder at the chain of circumstances that would lead a man from the north light and nude models of an art-school studio to the fluorescents and dumpy uniformed matrons of Detroit Police Headquarters.

"You say you didn't see if he came by car?"

Littlejohn shook his head. "You thinking he the one kilt Russell?"

"Do you think someone killed him?"

"You do, or you wouldn't of took us back here to talk. Nobody done that when my brother got kilt."

Battle's chair squeaked. "Your brother was killed?"

"During the riot it was."

He sat back. "Sixty-seven?"

"Hell, no! That wasn't no riot. I'm talking about nineteen forty-three. At Paradise Valley it was. The dance hall, you know?"

Battle didn't know, but he nodded anyway. It seemed the quickest way to get back to business.

"It started on Belle Isle. They was some kind of fight. Blacks said a black woman and her baby got throwed off the bridge. Whites said a white woman was raped. Wasn't none of it true, but it got around. They mixed it up in front of Paradise Valley downtown. My brother Earl got his head stomped in the middle of the street. Cops that come told my mother what happened said it was more like a hurricane than a murder, and that's the last we seen of them till the funeral."

"They came to the funeral?"

258

"Oh, they come to all the funerals. Twenny-five of them there was. *Black* funerals, that is. I think maybe nine or ten whites got kilt. Cops figured we'd get out of hand if they didn't come to pay they respects. 'Course, they took along guns and sticks."

"Things were different then," Battle said.

"Yeah, they got on different uniforms now."

He returned to the subject. "Were you aware your son used heroin?"

"No," said the woman. "Yes," said the man. The responses were simultaneous. Littlejohn said, "I figured he was using something. I didn't know heroin."

"You didn't figure anything of the kind," his wife said. She was holding a handkerchief twisted in one fist, but had yet to use it. Shock, Battle thought; or maybe she'd run out of tears a long time before. "If you did, you'd of said something."

Littlejohn was looking at Battle. "You know everything the little woman and I said to each other in the past year?"

Battle waited.

"She say" — screwing his voice up high — " 'Dwight, get out of that toilet, *Mannix* is on.' And I say, 'Well, he just have to wait, my bowels don't just up and move with that

259

big old minute hand.' Thassit."

Battle could see this wasn't going any further. He stood. "Thanks for coming down, Mr. and Mrs. Littlejohn. I'm very sorry about your son. Just so you know, we're not treating this one as a hurricane."

The old man — he was old now legitimately, too many notches past middle age to claim it — moved one of his thick rounded shoulders. "It don't matter. Earl and Russell, they never knowed each other, but they might just as well be one and the same. It don't matter when you lived. Once you dead, you dead all the time."

Battle said nothing. Dwight Littlejohn sat working his hands in his lap for a moment, like a warrior steeling himself for some dramatic act. Then he got up and scraped his heels going out, without looking back to see if his wife was following.

Chapter Twenty-Two

Kubicek lit about his hundredth Pall Mall off the butt of the last, shook out the match, and flipped it in the vicinity of the heaped ashtray, a homemade clay job left over from some proud papa's stint at 1300. By now that kid had probably turned in his summer-camp trunks for a bandanna and Old Glory on his butt. Kids today were pukes.

The interrogation room, steeped as were its lath-and-plaster walls in the sharp sweat-and-vomit stench of fifty years' worth of accusations, identifications, commiserations, refutations, genuflections, and the occasional confession, held no terrors for him. He knew where the mikes were hidden, the location of the dents in the floor where heads had struck in simpler days when the Supreme Court was just a building on the D.C. tour, where was the best place to stand on the other side of the two-way glass so the perp at the table couldn't see you watching him.

He was pretty sure this was the room where he and Silverman cracked the Krikor Messerlian murder in '67 when they obtained a confession from the young looter who had bashed in the Armenian shopkeeper's skull with a baseball bat. Messerlian had been the first person killed during the riots. That was the week the city went to shit and it hadn't been back since.

The sergeant felt no loyalty to the city, its residents, or his superiors. The first was just a collection of buildings, most of which needed work they wouldn't get from the people who lived in them, and the people themselves were animals who fucked and shit and stole to pump shit into their veins. If they were anything more than that they'd move out. His superiors spent their time at the office shuffling all the Kubiceks from one duty sheet to another, striking Kubiceks from the sheets when they got killed, sending their dress uniforms to the cleaners between funerals, then going to their real homes in the suburbs, stopping off on the way to pick up their mail at the addresses they maintained in the city to fulfill the department residency requirement. Kubicek felt protective toward his house and wife and daughter, but STRESS was home. The squad and he understood each other. Punch in on time, punch out at quitting, let it know where you were when you went out on a call, pick up your three hundred minus withholding on Friday, and you were both square. Run down the wrong alley too fast, turn too slow, and your wife got a pension and Old Glory from the captain of the Color Guard, folded into a neat blue triangle. What could be more tidy?

He'd been thinking these thoughts when Charlie Battle walked past the interrogation room door, purposely left ajar lest Kubicek get the impression he was being detained. With him was an older black couple the sergeant didn't know from a thousand he'd seen on sidewalks and in numbers parlors and in shabby living rooms where they laced their stained fingers together in their laps and swore on the Bible that little Tyrone was home with them eating the Colonel when poor Mr. Aboud was getting his brains blown out for the $63.50 in his till. The man, rounded all over like a stone from a stream and beaten-looking, paused and looked in at Kubicek for a long moment, then moved on with the others, shaking his head. Kubicek felt the corners of his mouth tightening in a wolfish smile. Rookie, he thought, and he went ahead and said it out loud. If you were going to pull off the old hidden-ball play, it helped to coach your players first. Back on Riopelle he'd been a little worried when the black officer pulled out his Miranda card, but he saw now things were going to be all right.

He wondered why he felt disappointed.

A long time later — just twenty minutes by his heavy-duty wristwatch, but clocks had a way of moving slowly in those rooms — Battle returned alone, closing the door behind him. Another tip-off that he didn't know what he was doing; did he think the sergeant would take that to mean no one was listening in?

Well, play the part. "About fucking time," Kubicek said, squashing out the butt in an old burn-hole on the scarred wooden table. "You through showing your mammy and pap around the office?"

"That's raw even for you." Battle leaned back against the door, folding his arms. "But I shouldn't be surprised. You killed Junius Harrison because he happened to be black at an all-white party in Grosse Pointe."

"Know that for a fact, do you?"

"There's nothing to link him to Kindu Nampula and Leroy Potts, nada. Nampula and Potts were heavyweights. Harrison's record squeaked except for a penny pop for selling joints. Just on the off chance he made some kind of contact with Nampula when they were both in Jackson, I checked with Records there. Since about two weeks into his orientation, Harrison worked as a file clerk and errand boy for the deputy warden; slept in the bedroom the deputy didn't use because he had a house and family in Albion. Both the warden and the deputy warden provided references when he was released. Those references helped land him his job in the legal firm that sent him to the Ogden party that night with a message for one of the Ogdens' guests. Harrison never mingled with the general population all the time he was behind bars. If he saw Nampula at all it was in passing. Not much opportunity to forge a criminal partnership there."

"Harrison's old man beat his old lady. He didn't grow up no Ricky Nelson."

Battle stared. "Who told you that?"

"I'm a cop. Lessons cost extra."

"Never mind. I can guess. Okay, he had a bad childhood. You didn't know that when you shot him. All you saw was the color of his skin."

Kubicek shook a cigarette out of the pack and tapped it against the back of his hand. "I'm out on the streets, pal. I don't see a whole hell of a lot of Swedes running away from smashed plate-glass windows with color TVs under their arms."

"What if one's a TV repairman running to catch a bus?"

"Shit." Chuckling, he lit up. "Say Harrison had a legit reason to be there. Even the Grosse Pointe cops said there had to be someone inside."

"Inside men know the layout. New Year's Eve was his first visit."

"Anybody can get hold of a floor plan. They needed a layoff man to watch their backs."

Battle counted a beat. "What if I told you the Grosse Pointe police have the inside man in custody?"

Kubicek extinguished his match by pressing it between thumb and forefinger. The stinging burn established calm. "What if I told you Nixon wore Pat's panties to the Kremlin? Buddy, you stink at this."

"Inside woman, actually. Cops up there found men's clothes and Kindu Nampula's fingerprints all over the apartment of a server who worked for the company that catered the party. She'd worked the house once before, last Easter. The public defender's cutting a deal: No jail time if she testifies."

"Stupid fuckers, them Pointers. Heist guys don't tell their cunts shit."

"But if she plugs the hole, where's that leave Junius Harrison?"

"Back-up, like I said. Most messenger boys don't pack a piece, even in Detroit."

266

"Harrison never saw that thirty-two. You dropped it next to his corpse. It was a throw-away piece you carried around just in case you shot an unarmed man."

"Prove it."

Battle straightened, walked around the table. Kubicek blew an elaborately unconcerned plume of smoke and flicked ashes at the overflowing tray. Gently, the black officer took the sergeant's wrist and turned up the knuckles. Kubicek snatched his hand away.

"That's a bad scrape," Battle said. "Were you in some kind of fight?"

"Banged it on a doorjamb putting on my coat. Keep your fucking mitts off me, by the way. I didn't come here to hold hands with no" — he took a drag — "rookie."

"Sure you didn't bang it on Russell Little-john's hard head?"

For a bad second he thought he was going to choke on a lungful of smoke. He felt his face grow red. But he let out a shallow hack and cleared his throat and the moment passed. "Who the fuck's that?"

"You probably heard the name and forgot it. Just another OD they pulled out of a culvert out in the neighborhoods. The ME said he'd been roughed around some shortly before death. Life's never easy for an addict, I guess. Especially not the last part."

"Don't bleed all over the floor, son. Maintenance don't like it."

"Bad break for you," Battle said, "if you're telling the truth. Littlejohn was the pilot of the speedboat that was supposed to carry away Potts and Nampula and the plunder from the Ogden place. If anyone knew whether Harrison was in with them, it would've been him.

"He had pork in his stomach, and rice. After his Bronco turned up on Chicago, I beat a little leather near there and wound up at Greenleaf's on Linwood. A waitress there who knew him slightly thought she saw him come in around six P.M. the evening before his body was found. Assuming that's where he ate — Greenleaf's famous for its hamhocks and rice, did you know that? — he stopped digesting somewhere between seven and nine. Would you happen to know where you were about then, Paul? Can I call you Paul?"

"You can call me Sergeant Kubicek. And you got to tell me what night it was before I can tell you where I was. That is, if I even want to."

"You're right. I didn't really think you'd trip over one as old as that. Just boxing the compass. Like when I bothered to read you your rights before I took you in for questioning. I want to make sure nothing gets overlooked when I pull you down." He was leaning over the sergeant's shoulder, close enough to smell his aftershave.

Kubicek spat a grain of tobacco off his lower lip. "For what, wasting some junkie puke accomplice to armed robbery? Make it stick, Sambo. That didn't look like no positive ID from the coon in the hall. Littlejohn's old man, right? As much as any of you knows who's whose old man."

"I'll make it stick. If Littlejohn could've told us Harrison was in with Nampula and Potts, he could've told us he wasn't. And if he wasn't, he didn't pull a gun on you any more than you scraped your knuckles shadowboxing in your bedroom. So you took out Littlejohn. If I *don't* make that stick, I'll make Harrison stick. I'd rather it be the junkie puke: That's Murder One. But I'll settle for the messenger boy. It'll get you out of the department anyway, and put one more nail in STRESS's coffin."

"*That's* your wagon, ain't it? Just like a nigger. Burn down the whole fucking barn to clean out the rats."

"I'm glad you see it. It's not every rat knows what he is."

"You ain't no cop. You don't know what being a cop means."

Battle blinked. He unfolded to his full height. "That's rich. Coming from someone who's no better than Leroy Potts or Kindu Atticus Nampula Geary. Hell, you're worse. They never pretended to be anything but the punks they were."

Kubicek stood suddenly. His chair skidded back and clattered over. Facing Battle, he was shorter by several inches but broader and, despite his apron of beef fat and doughnuts, harder. "Unless the oath changed since I came through, it don't say nothing about putting your black skin ahead of the shield. Why'n't you just quit and join up with Quincy fucking Springfield?"

"Probably because that would leave the department in the hands of guys like you."

The door opened and Walter Stilwell came in, brows arched to the roots of his carroty hair. Battle and Kubicek turned to look at him.

"Chance meeting?" Stilwell asked.

"Shit." The STRESS sergeant pushed out past Aaron Bookfinger standing in the doorway.

Stilwell put his hands in the pockets of his plaid polyester slacks, eyeing Battle with his tongue bulging his right cheek. "You're just a team all by yourself, aren't you? I guess me and Aaron missed a memo."

Battle's jaws ached from clenching. Willing them to relax, he took a deep breath and looked from Stilwell to Bookfinger and back.

"Which one of you told Kubicek about Harrison's father?" he asked.

PART FOUR

The Slaughterhouse

Chapter Twenty-Three

O, the life of a public enemy.

Every evening at sundown — with certain minor variations in detail — Wilson McCoy put on his good brown leather hip-length coat, bent to tuck his mottled jeans into the tops of his freshly oiled stovepipe boots, plucked lint off the short springy nap of his black beret, and cocked it at a precise angle over his left ear, monitoring the operation in the shaft of clouded mirror over the basin in the little toilet where he'd performed all his ablutions for three years. Finally he ran his pocket pick through his stringy Ho Chi Minh goatee and headed for the stairs, whistling "Thank You Falettinme Be Mice Elf Agin" through the gap in his front teeth and picking up swagger as he went.

Once on the street, he turned his collar up Elvis-style against the Arctic blast and started north to Edison with his hands in his coat pockets. There he exhaled the stale brown air of the empty blind pig where he lived and sucked in the midnight-blue oxygen of the street, heady as cold ether. Quite apart from the fact that it was the one time of day when he felt safe going out, McCoy liked that hour the best. It was the only time when you could actually see the complexion of the town changing from white to black, when the fat honkies in striped suits threw their briefcases into their cars for the drive home to the suburbs and the brothers and sisters changed from coveralls and baggy bellbottoms to sunset colors and skirts so short you could use them for napkins; and in the past he had, boy, he had. He told people that making the Most Wanted list was the best way he knew to get women. Just plant that old suggestion in their heads that a team of FBIs might bust through the door any second, he said, and they came to a screaming climax in about eight point four seconds.

In truth, though, women entered his world rarely, didn't stay long, and left unsatisfied and disgruntled. It was a tiny planet, to begin with: ten blocks square, bounded by Edison to the north, Woodrow Wilson to the west, Hazelwood to the south, and good old Twelfth Street to the east, the one he was walking on now, in better days the Black Broadway of Detroit, now a windswept desert of dirty snow, skittering Want Ad sections, charred timbers, and the echo of angry voices, five and a half years old now and losing shape, sounding more and more like the hollow keening of monotonous despair. When a woman did penetrate its orbit, she did so for money, and if the name Wilson McCoy meant anything to her at all it meant getting paid up front, a John who was shot full of federal holes being notoriously difficult to bill. Then right in the middle, just when he was starting to have a good time, he would wonder if she was some kind of undercover operative, a dusky Mata Hari dispatched to divert his attention until he was helpless with orgasm and unable to struggle against an invading horde armed with greaseguns and handcuffs. Then he would become flaccid, and when the bitch failed to get him back up she would yank on her panties and flounce out to spread the word on the street that the great Wilson McCoy was a limp wad. The risk to his reputation was too great, and so he had told Wolf to cool it on the sporting ladies for a while. A while having been ten months and some days as of this last week of January 1973.

The old man who sold papers in front of the burned-out bakery on Edison solemnly handed a copy of that day's *Chronicle* to

McCoy, who never paid; in 1969 the old man's daughter, a sophomore at Wayne State University, had been walking past a safe house on Cass on her way to school when a bullet shattered her spine. The slug was eventually traced to a .30-30 issued to a Detroit police officer backing up an FBI raid on the Black Panther hideout, which at the time had been unoccupied for several weeks. The last McCoy had heard, the girl was in a state-owned nursing home in Monroe or somesuch place, getting spoon-fed Malt-O-Meal and watching *Days of Our Lives* during the hours when she would have been studying for her master's.

Paper tucked beneath his arm, he walked east to the corner of Woodrow Wilson, where he slapped five with a couple of brothers he knew by their nicknames only from the rib place on Hazelwood. One of them had a transistor radio, over which McCoy learned that the Pistons were taking a beating from the Lakers in the second quarter.

Which what else was new.

"Hey, man, turn on the news."

Obediently the brother with the radio, a long drink of water with a Wilt Chamberlain Vandyke who looked as if he must have played a little roundball in his time, thumbed the wheel over to CKLW, the Windsor station, just in time to hear Grant Hudson announce that two "punks" had been taken away in a "meat wagon" from the scene of the botched robbery of a drug operation on Sherman earlier that evening. McCoy, who liked the stentorian-voiced news reader's snide copy even if he wasn't a brother, didn't recognize the name of either of the robbers-turned-victims. When the headlines gave way to a traffic report with no mention of McCoy, he concluded that an FBI blackout was in force. They were planning some kind of maneuver. He made a mental note to put Wolf to work on it. For an Indian he was plenty good at sniffing out the scuttlebutt on the street. McCoy himself was piss-poor; pushed too hard, tipped his hand. Didn't matter what kind of hero you were in that situation, when people found out you wanted something, really wanted it, they stood on it like it was the only thing holding them up.

He took his leave of the pair and started down Wilson, wondering if one or both of them were reporting to the feds. He'd learned at lot about people since his late teens, when he'd first put on the black beret to get himself out of his mother's house. In those days things had seemed pretty clear: black to black, white to white, and no overlap. That was before one of his closest friends had turned state's evidence to indict him and a half-dozen others in return for immunity, and before a white attorney in a five-hundred-dollar suit had sprung him clear of a homicide charge when the only question among those who followed the case was whether McCoy would go to Jackson or Marquette for his life stretch. Wising up was the shits.

In 1967, before the riots and shortly after beating the rap for the ambush slaying of four men in the elevator of the Penobscot Building the previous summer, Wilson McCoy had been busy composing a letter to the local media in a second-floor bedroom of a condemned house — ironically, it was the same one in front of which the Wayne State sophomore was shot two years later — when the floor shook and a pane popped out of his window overlooking Cass. McCoy had been smart enough to quit the premises immediately, and dumb enough to leave the letter behind. Its threatening tone made it Exhibit A at his Grand Jury hearing, resulting in his being bound over for trial for conspiracy to endanger the public and commit property damage in excess of ten thousand dollars and two counts of manslaughter. The two counts belonged to a Panther named Cameroon and a fat nineteen-year-old slut of a Symbionese Liberation Army recruit who had been packing C-4 into a galvanized pipe in the basement of the house when it went off, blowing out the ground-level windows and plastering a surprised blue eyeball against the foundation of the restaurant next door.

The white attorney who had won McCoy's acquittal in the homicide case, a Panther retainer, argued his bail down from a million to a hundred thousand, whereupon McCoy's aged deaf mother put up her house as collateral to a bailbondsman named Ance. McCoy was out about two hours when he hot-wired a new frost-green Impala on a Chevrolet lot on Gratiot and took off for San Francisco. Transporting a stolen vehicle across state lines brought in the FBI, and he'd been on the run ever since; if you could call festering in attics and basements and shitholes like the condemned building on Twelfth *on the run*. He'd only come back to Detroit because he was sick of flower children and earnest revolutionaries, and curious about what would happen when he turned up in the old neighborhood.

He had never for one moment thought the feds would do nothing.

His first glimpse of Twelfth Street after the riots shocked him to the soles of his feet. He'd bitterly regretted missing the excitement, had applauded the flames and destruction on the portable black-and-white TV set where he'd followed it in his little room at the top of a row house in Haight-Ashbury, but hadn't been prepared to find that nothing had been done three years later beyond clearing the rubble from the streets and boarding up the shattered windows with plywood. Quincy Springfield's blind pig was gone, burned to the ground. The juke boxes that had belted out Aretha and the Temptations — "Ball of Confusion," man — were silent. The street that had glowed pink and green of neon noon the whole night through, Saturday night after Saturday night, was dark, deserted by even the ghosts of big boatlike Cadillacs, super-bored Dusters, and junked-up Harleys whose rumbling carburetors and mashing gears had made the whole neighborhood tingle like an electric charge. Now the unobstructed wind slapped at the shreds of old election bills. Terns swooped at flutters in the patches of untended grass and shat from the disintegrating gingerbread on the empty buildings. At twenty-two, he'd felt like the old man who had outlived all the friends who could serve as his pallbearers.

He remembered where he was when he found out he'd been named among the Ten Most Wanted. It was in the rib joint on Hazelwood, and he was wiping his hands on a steamed towel after polishing off a rack as big as his head when Tino, the restaurant's bull-necked owner and one of Joe Louis's early victories in the string that had led him to the championship, came over and informed him that as a celebrity McCoy was now entitled to have a meatball sandwich named after him. That night on Channel 4, Ted Russell confirmed that he had made the list.

That was how he learned the FBI knew where he was. He'd heard they didn't swing that spot on someone until they were ready to bring him in, thus maintaining the legend.

For a week after the announcement he didn't stir from his building. He salvaged a dozen Campbell's soup cans from the dumpster out back and stood them in front of the door and on the windowsill in the room upstairs where he slept and scattered crumpled newspapers around his bed, just in case they got past the cans without making a racket. He tucked a .22 magnum inside the top of his right boot to back up the big .44 in the web canvas holster under his left arm. He quit marijuana cold, wanting to keep his reflexes sharp for when Efrem Zimbalist, Jr. kicked out his lock. When the week was up and cabin fever forced him outside at last, he almost shot a kid on a skateboard when he whizzed around the corner from Atkinson, narrowly missing him. The kid, who was no more than thirteen, fell on his butt on the sidewalk and goggled at the big nickel-plated muzzle staring him in the face. Mortified, McCoy snarled at him to split and threaded the long barrel back into its scabbard.

Nobody came up and arrested him that day. Or the next week. When after six months he was still at large, McCoy had realized there was no incentive for the feds to take him into custody as long as he stayed put. If their information system was half as good as they made out, they knew the esteem in which he was held by the rebellious black community where he'd spent most of his life. He was *their* fugitive from justice. Hoover's Heroes weren't about to risk a civil disturbance on the scale of 1967 by going in after him. He was a free man — provided he remained within the ten blocks contiguous to the safe house he had selected. One step outside would be his first on the short straight path to the federal correctional facility at Milan, Michigan, or more likely the hardcase specialty center at Marion, Illinois, where he'd have the opportunity of being butt-fucked by a much more exclusive class of convict. Given that choice, he'd go on swimming between and around the rib cage of the skeleton of what had been Twelfth Street. He couldn't even bring himself to take a suppository.

By the time he got to Tino's on Hazelwood he was hungry enough to devour the aroma of sweet barbecue sauce that permeated the establishment. His favorite table was unoccupied — no surprise, as it was always reserved for him, and in any case the place hadn't been full since Johnson was in office — and he sat with his back in the corner just like Wild Bill as Tino boated in from the kitchen mopping his big broken-knuckled hands on an apron stained the color of blood.

"What's it tonight, the McCoy?"

"No, bring me the Redd Foxx. Extra sauce."

"I got the Thurgood Marshall on special. Cajun chicken stuffed with crab."

"The Foxx."

Tino ducked his head, a tic left over from his former profession. "Oh, the Indian called. Said he'd try again."

The call came while McCoy was eating his slaw. He walked down the short hall that led to the restrooms and lifted the receiver dangling from the pay telephone.

"I picked up that delivery," Wolf said.

"Delivery? What the fuck you —"

"At the hospital, remember? We talked about it." The Indian sounded resignedly patient.

"Oh, yeah. No busted parts?"

"It's intact, kind of. How soon you want me to collect?"

"Give it a couple days."

"These goods are a little more perishable than I thought. If we don't make delivery soon it may lose all value."

"Couple days, I said. You got to make them want it bad enough to pay what we ask."

"I may have to bring someone in," said Wolf after a pause.

McCoy belched. Paranoia brought out his chronic indigestion. "What kind of someone, Dick fucking Tracy? You screwing me over, Cochise?"

"Wilson, I put this together. I'm the one taking the risks. I'm not asking your permission, I'm telling you I'm bringing someone in. Otherwise in a couple of days there won't be anything left worth paying for."

"How come I didn't hear anything about it on the radio?"

"They're sitting on it. If anyone knows how they do things it's you."

"Just don't screw me over. I don't think Michigan ever lifted the bounty on redskin scalps."

"Call you tomorrow."

"Wolf?" Dial tone. McCoy slammed the handset into its cradle. "Goddamn Squanto."

He chased down his meal with Bromo as usual, left according to his custom without paying, turned the corner, and started up Twelfth for home, hooking it now. The cold burned his face and frosted the hairs in his nose. Minus readings tonight. On the stoop in front of his door he pretended to hunt for his key while he checked out the two vans parked down the street. One was a rust-bitten VW bus crusted over with peace signs and old McGovern/Eagleton bumper stickers; the other was spotless silver and bore the Highland Electronics logo on its side panels. Guess which vehicle was wired to D.C.

Shivering in the danker air of the unheated ground floor, he checked his watch, an unconscious military habit from his Panther training. Forty-minute walk, not counting supper. He figured he'd been photographed — what, fifty or sixty times? Price of fame, Wilson. Hope Kmart soaks them good for extra prints.

Chapter
Twenty-Four

Wolf wondered how it had come to this.

What had started with an awakened sense of pride in his blood had turned into something else.

He knew now that there was no special reason to be proud of something one had been born to, that he couldn't change; and God knew that what he'd seen of his people up North and at Alcatraz scarcely lived up to the old legends. If he still clung to a cause, that cause was Wilson McCoy; and if Wilson McCoy in the flesh seemed hardly worth the grief of self-denial, then that great abstract, Loyalty, served. A man had to commit to something to justify his birth.

But how justify an existence that placed an innocent in jeopardy for the sake of an abstract?

Had he for one moment stopped to consider the state of the little girl's health, he'd have waited until she was out of danger before taking her. He'd been so pumped by the phenomenal good fortune of a development that had removed the object of his quest from the security of the mansion in Grosse Pointe to the relative chaos of a hospital environment — where, for chrissake, rapes took place, babies got switched by accident, and patients had the wrong organs removed — that certain incidentals had escaped his attention, such as the importance of keeping Opal Caryn Cooper Crownover Ogden alive long enough to collect fifty thousand dollars from her parents for her return.

True, her condition had not been thought serious enough to place her in intensive care. That would have made the snatch much more difficult, with only one door leading to the ward from the public part of the hospital and two nurses seated at the monitors inside at all times. Her placement in an ordinary private room for observation only meant that he had merely to duck into a vacant room nearby when visiting hours ended and wait for things to quiet down. Mother Caryn's decision to remain by her daughter's side complicated things somewhat, but he'd felt confident — and he'd been right — that sooner or later she would step outside the room, if for no other reason than to clear her head of nighttime horrors. A lifelong insomniac, Wolf was intimately acquainted with those horrors. Should worse come to worse he was armed, but that was a scenario he chose not to entertain. If nothing presented itself that night, it would on the next. Hospitals didn't dump the children of the wealthy out of their beds after just twenty-four hours.

But Caryn came through for him early the first morning.

The girl was groggy and offered no struggle when he disconnected her from the tubes and monitor wire and carried her out, bundled in the thin hospital blanket. He moved fast, before the nurse at the station could react to the flat line, taking the fire stairs at the opposite end of the corridor to the first-floor exit. But the exposure to the below-zero air of the parking lot during the brief walk to his car must have aggravated Opal's condition, because she coughed and cried all the way to the motor home park in rural Oakland County where he'd put down a month's cash deposit on a seventeen-foot trailer. By the time he'd tucked her beneath the cheap polyester Kmart quilt he'd bought in Troy along with the other incidentals required for a short stay, the shallow hacking had deepened and she was spitting up fluid. And for the first time in his life he knew true terror. It was one thing if he traded a healthy child for money, quite another if she died in his charge. He knew what happened in prison to the murderers of little girls. He was pretty sure the conviction of his own loyalty wouldn't be enough to see him through that.

After he'd called Wilson from the open-air booth at the Shell station across the road, he pumped the cradle and asked Information for the number of Mary Margaret Whitehorn in Rochester Hills.

She came, prosaically enough, by taxi, carrying an old scuffed beige-and-blue suitcase with tarnished brass latches; but if Wolf found these details disappointing, he was heartened by the sheer physical presence of the woman. Standing well over six feet in two-inch cowboy heels, she could have been fifty or seventy-five. Her hair, tied casually at the nape and fanning out below that to her waist, was iron gray, but her face, lightly rouged and painted, bore no lines. She wore an ankle-length cloth coat open over a brown corduroy dress whose hem reached the tops of her worn tan boots. The ancient-looking polished black bear's-claw necklace that hung around her neck had to have cost a fortune; beyond that there was nothing on her person that couldn't be redeemed out of Wolf's pocket. He had to wonder what she did with the legendary fees she charged for her special services.

Respect was crucial. He stepped onto the flight of wooden steps that led to the trailer's door, holding it open for her. "Mrs. Whitehorn, I'm very grateful —"

"Give the driver fifteen dollars." She went inside.

He saw to the chore. The cabman, a lean black crowding sixty with a CORE button pinned to his Tigers cap, said, "She like a gypsy?"

"Shaman," the Indian corrected. "A Creek medicine woman. She practices all over Michigan and Wisconsin. Why, what'd she say?"

"She don't like the moon. She say it all bloody."

Wolf searched the overcast sky.

"I can't see it neither, but I didn't argue with her. You see her eyes?"

"I didn't get a look. Something wrong with them?"

"All I'm saying is I'm sleeping with the lights on tonight."

When Wolf entered the trailer, Whitehorn was bent over Opal. She pried open each of the girl's eyelids with a square thumb. "How long has she been unconscious?"

"Couple of hours. I'm thinking she needs the sleep."

"The child's in a coma."

Shit.

The woman peeled the quilt down to the foot of the bed, exposing the tiny body in its cotton gown. Her feet looked blue in the light of the fluorescent tube mounted above the headboard. She placed the back of a hand against the girl's forehead and cheeks, took her wrists gently and pumped them up and down twice slowly, as if performing artificial respiration, then laid both palms inside Opal's armpits and slid them all the way down to her ankles, tracing her outline into the sheet beneath her. It all looked pretty theatrical to Wolf, who began to wonder if he shouldn't have risked calling a legitimate doctor.

Whitehorn straightened suddenly, removing her coat in the same movement, and threw it into the armchair by the bed. As she lifted her suitcase from the floor to the chair, Wolf saw her eyes. The pupils were vertical slits, the irises large and mahogany-colored, almost obliterating the whites. He could actually see the catlike apertures opening to let in light as she lifted the lid of the suitcase.

It contained nothing but a bundle wrapped in what looked like deerhide, the size of a swaddled infant, painted all over with geometric shapes in faded primary colors and tied with sinew. She lifted it gently, laid it on the bed near the foot, untied the knot, and spread out the hide. A pungent aroma filled the room when the contents were exposed to the air: a combination of herbs and chlorophyll and something much more basic, which reminded Wolf instantly of his first visit to Mackinac Island, where bicycles and buggies were the only wheeled traffic allowed by law. And he wondered what plain horseshit had to do with the process of healing.

Moving with assurance — there seemed to be order to the arrangement of the items in the bundle — Mary Margaret Whitehorn pushed back her corduroy sleeves, selected a tiny sprig of green leaves bound at the stems with something that resembled a strand of hair, crushed them between thumb and forefinger, and held them beneath the girl's nostrils. Although Wolf himself detected the acrid stench, Opal showed no reaction. Whitehorn grunted and returned the sprig to the bundle. She slid a hand behind the child's head, lifted it, and undid the tie behind her neck with the other hand. Wolf turned away when the gown was removed, feeling like a child molester. But he turned back to watch the rest of the procedure.

The medicine woman unrolled a small oil-cloth cylinder, picked up one of the matches inside, struck it on the steel bedrail, and lit a small stump of dirty yellow candle. Wolf smelled tallow. Chanting gutturally, she offered the flame to the earth and the sky and the four directions, then tilted the candle over the cheap nightstand until a puddle of melted tallow formed on the surface, whereupon she stood the candle in the viscosity. She turned the switch to the fluorescent light. Now the greasy orange glow of the tiny flame was the only illumination in the trailer. Chanting still, Whitehorn removed the lid from a clay jar. The manure stench sharpened as she rotated her fingers inside the jar, then bent once again to the naked child and smeared the greenish contents all over the narrow undeveloped chest, taking special care to draw circles around the nipples.

She called for a damp cloth. He went into the claustrophobic bathroom, wet a hand towel in the sink, and brought it to her. She wiped the shit off her hands and gave it back. Holding the towel by a clean corner, he opened the lid of the trash canister in the kitchen end of the trailer and dropped it inside. When he returned to the bed, Whitehorn was pouring white powder from a glazed-pottery bottle into a matching saucer. She set the bottle down, struck a fresh match and, holding the saucer directly over Opal's chest, dropped the burning stick into the heap of powder. There was a snap and a blinding blue flash and black smoke filled the trailer, stinging the membranes inside Wolf's nostrils. He swore and reached for the window crank. Iron fingers clamped his wrist. He relaxed his biceps.

The smoke dissipated. Now the medicine woman let go, and Wolf tilted the glass louvers to let out the sharp sulphurous stink. Whitehorn plucked a fresh sprig from the supply inside the bundle, squashed the leaves, and held them to the child's nose. The nostrils twitched, the nose wrinkled.

Grunting again, Whitehorn dropped the sprig, switched on the light, blew out the candle, and rolled it back into the cylinder of oilcloth along with the matches. She rewrapped the bundle, making sure the side with the painted symbols remained on top, tied it tight, and transferred it to the suitcase.

"That's it?" Wolf asked.

"If you expected me to dance around the bed and shake a rattle, you went to the wrong tribe. You want Comanche." She shut the lid and snapped home the latches.

"What about the horseshit?"

"It's not just horseshit. But you can wash it off as soon as she regains consciousness."

"What if she doesn't?"

"See for yourself."

He looked down. Droplets of sweat glittered all over the six-year-old's body. He put a hand to her forehead. It felt cool.

"I'll be damned."

"More than likely." She snapped her fingers and held a palm under his nose. It smelled of herbs.

He fished two hundred dollars out of his wallet and laid the bills in her hand. Ten minutes, and she had collected as much as he made in a week excavating basements for the construction firm where he worked during Michigan's brief building season. She counted them quickly, stuffed them down the front of her blouse, and shrugged into her coat. "Can I pick up a cab at the park entrance?"

"There's a Shell station across the road. You can call. If I knew you wouldn't be here any longer than this I'd have told the cabbie to wait."

"There's no telling. Sometimes it takes hours, or days. She's young, she wants to live. The dark spirits never had a chance."

"Was all that stuff necessary?"

Her pupils shrank, and he thought he was in for a lecture. Then she moved her shoulders. "Some of it's show. You can try to guess which part. The two hundred's for healing, not lessons on how to be a shaman."

"I'm guessing it was the magnesium powder."

"That was the most important part."

Before leaving she spread the quilt back over Opal. The girl's breathing was ragged now, more like troubled sleep than cataleptic torpor. Wolf walked the woman to the station. He didn't know why, apart from the fact that she fascinated him. She was more than big enough to take care of herself and he suspected she was in better condition than he. He offered to carry the suitcase, but she ignored him.

"I'll wait with you till the taxi comes," he said when they reached the booth.

"Be with the child. Coming back from the shadows is hard enough without a familiar face waiting." Her pupils were huge and shining in the gloom beyond the lights of the station. He had the impression they would reflect direct light with a green glow. "*Is* your face familiar?"

"I'm a family friend."

She went on watching him while a tractor-trailer rig advertising New Tide with Enzymes ground down for the turn into the driveway, air brakes farting. Then she lifted the receiver from the telephone. "She'll be hungry when she wakes up. Lots of protein and liquids. Orange juice."

"Now you sound just like the A.M.A."

"Where do you suppose they picked it up?" She started dialing.

The walk back was bitterly cold. He'd neglected to put on his quilted vest and he felt it in his bones, just the way the old ones used to complain about when a big snow was coming. The built-in electric wall heater cut in with a whir when he opened the trailer door, welcoming him like a happy dog. Opal was propped up on one elbow, digging sleep out of her eyes with a fist.

"Someone pooped," she said.

Chapter
Twenty-Five

"*Detroit P.D.*, that's what they was calling
it," Horace Hyde told Mac McDowell, the
night sergeant at the First Precinct.

"Yeah?" McDowell grinned, anticipating.
Wednesdays behind the front desk were flat
as piss and he'd been glad as hell to see the
sixteen-year Traffic Bureau officer stop by
for a cuppa on his way home. Horace —
they were calling him "Hollywood Hyde"
now, on account of his brief exposure before
the cameras in the movie shoot going on
downtown — was a good storyteller, which
as far as McDowell was concerned was the
most important thing once a cop proved himself on the street.

"Well, that got the mayor's juices going,
Detroit being in the title and all. So he opened
up all kinds of doors: issued permits, waived
the disaster bond, put cops on the barricades
— shit, I bet if that hippie fuck director took
a dump in the middle of Gribbs's office

Hizzoner'd wipe his pimply ass for him. Public image, tourist revenue, show the country we got crime in hand; you know the drill."

"Sure do."

"So in the Freep this morning, Doc Greene starts his column with the scoop that they're changing the name of the picture. You want to guess what they're calling it?"

McDowell shook his head. He lifted his mug but didn't drink from it. If this was as good as he suspected he'd be squirting coffee out of his nose in another minute.

"Murder City."

The sergeant roared, spilled coffee on his blouse anyway and jerked a napkin out from under his chocolate fried cake to mop it up before it stained. "Jesus!" There were tears in his eyes.

"Gribbs shit a brick, Nichols too. They're holding a press conference tomorrow."

"Give Hollywood the old heave-ho."

"Oh, hell no. They want that studio money. What they'll do is make faces and write letters and fall all over themselves kissing Ryan O'Neal's or whoever's ass next time they come to town looking for a cheap shoot. Shit, if I had a daughter and she came to me and said she wanted to be mayor, I think I'd buy her a pair of them go-go boots and set her up on the corner of Michigan and Third.

301

At least when you tell a hooker to roll over and spread 'em she don't make no speech first."

"Sergeant."

"Just a second." McDowell gave the citizen who'd come up to the desk a grazing glance and returned his attention to Hyde. "You figure this joker Young's going to be any better?"

"Shit, I don't know. Maybe it's time this city *had* a black mayor; make the collar match the cuffs."

"Charlie Battle. I'm with 1300." The man standing in front of the desk held out a palm with a shield on it. "If you're Sergeant McDowell, you called me earlier tonight. About my uncle."

"Oh, yeah. Sorry. I thought you was some drunk looking for a hole for the night." He gave Battle the once-over, to show it was an honest mistake. The black officer had on a gray overcoat that needed brushing on top of a rumpled shirt with a dirty collar that looked as if he'd rescued it from the hamper. He carried a paper shopping bag with handles. His face was haggard. "Watch the desk, will you, Horace? Come on back." He climbed down from the platform and held open the swinging gate that separated the reception area from the rest of the building.

Battle followed him down the aisle that ran between the desks, only three of which were occupied by a skeleton crew that wasn't even bothering to look busy; one, a balding uniform with a Clark Gable moustache, was setting his wristwatch according to the recorded voice rustling in his ear from the telephone receiver he had tucked under his chin.

"Figured we had us a drunk at first," McDowell was saying, "then a psycho case. We were all set to call Ypsi State to send some guys with a happy jacket when he started talking about you. Matt Kellog happened to be around. I guess he knows you. Anyway that's where we got your number."

The holding cell, seven by six, contained a plain army cot, olive-drab canvas on a wood frame. Anthony Battle sat on its edge with a blanket over his shoulders, staring somewhere into the middle distance. His big bare feet were dark against the worn green linoleum tiles on the floor.

"Matt's civvies fit him as to pants. Couldn't find a shirt he wouldn't split the first time he raised his arms. Forget shoes. Your daddy's a big man."

"He's my uncle."

McDowell looked sympathetic. "We had to pull him in. Buck naked running down the street — he'd of froze to death if some old lady didn't stab him with her umbrella for attempted rape. You ought to put him somewhere."

"Can I talk to him in private?"

"Hell, you can take him on out of here. We only locked him up for his own protection." The sergeant unlocked the cell with a key attached to the case on his belt.

"I'd like to talk to him first."

"Sure."

Alone with the old wrestler, Battle smiled. "You sure had Thea worried. She thought you were in your room watching *Medical Center*. How'd you sneak past her?"

"Ginny, that you?"

He felt a lurch. Anthony's wife had been gone eight years. Ovarian cancer. "No, Uncle. It's Charlie."

"Charlie ain't coming out. Don't know why he done went and kilt that man. He don't neither, I'm betting. Stick that shit in your veins and stop thinking. I know we can't afford to bring up his boy. It's just till Social Services finds someone to take him in. I don't want my flesh and blood in no state home."

"You did a good job, Anthony. You and Aunt Ginny. I never felt like I didn't have a mother and father."

A grin transformed the brutal face. "It won't take long. That boy sure looks cute in that Davy Crockett hat."

"I've still got it somewhere. Ginny kept it in her hope chest along with her wedding hat."

"What you talking about, boy? Your Aunt Ginny's been dead for years." Anthony's grin was gone, his eyes in focus. "Get me out of here. I never done a day in jail in my life. This is a damn disgrace."

Battle held out the sack. "I brought some clothes. It's two below. You'll freeze your nuts off."

"I never took one penny didn't belong to me. Not when I carried a hod for fifty cents a hour, feeding three mouths. Not even when I was getting my brains beat out at lunch for bets." He bent to pull on his socks. The blanket slid off. His build was still impressive, despite the slackening muscles. Battle envied him his shoulders.

"You didn't get them beat out much. That's why Charlie Balls offered you that wrestling contract."

"Wrestling? Shit. Monkey-training's more like it. Airplane spins. Atomic drops. We had us a script. Otherwise I'd of throwed the Peruvian Giant clear acrost Olympia."

Battle knelt to tie his uncle's shoes. "You make it how you can. That's what you always told me."

"Not you, Charlie."

He raised his head. Anthony was looking at him.

"I bust my buttons when you took that oath," the old man said. "You come a far piece, boy. Mother run off, your daddy dead at twenty-seven with a shiv in his ribs in the shower at Jackson. Everybody said you'd end up the same way."

"Not you."

"They was times. When you cut up them bus seats your aunt and I thought we lost you for sure."

"Reggie Cleveland dared me. It was his scout knife."

"Walking them eighteen blocks to school and back for the rest of the semester cured you of that. Ginny said I should drive you, but I said no, walking gives a boy time to think."

Battle helped him button his shirt. "Anthony, we've got something to talk about."

"I know."

The old man's tone was suddenly grave. When his nephew looked at him, his eyes were watering. He hoped this wasn't going to be another uncontrollable jag. Sometimes the wires in his head crossed and he started blubbering.

"Hey, Battle!"

306

"We're on our way, Sergeant." Battle threaded his uncle's arms into the sleeves of the old coat he'd brought.

"You know these women?"

He looked beyond the gate. Thea was standing there with a black woman he didn't recognize. She wore a heavy woolen cape, a black slouch hat secured with a scarf tied under her chin, and that tragic, big-eyed expression that went with the professional caregiver.

Shit.

He told McDowell they were okay. Thea opened the gate without waiting and approached the cell, followed closely by the woman in the black hat, who was carrying a leather portfolio.

"Is he all right?" Thea asked. Unlike her husband, she looked put-together. No one would have known she'd been up half the night like Charlie. She had makeup on and a pressed pants suit under her belted trench coat.

"H'llo, Thea. My, don't you look pretty. Tell her she look pretty, Charlie."

"He's fine," Battle said. "Just got a little turned around."

"A woman gots to hear these things," Anthony insisted.

"Charlie, this is Bianca Ferguson. She's

with Social Services."

"Hello, Charlie." The woman pulled off a glove to grasp his hand. She had strong fingers. "How you doing, Anthony?"

"You the social worker?"

"Yes, I am."

"Sorry you come all this way, ma'am. Truly I am. Ginny and me, we done decided to keep little Charlie. Blood gots to stay with blood."

"Mrs. Ferguson specializes in geriatric cases."

"You work late." Battle felt his gorge rising.

"We have a twenty-four-hour line at the office. Thea called there and they called me. I was visiting a case not far from your neighborhood. One near you, as they say." She smiled.

"Honey —"

Thea interrupted him. "Charlie, we talked about this. What if no one got to Anthony? He could have frozen to death."

"He wouldn't have got out if you kept an eye on him like you were supposed to."

"Charlie?" Mrs. Ferguson said.

"We've been through this. I can't watch your uncle every minute of every day."

"Charlie, if I may say something."

He gave the social worker an expression

308

of exasperated patience.

"Everyone in your situation thinks their problem is unique. Believe me, I see it a dozen times a month. I understand your uncle raised you, and now that he can't look after himself you feel obligated to take care of him."

"It's not an obligation."

"I didn't mean it that way. It happens all over. You're adults, you have your own lives to lead, but you don't want to abandon your older loved ones to an institution. Meanwhile the tension grows. Your wife resents the demands on your time and emotions, you resent her objections, and you both resent the person in need — you more than Thea, because you remember when your uncle was young and strong and able to look after himself and his family, and you're constantly reminded of the disparity. And you feel guilty for feeling resentful, and take it out on your wife. Institutionalization —"

"Got it all figured out, huh?" Battle said. "Just another case history for your folder."

"Charlie, that's not what she's saying at all."

He ignored her. "Bianca, is it? I mean, since we're all getting on so tight, first-name basis and all. Well, Bianca, you're right. This all happened before. Only with us, the last time *I* was the person in need, and somebody from your department tried to talk Anthony into putting me in a home because he was making thirty bucks a week and already supporting himself and my aunt. And he said the same thing I'm saying to you. No. Not on your life."

The blow, coming from beyond the corner of his eye, nearly knocked him off his feet. A blue light exploded and he staggered, grabbing one of the bars.

"Hey!"

All five of the uniformed officers in the room converged on the cell. Sergeant McDowell had snaked a baton from the socket behind the front desk. Battle stuck out a hand, stopping them. He looked at his uncle, who was kneading the stinging palm of his huge open hand.

Anthony said, "You don't talk to no ladies that way, no sir. Didn't I raise you no better than that? You tell her you's sorry."

Bianca Ferguson smiled. The whites still showed all around her irises. The old man could still move swiftly for his bulk. "It's all right, Anthony. He wasn't being disrespectful."

"It ain't all right. He ain't so big and I ain't so far gone I can't take him over my knee like I done that time I caught him spitting on a girl when he was nine. Charlie, you tell this fine lady you's sorry and it won't never happen again."

He told her, smiling a little despite the numbness. The side of his face had begun to swell.

Anthony grunted surly satisfaction. "Now, you listen to what the lady gots to say. She making sense if you just open up your ear-holes."

"I was about to suggest our foster home program." Mrs. Ferguson was addressing all three of them now. The other officers had begun to disperse. "Anthony will have to undergo a complete physical and psychological examination to determine he doesn't need advanced nursing care. I'm inclined to think he doesn't. In that event we'd place him in a group home, which Charlie and Thea may select after visiting a number of them in the area. He'd be free to come and go as he pleases, with some supervision purely for his own safety, and he'll receive all the medical care he requires. You may visit him at any time, and sign him out whenever you want him to stay with you at your home, or accompany you on a family trip."

"I've heard some bad things about foster homes," Charlie said.

"There have been serious abuses. In every

case, the elderly victim had been dumped at the facility by relatives who never stopped by to see how they were getting on. I don't deny that Social Services slipped up badly in those cases, but it shared the blame with the families. Very likely the victims would have been subject to the same abuse and neglect at home. I think I can state with assurance that these circumstances are very different."

Thea moved close to her husband inside the cell's open door and took his hand. He squeezed it. "I can't make this decision," he said.

"This place black folks only?" Anthony asked.

The social worker shook her head. "We're forbidden by law to discriminate. However, in this area, the guests are predominantly black."

" 'Guests.' " The old wrestler beamed. He had all his own teeth. "I likes the sound of that. How soon I move in?"

Battle laid a hand between the great bunched muscles high on his uncle's back. "We'll talk about it tomorrow."

A ditch appeared in Mrs. Ferguson's brow. "I'd like your consent to check Anthony into Detroit Receiving tonight. When someone his age has been exposed to extreme cold he should be held overnight for observation. Pneumonia is the greatest killer in his age group."

"We'll keep him warm."

"Charlie," Anthony said, "I'm awful tired."

Thea said, "Of course we'll check him in. Charlie?"

Anthony winked at his nephew. "I be back for my things, so don't you sell 'em."

Charlie embraced his uncle. After a moment the old man's arms closed around him and squeezed. Charlie gasped for breath, choking on tears and the rough wool of his uncle's shirt.

The telephone was ringing when they got back to the apartment, loud in the emptiness of the place with just Charlie and Thea Battle in it. He hurried to answer. It was twenty past three, way too late for good news.

"Sergeant, this is Lieutenant Zagreb. I've been trying to reach you all night."

"Sorry, sir, I had an emergency." He dropped into his worn easy chair, then rolled over on one hip to finger his keys out of his pocket. Thea, satisfied the call wasn't from the hospital, went into the kitchen. He heard cups clinking.

"I just wanted to tell you to report to the City-County Building tomorrow instead of

313

1300. You've been reassigned. You're back on City Hall detail."

"How come?"

"We're closing the Crownover-Ogden investigation and reinstating Kubicek. He's back on STRESS starting tomorrow."

"What about Junius Harrison?"

"We have a gun and a dead man with a criminal record. Thanks to you we have an unstable early home life for Harrison, an abusive father who beat his wife and probably his boy as well. That's a breeding ground. Damn fine detective work, Officer."

"It doesn't make Harrison a criminal."

"It's enough to make Quincy Springfield and his American Ethiopian Congress go looking for a more suitable martyr. Anyway with Russell Littlejohn out of the picture we have nothing to prove Harrison wasn't involved in the robbery and that Kubicek wasn't justified in using deadly force to stop his flight." He cleared his throat. "I'm putting you in for a commendation. For a novice investigator you did an impressive job."

"Trouble was I impressed all the wrong people."

"What? I'm sorry."

"If it's all the same to you, sir, I wish you'd forget the commendation. I was just an extra hand on this one. Bookfinger and

Stilwell should have all the credit for the way it turned out."

"Don't be coy, Officer. The department doesn't appreciate modesty."

"I'd consider it a favor."

"It's your career. Good night."

"As a matter of fact, it's been shitty all around." But he was talking to a dial tone.

Chapter
Twenty-Six

Twenty-four hours after Opal Ogden disappeared from Hutzel Hospital, the Detroit office of the Federal Bureau of Investigation released an Identi-Kit reconstruction of the face of the man believed to be her abductor to the Associated Press and every television station exceeding ten thousand megahertz in Michigan, Wisconsin, Ohio, and Indiana.

Four hours after the drawing first aired, during the six o'clock EST TV news reports, all the circuits in the switchboard of the Federal Building on Cass Avenue were loaded. One citizen, an elderly woman from the sound of her voice, insisted that the dour Indian features belonged to her milkman — a report that was discounted when it developed that there had been no residential milk delivery to her neighborhood since 1963. Another forty or so were circular-filed immediately when the callers drifted off on tangents to extraterrestrial conspiracies, the

Second Coming, and in one memorable instance the somber assurance that the suspect was in fact Art Linkletter rigged up in a diabolical disguise.

(The caller was well known to most of the operators, who had for years been directing his singular theories concerning the children's talk-show host to Bureau offices upstairs. He was a retired tool-and-die foreman living in Inkster whose son, a guest on the show at age five, had run away from home when he was sixteen. Mr. Linkletter had changed his telephone number twice to discourage the man from calling him and demanding to know the whereabouts of his son.)

Approximately twenty of the callers were considered serious enough to warrant putting an agent on the line. Seven of the callers received personal visits. The information in each case was found to be faulty, although the superintendent of an apartment building in Harper Woods, a three-quarter-blood Cheyenne who had come east from Oklahoma in 1954 to take a job in the Ford Rawsonville plant, was brought in for questioning. He was released when the Wayne County Sheriff's Department confirmed that he had been in jail awaiting arraignment on charges of assault and battery and malicious destruction of property in connection with a disagreement in a downtown Detroit bar the night of the abduction.

Stephen Grunwald, Special Agent Francis Riordan's number-two man, adjusted his black-framed glasses when he entered Riordan's office. The senior field operative looked as close to disheveled as Grunwald had ever seen him. He was in his shirtsleeves, and a comma of uncombed hair dangled over his right eyebrow. Both conditions were a clear breach of Bureau regulations, such as they were amid the shambles caused by Hoover's death and the assumption to the national directorship by L. Patrick Gray — aptly named, pale nonentity that he was. And the knot of Riordan's silk necktie was slipping. But then he had been at his post since eight o'clock that morning, or rather yesterday morning, with no hope for relief in sight.

"Yes, ma'am," he was saying into the telephone. "If we should run across your husband while we're looking for the kidnapper, we'll be sure and tell him to run along home. It's lucky you haven't moved in the twelve years since he left. Yes, that would be inconvenient. Thank you for calling." He banged down the receiver. "Bitch. Is anyone screening these calls?"

"Everyone is. You're getting the cream."

"Anything from the reservations?"

Grunwald shook his head. "Custer has a lot to answer for."

"I'm still waiting for feedback from Quantico. The computers are mucked up. Hoover had all the access codes in his head. I could get the Flying Nun to put out faster."

"I don't imagine Watergate's greasing any gears either."

"Please. I'm just hoping nothing important winds up getting shredded in the confusion."

"There's someone outside you might want to talk to," Grunwald said. "He says he's on his break and he can't hang around long."

"At least that lets out the Art Linkletter guy. He's retired. Did you check his shoes for Mars dust?"

"He seems stable enough. I can run interference if you want to go home and catch some sleep."

Riordan stood and hooked his jacket off the back of his chair. "Remind me to recommend you to this job when I quit to open a haberdashery." Then his resolve faltered. He caught sight of his reflection in the night-backed window at the end of the desk, smoothed the comma of hair back into place, straightened his tie, and sat back down. "Cripes. Shoo him in before I change my mind again."

Grunwald opened the door and held it.

319

"Please come in, Mr. Mapes."

The visitor, a lean black crowding sixty with a CORE button pinned to his Tigers cap, came in and goggled at the room, mahogany-paneled with a lighted ceiling well and the Great Seal of the United States embossed six feet across on the wall behind the desk.

"Nice dump," he said. "I wondered what become of that nine hunnert bucks you fellows withheld from me last year. You got any smokes?"

"Sorry, I don't use them. Do you have some information for us?" Riordan lifted the sketch from the desk. He had done that so many times in the past fifteen hours the sheet had begun to curl away from the surface.

Mapes glanced at it briefly. "Him okay. Nose was bigger."

"Where do you think you saw him?"

"Oh, I seen him all right. I don't guess you know I'm a hackie. Picked up this fare earlier tonight. Rochester Hills it was. Sitting Bull there is waiting for her. He paid for the cab. It was this little shit trailer park way out on Northwestern."

Riordan wrote the information on a legal pad. "Did you notice anything else about him?"

320

"No. Well, he smelt like he took a bath in Brut."

Riordan stopped writing and stared at him.

"Brut, yeah." Mapes nodded, apparently to himself. "You get to be a expert when you lock yourself up in a car all the time with folks. You be surprised how many ways a person can stink."

He stopped and grinned, recognizing a rapt audience in the two agents. "I don't guess either of you fellows know what's a shaman."

Before Mapes left, Riordan's secretary, a tall redhead awaiting the results of her bar examination, with aspirations to enroll in the field training course at Quantico, entered and placed a green-and-white computer printout on Riordan's desk. He left it there unread while he stood to shake the cab driver's hand.

"You're a good citizen, Mr. Mapes. I'm going to ask you to be even better. Will you remain available? We may need you to identify the suspect."

"You mean, be in on the bust?"

"We'll keep you out of harm's way. And you'll be reimbursed by Washington for the time off work."

"I'll give you my hack number. Dispatcher knows where to find me."

"Fine. Leave it with Miss Green."

Alone with Riordan, Grunwald said, "A medicine woman?"

"It's too nutty even for the crackbrains to have dreamt up. And the girl is sick. Ring in the sheriffs on this one. Detroit too; the snatch took place in their jurisdiction. We need their good feelings if we're ever going to clean up our rotten record in this town."

"The Chief wouldn't approve."

"The Chief's deader than the Nehru suit. Oh shit." Riordan was reading the printout.

Grunwald, who had never heard his superior curse, said, "Don't tell me they deleted a file."

Riordan handed him the sheet.

SUSPECT IDENTIKIT GEO-MATCHES PORTERMAN ANDREW NO MIDDLE A/K/A WOLF B ALLENVILLE MI 9/12/46 BELIEVED ACTIVIST ALCATRAZ 1969 PHOTOS TO FOLLOW CRIMREC 6MOS WCJAIL DETROIT MI MDOP REL 2/09/70 KNOWN ASSOCIATE WILSON MCCOY SEE MCCOY WILSON FRANKLIN MOSTWANT FILE G315442/004

Chapter
Twenty-Seven

Wolf figured he'd picked the wrong place to pull off a kidnapping.

Had he been spotted someplace out West, Oklahoma say, or even in his own North country, his face all over television and in the newspapers wouldn't have concerned him; but this was Detroit, where being invisible meant being black, not Indian, and he stood out like a redskin peanut in a bowl of raisins. At the hospital he'd been especially careful not to show himself too much to the nurses behind the desk, but the God's own truth was when you looked like him, one sighting was as good as three.

Ever since the kidnapping story broke the night before, he felt as if he were being watched; a sensation he knew well from his visits to Wilson McCoy, all of whose callers had been photographed by an FBI long lens so many times the file of their pictures alone would fill a Time-Life series: *Dastards,*

Douche-Bags, and Desperate Characters. But then this was his first experience as a fugitive from justice and he wasn't sure how much of that was mere projection, as the government-paid shrink who used to drop by the tribal council chamber in St. Ignace explained the term. Indians, according to him, were notorious projectors. In any case the wheels were in motion and he had to see the thing through. If the ransom came off and things got hot he could always nick a little and take to the mountains.

Which of course was what the old ones up North dismissed as making dreams. He was tied to Wilson, if for no other reason than that a man who wasn't tied to something risked having his spirit float away.

Opal's condition was a good omen. Whether because of Creek medicine or the healing properties of time and her own youth, the little girl had improved steadily since Mary Margaret Whitehorn's visit, sleeping comfortably when she slept and from fatigue alone, and asking questions non-stop when she was awake: "Who are you?" *I'm a friend of your mother's; she asked me to look after you while she's busy.* "Are you really an Indian?" *Yes, I'm an Ottawa brave. I'd show you my bow and arrows, only I loaned them to a neighbor.* "Did you see *Jeremiah Johnson?*

You look like the Indian in that, the one at the end. Can I have something to eat?"

That one came up a lot. He hadn't realized a small child could put away so much food. Fortunately, he'd laid in a sufficient supply of kid-pleasing dishes, franks and beans and all kinds of canned fruit and puddings, and there was plenty of propane in the tank attached to the little four-burner stove. It beat all hell out of forcing C-rations between stubborn young lips, as he assumed most kidnappers did. He held that fifty-thousand-dollar packages should be treated with some care. Anyway he wasn't capable of burying a child alive or binding and gagging it and locking it in a dark closet, or committing any of the other excesses that had given the simple practice of person-stealing for profit such a bad reputation going back to the Lindbergh case.

She could identify him, of course. He didn't dwell on that. The die was cast, had been when his capital-raising scheme had shifted from robbery to ransom, and his part in it from supernumerary to major player. He'd been lost so long, wandering between worlds like the slain warrior in the old legends whose eyes had been poked out by his enemies after death, and now he had found his place. If that meant a lengthy prison sentence, he felt he could face it as a man who had made his choice and seen it through. This aimless meandering from one pale cause to the next; *that* was confinement of the cruelest sort.

His only fear — and it gnawed at him — was that he would be interrupted before the thing was finished.

It was dark outside. Nearly forty-eight hours had passed since he'd taken the girl; time enough even by Wilson's schedule for her parents to submit readily to the instructions the pair had worked out. In his pocket was a scrap of paper containing the Ogdens' unlisted telephone number, courtesy of Kindu Nampula's caterer girlfriend. He sure didn't miss Kindu. The man was an ambulatory volcano, even less predictable in his moods than Wilson. You never knew who he was going to erupt all over or what would set him off.

Opal was sound asleep. Noiselessly, Wolf slipped on his quilted vest and pulled out one of the trailer's built-in storage drawers, peeling back his shirts and underwear to expose the big nickel-plated .357 magnum Wilson had given him. That had been a special moment, although the former Panther had tried to play it down by saying that he was sick of seeing the Indian run around half-naked. The gift meant that Wilson, who trusted no one, trusted Wolf. The Indian checked all the chambers and slid the revolver down inside the waistband of his jeans, shifting the walnut grip so that the vest concealed it. The metal felt cold through the thin cotton of his undershorts.

With one hand on the doorknob he stole another look at the six-year-old. She'd lost a lot of strength during her illness and slept hard, snoring a little, like a puppy.

In the old times, Wolf had read, braves preparing for battle stripped down so their wounds would bleed clean; but the braves of old never did battle in winter. Certainly not in winter in Michigan.

Anyway, he was just going out to make a telephone call.

"How sure are you of your man on the roof?" Riordan asked in a low voice. There was a stiff, freezing wind and he had to bring his lips almost to Inspector Boyer's ear to keep his words from being snatched away.

The sheriff's inspector, a red-faced walrus in winter uniform with a pile collar and Tibetan-style cap, simply shouted over the wind, which made Riordan wince, although he was pretty sure nothing could be heard inside the trailer. "He's been in this situation a hundred times. He won't fire until he has a clear target."

"Just so he understands 'clear' doesn't mean

pacing past the window. A thirty-thirty can pass straight through his target and bounce around inside a metal box like that from now till Sunday."

"We don't even know the girl's in there with him."

"We don't know she isn't."

They were silent for a little, watching the restless silhouette moving in the window. Riordan and the other agents, wearing long-billed caps and loose windbreakers emblazoned with the FBI legend in bright yellow lest they be shot by their own allies, were crouched behind decorative evergreen bushes and nearby trailers, working their toes and fingers from time to time to keep the ice out of the joints and expelling vapor as thick as hoarfrost. Riordan hoped the guns carried by the borrowed Oakland County sheriff's deputies and Detroit city police weren't seizing up in the cold. Bureau firearms were lubricated with a polymer composition laboratory-tested to perform efficiently in temperatures as low as -40° Fahrenheit.

Squinting against the stinging wind, he peered toward the battered red taxi parked on the edge of the trailer park drive, and was annoyed to see exhaust smoke boiling from the tailpipe. He'd specifically instructed Mapes not to start the engine unless he absolutely had to. But the cab driver was getting on, and the cold probably affected him severely. The FBI man hoped he'd be alert when Porterman showed himself. If he recognized the Indian who'd paid the medicine woman's fare the previous night, he was to inform the agents by flicking on his left turn indicator briefly. That would be the signal to close in.

"Who do we have across the street?" Riordan asked the inspector.

"Two Detroit plainclothesmen. STRESS. The best they've got, or so I hear tell."

"That's what I asked for. The farther we get him away from that trailer the better."

"What if he doesn't come out?"

"Look at the way he's moving around. He'll explode if he doesn't."

"If I were running this show I'd punch in the trailer and drag him out by his balls."

"That's one good reason why you're not running this show."

"Suits me fine. You can take the flak when he trickles through your fingers. I'm —"

Riordan shushed him violently. "He's coming out."

Wolf had to lean into the door to force it open against the wind, and hang on tight to the knob once he had it open to keep the gale from snatching it out of his hand and slamming it against the side of the trailer. Bits of crystallized snow stung his face like ground glass. At the bottom of the steps he tugged his cap down over his ears and turned up the collar of his flannel shirt. The shirt and the down-filled vest might have been made of cheesecloth for all the protection they gave him. The wind chill must have been down around twenty below.

As he trotted across the drive, a glint of orange caught his eye. A car parked down at the end had its turn signal flashing.

He picked up his pace, crunching through the frost-killed grass that separated the park from Northwestern Highway, paused to check traffic, and sprinted across both lanes, hands tucked inside his armpits.

No one was using the telephone at the Shell station, a break. He'd been afraid someone might be calling home to report a delay caused by a rundown battery.

When he stepped under the light mounted above the telephone, something struck sparks off the instrument's steel cowling. The rifle report reached him an instant later, warped and drawn out by the wind. Seeing movement in the corner of his eye, he pivoted, drawing the .357, and fired. There was a loud, breathy gasp and a man in a tan coat with epaulets fell forward, skidding on the icy asphalt nearly into his feet.

A boulder struck Wolf in the chest then. His legs jerked out from under him and he sat down hard, jarring his tailbone. The big revolver spun away. When he opened his eyes a thickly built man in a long topcoat, hatless, his coarse graying hair moving in the wind, was standing over him with a big .45 army automatic clamped in both fists. The wind caught the smoke twisting out of the muzzle and tore it apart.

"Guess who, cocksucker," he said.

Chapter Twenty-Eight

Funny, the things you think of when you've got someone else's finger up your ass.

Leaning forward on the examining table with his drawers down around his knees, Joe Piper considered that the cutaway schematic drawing of the male urinary tract pinned to the bulletin board across from him resembled the map of California.

But then it occurred to him that after clouting his way down Telegraph Road to the doctor's office through two-foot drifts in the middle of a raging fucking blizzard, almost anything would.

Lowell Ridgley, M.D., urologist, Knights of Columbus sergeant-at-arms, and one piss-poor cribbage partner at Joe Piper's old house in the city back when they'd both had time for such things, skinned off and disposed of his rubber finger and washed his hands in the stainless-steel sink.

"Well, pull 'em up Joe. What are you waiting for, a tattoo?"

He pulled them up. "No, and if I was, it wouldn't be you I'd be getting it from. You got a touch as light as a punch press. So what's the verdict, do I go ahead and get dressed, or is it just going to slow things up at the autopsy?" He sat down on Ridgley's stool and tugged on his socks.

"Oh, you'll be around for a while yet. How long depends on whether you follow up on what I've got to tell you."

Standing now, Joe Piper paused in the midst of reaching for his shirt. Jesus, he loved physicals. They beat Vincent Price and the rollycoaster for scaring the shit out of you.

Ridgley paged through the sheets on his clipboard. He was a tall skinny fifty or so who appeared to have grown right up through his ring of black hair. "I won't load you down with numbers. Blood pressure's high, cholesterol's high, you could lose forty pounds —"

"Cholesterol, what the fuck's cholesterol?"

"Too much of it's bad news, trust me. Your stool's okay. I wish I had your prostate."

"What about the chest pain?"

"No sign of serious heart disease or angina. Your EKG shows some arrhythmia, but you've had that since you were a kid. We'll continue to keep an eye on that. Off the top of my head —"

"Yeah, that's what I want for my sixty bucks besides the chance to pee in a cup and cough when you grab my nuts: Your best guess."

The physician peered over the tops of his reading glasses. "You want to hear this?"

Joe Piper flicked a hand and went on buttoning his shirt.

"The pains are stress-related. You weren't always this irritable and short-tempered, so I assume you're under a great deal of pressure. What kind isn't my business."

"It sure as hell is mine."

"Medical science is just waking up to stress and its effect on health. It's inevitable, you can't duck it; just trying makes it worse. But you can step back from it now and then. When was the last time you took an honest-to-Christ vacation?"

"That'd be my honeymoon. We spent the weekend in Chicago."

"That was it? One weekend — what, seven or eight years ago?"

"No, no. Dolly and me ain't got around to a honeymoon yet. We were too busy building that fucking house. I'm talking about Maureen."

Ridgley took off his glasses. "You haven't left work in twenty years?"

"Twenty-three, come May. Hey, it takes time to get a successful cement business off the ground. My old man ran it into nothing before he died."

"You're in worse shape than I thought. According to all the actuarial charts, you died in 1960."

"Charts, shit." He stepped into his trousers. "Gimme something for my dough. A prescription."

"Have you considered retirement?"

"Only every day for the past five years. Who's going to buy me out, you?"

"Would that be so ridiculous?"

"Oh, no. 'Doc Ridgley's Better Cement.' Good for what ails your sick foundation. C'mon, Lowell."

"Not the business. You still own that place up in Pontiac?"

"Detroit Manufacturers owns it. They let me live there as long as I keep sending them fifteen hundred a month." He pulled up his suspenders. Dolly had been after him to switch to a belt; she said he was starting to look like an old potato farmer. He was considering it.

Ridgley hiked a hip up onto the examining table, scratching his ear with the eraser end of his gold pencil. "The investment group I belong to is looking for residential property in all the northern suburbs. We're speculating that the white flight from the city that's been going on since the riots is just the beginning. If Coleman Young wins in November, property values above Eight Mile Road could double the first year. You've got a pretty nice lot, as I recall."

"Pretty nice mortgage, too. I got twenty-four years left to pay."

"We'd pick it up, of course."

Joe Piper zipped his coat. "So I get out clean, and you and the orthodontist and the gynecologist and the ear, nose, and throat man make a killing. What's to stop me from hanging on till the values go up and cutting my own deal without you guys?"

"Nothing. In fact as your friend I'd recommend it. But as your doctor . . ." He pointed his pencil at the clipboard on the sink counter.

"My Uncle Seamus had a saying," the gun dealer said. " 'Don't sell your sheep to the same guy who tells you wool's down.' Suppose after I sign the papers I get a check-up from another doc who says I'm going to live to be a hundred?"

"That's a fucking insult." Ridgley spoke mildly. "You're free to get a second opinion. I wasn't thinking real estate when I was going over the results of your examination."

336

"Don't get your shorts in a wad, Lowell. I got to have some fun. I got a hundred and thirty-two thousand tied up in the place. How much you offering over that?"

"I'd have to talk to my partners. They'll want to look at the house and lot."

"Yeah, yeah. How much?"

"Say fifty thousand."

His heart thumped against the wall of his chest. "Hell, I can say fifty thousand with my eyes closed."

"I'll call you."

Joe Piper turned toward the door. "Now I just got to find a buyer for the business."

"I'm sure you will. Everybody needs guns."

He turned back.

Ridgley hoisted his eyebrows toward his bald crown. "We played cribbage. You never could bluff for shit."

The drive home took two full hours. The snow had stopped falling, but the wind had increased, blowing the powder into big pillowy drifts. He got stuck twice and had to detour via Square Lake Road and I-75 for a fender-bender involving a Gremlin and a VW Super Beetle on Telegraph. The radio was jammed with commercial spots extolling the virtues of cruises to the Bahamas and barefoot strolls along Malibu.

Unwinding at last in front of the big color console TV in his living room, with his feet propped up in warm dry socks and his hands wrapped around a glass of the Irish whiskey he'd been saving since Christmas, Joe Piper watched the man he knew as Wolf being rolled on a gurney from the box of an EMS van through the wide emergency-room doors at Detroit Receiving Hospital. Although he only got a brief glimpse of the Indian's face behind an oxygen mask before it was obscured by a gang of paramedics, nurses, and Detroit police officers, the gun dealer immediately recognized the man who had frisked him in McCoy's quarters on Twelfth Street nearly a month ago.

The scene shifted abruptly to another emergency room at another hospital, Harper-Hutzel, where a man in FBI cap and windbreaker was shown carrying a little girl wrapped in a yellow blanket into the building from an unmarked sedan.

". . . six-year-old was reported in good condition," announced Channel Seven newsman Jack Kelly. "The name of the slain Detroit police officer is being withheld pending notification of relatives."

The doorbell startled Joe Piper. He got up, turned off the set in the middle of a scene of snowy vehicular mayhem on Outer Drive, and opened the door to Homer Angell.

The former militiaman filled the doorway in a huge inflated army-issue parka whose hood framed his face in thick fur, dyed olive-drab to match the material. Below this were jodhpurs and black leather boots laced to his knees. His fair skin was flushed cherry-red.

"Jesus Mary," said the gun dealer. "I thought you were Bigfoot come to call."

"Well, do I come in or what?"

Joe Piper moved out of the way and closed the door behind his visitor. Standing in the entryway, Angell stripped off his big mittens, the coat, the boots, an insulated Korean War–surplus jacket whose insignia had been removed, and six feet of green knitted scarf wound around his telephone-pole neck. His host hung the garments in the hall closet and left the boots in a puddle of melted snow on the floor. Angell had to duck to clear the living room archway. He looked around with bright blue eyes. "You're alone?"

"I was till you came. Dolly's stuck at her sister's till the plows get out. How'd you get here, by helicopter? I thought everything was shut down."

"The Cherokee eats this stuff up. When was the last time you swept the place?"

"Sunday. This too hot for the phone?"

"We've been using the same code for too

long. Six weeks is my limit." The big man occupied Joe Piper's chair. "What've you got to drink?"

He named Scotch and bourbon. He wasn't going to waste his good Irish on this company.

"Tea?"

"Lipton's okay?"

"If you haven't got camomile."

"Jesus. I'll check the pantry."

He didn't have a pantry. He didn't have camomile tea either. What he had was two bags left in a box with the guy who looked like a seagoing Colonel Sanders on the lid. He filled a pot from the tap and set the burner on high. When he returned to the living room, Angell was flipping through a copy of *TV Guide* with the cast of *M★A★S★H* on the cover.

He flipped it onto the coffee table. "In my unit we'd've busted out a bleeding-heart pinko like Alan Alda the first week. Hollywood doesn't know shit about the military."

"I heard they couldn't get Sergeant York. Dead." Joe Piper sat on the couch. "What's the rumpus?"

"Tomorrow's the first."

He pulled a frown, turning that one over. Then he got up and checked the calendar in the niche by the fireplace. "Damn, you're right." He went back and resumed his seat.

"Don't know why you couldn't have told me that over the phone. ATF knows tomorrow's February." He pronounced both *r*s. He hated it when people made it rhyme with "January."

"When I didn't hear from you I thought maybe you forgot. You were going to buy those Ingrams from me tomorrow. Twenty guns at fifteen hundred apiece."

"Oh, them. That deal went south."

"When?"

"Last night, around midnight. Did you see the news?"

"I sold my set when they canceled *Combat*."

"My customer's under arrest for kidnapping a girl and killing a cop. Plus he's got a bullet in his chest. I consider that a bad risk."

"That's your problem. We had a deal."

"Bullshit. This ain't Wall Street. Everybody loses when the customer takes a fall."

"He'll have company if I get nailed with two cases of hot guns."

"What happened to the Perón deal?"

Angell ran a freckled hand over his buzz cut. "There wasn't exactly a Perón deal. I made it up."

"Homer, Homer."

"Well, you were dragging your feet. You've been doing that a lot lately."

"Yeah, the kicks went out of it for me a long time back. I think it was the Bay of Pigs done it. All that ordnance shot to shit, and for what? A ratty little piss-hole of an island we already got rid of once. And we didn't get it then. Fucking Kennedy."

"One of yours."

"Uh-uh. Wrong county. The business was different when I came to it. My Uncle Seamus really thought he was making a difference. The Irish Free State came out of the guns he smuggled over there. It didn't matter that he got stinking rich doing it." Perched on the edge of the sofa, he realized he was gesturing like some broken-down drunk from the Old Sod. He let his hands fall between his knees. "Hell, I don't know. Maybe the business has always been rotten. Maybe it just took getting my throat cut to see it."

The tea kettle whistled. Joe Piper went into the kitchen, filled a mug, sank a tea bag in it, and went back out pumping the bag up and down by its string.

Angell reached up and took the mug. "You're wrong."

"Hey, fix your own fucking tea." He scooped up his glass of whiskey and slung himself back onto the sofa.

"I mean about the gun business. I think it's whatever you bring to it. To you it's just a living and to hell with it. To me it's all those beautiful guns."

"I hate guns."

"Oh, but you shouldn't. They're the only true precision instruments still in mass production. Cars are crap. You bring home a TV set or a radio, watch it until it breaks, then throw it away and buy another. Not a gun. Why do you think so many killers get nailed with the pieces they used still in their possession?"

"That's easy. They're stupid fucks."

"Wrong. It's because they can't bear to part with them. Guns are history. They've won wars and freed nations. The man who sold Hitler the gun he used to blow his brains out made more of a difference than the six hundred thousand men in the *Wehrmacht*. Every time I handle an Ultra Light Reb Hunter or unpack an L71A British FN MAG, I wonder where it's been and where it's going. And when I open a newspaper and read some thug dictator in some country I never heard of took one in the melon, opening that country up to democratic government, I wonder if I had a part in it."

Stretched full-length on the sofa, Joe Piper studied Homer Angell inside the *v* of his stockinged feet. He'd been about to inform the gung-ho prick that he knew for a fact he'd unpacked and handled the gun his first wife had used to blow out her brains, but as the speech went on he'd grown thoughtful.

"I got two hundred thousand bucks' worth of guns, ammo, and C-4 sitting in a barn just outside Saline," he said. "I can let you have the lot for half that."

Angell looked at him, seemed about to say something. Then he sat back and sipped tea. Joe Piper went on.

"I could get the full amount piecing it out, probably more, but that takes time. This is virgin stuff. It's a sweet deal, one time only. A going out of business sale."

"I'd have to see it."

"We'll run out there soon as the roads are clear."

"I don't know if I can lay hands on that much."

"How much can you?"

Sip. "Twenty thousand." Sip. "Maybe twenty-five."

Joe Piper swirled the golden liquid in his glass. "That'll do for the down. After that you can send me a couple thousand a month for three years. Well, thirty-seven months. You get good at doing arithmetic in your head in this game."

"How do you know I'll send it?"

"You'll send it. I know a lot harder guys

344

in cement contracting than I ever met dealing guns."

"Why me? I always thought you had a pretty low opinion of my type."

"That's your imagination. Your type is the future of the gun trade."

"Where will you go?"

Joe Piper unwound himself from the sofa, set down his glass, and carried the United States Atlas he'd had on the coffee table over to Angell, spreading it open on his lap to the page he had marked with a swizzle stick. He ran his finger down the coast of California and stopped just short of Santa Barbara.

Angell squinted. "What's at Point Conception?"

"The Pacific Ocean."

Chapter Twenty-Nine

By turns the feral Michigan winter stalked and slew throughout February, slunk away during the second week of March, then pounced with a primordial howl on St. Patrick's Day, dumping seventeen inches of snow on Detroit and blowing down power lines in the northern suburbs. In Toledo the lake effect heaped quays of white powder across U.S. 23, sealing off the Northwest Territory as efficiently as dynamiting a bridge. Dozens of hearts burst beneath the strain of digging out. Then came the thaw. The earth, liquefied, collapsed under city streets and expressway ramps, imploding the asphalt into craters that shredded tires, snapped axles, and crumpled suspensions like cheap foil. April stormed. The sky rolled down to the rooftops and sprouted fangs. Tornadoes and lightning gouged furrows through housing tracts in Westland and the factory towns downriver.

During much of this time a disturbance

considerably less elemental, but every bit as desperate, had taken place between the United States Department of Justice and the City of Detroit over who would receive custody of Andrew Porterman, a/k/a Wolf. The city attorney argued that while the FBI held jurisdiction in kidnapping cases, the fact that a Detroit police officer was killed during the suspect's apprehension gave priority to the city; moreover, since no ransom demand had been made at the time of the incident, the taking of Opal Ogden was not precisely a kidnapping at all, but an abduction, which was a civil crime and not federal. The U.S. Attorney General's office countered that because Porterman was approached by agents and officers while on his way to a public telephone, and because a piece of paper was found on his person bearing the unlisted telephone number of the parents of the girl who had been taken, it stood to reason that a ransom demand was forthcoming. Further, as a three-quarter-blood Ottawa born in Michigan's Upper Peninsula, Porterman was a ward of the government, and as such his fate belonged to Washington.

The debate wore into March, while its subject, recovering under heavy guard in a private room at Detroit Receiving Hospital from surgery to remove a .45-caliber bullet from the upper right quadrant of his thorax, remained unaware whether he would spend the rest of his life in the crumbling state facility at Jackson or the relative comfort of the Milan federal house. With no access to television or a newspaper, all he knew was what he overheard police officers and hospital staff discussing outside his door.

In fact, his first indication that any sort of decision had been reached occurred when a male nurse accompanied by half a dozen large men in plainclothes transferred him from his bed to a wheelchair in the meager hours of a sodden morning in late March and pushed him out to the curb, where two Detroit police officers waited to bundle him into the back seat of a city blue-and-white. Within twenty-four hours he had been arraigned in Detroit Recorder's Court on charges of child abduction and the homicide of a police officer, outfitted with orange coveralls, and assigned a cell in the Wayne County Jail.

As Wolf pieced it together later, the Justice Department had finally bowed to local demands so that it could attend to the far more pressing issue of damage control in the wake of Attorney General John N. Mitchell's resignation to face charges of obstruction of justice in the Watergate investigation. The Indian, who since his near-fatal injury had become something of a philosopher, supposed there was some solace in the knowledge that he shared his outlaw status with the highest official in the cabinet.

Trial was set for April. Two days after his arraignment, at which he was represented by a public defender, Wolf was visited in his cell by one Theophilus Carver Corbett, a trim young black attorney in a superbly tailored maroon suit who glittered when he moved. The Indian divined early on that this quality had less to do with the man's personality than his accoutrements, which included a gold collar clip, diamond rings on both hands, a gold Rolex and identification bracelet, and a special hairspray that made his impressive afro twinkle whenever it caught the light. Corbett explained that he was a junior partner in the firm that had represented Wilson McCoy in two criminal cases and that his fee was provided for by the defense fund set up by the National Black Panther Party.

"Answer me one question," Corbett said. "Then you don't say another word until after the trial, understand what I'm saying?"

Wolf nodded.

"You do the girl?"

"No!" He tasted bile.

"I don't just mean did you fuck her. You touch or fondle or say anything to her that could be described in any way as sexual?"

"I bathed her once."

"Why'd you do that?"

"I had to. She was covered with horseshit. The shaman —"

"I know all about that. She's a prosecution witness. Answer this one, then shut the fuck up. When you was giving her that bath, did you get a hard-on?"

"No. Jesus."

"Good. Now, seal up that hole and listen to me. They're going to slap you with two consecutive life terms on account of this here's political and there's nothing like current politics for putting folks' backs up; look at Nixon. But politics go stale faster than pork rinds. Give this thing five years and folks start wondering why they got so hot and bothered over that old thing. That's when I swing you a new trial, maybe get you off with ten years total. But if they ring in child molestation and it sticks, ain't no lawyer in this world can spring you any way but feet first on a plank. That don't never change."

"I killed a cop."

"You shot a guy coming at you with a gun. They shot first, from way up on a roof with a scope rifle. You didn't know if you was being busted or attacked by one of them youth gangs. Did they *say* they was cops?"

"No."

He nodded his glittery head once. Then his expression changed. "This one's just because I'm curious. You don't have to answer, it makes no difference. What were you planning to do with the money once you had it?"

"Buy guns."

"What for?"

Wolf hesitated. "You know, I don't remember if we ever got into it. Wilson just wanted guns."

"That boy's a handful. I'd sure like to know why he's worth so much grief."

Wolf started to answer, then remembered instructions and simply shook his head.

Corbett's grin illuminated the cell. "You're a quick study. I do admire that in a client. Now do everything I say and we'll have you out of denims and back in warpaint and feathers before your hair turns so white you won't be able to raise a whoop."

"The state calls Sergeant Paul Kubicek."

The courtroom presided over by Judge Del Rio in the Frank Murphy Hall of Justice, a judicial bandshell built of green-and-white Carrara marble with a vaulted ceiling and slightly dished walls, was laid out like a the-

351

ater. The stage belonged to the judge's high oak bench and the defense and prosecution tables facing it, behind which spectator seats climbed in graduated rows to just under the balcony. The last, separated from the proceedings below by a gleaming oak rail, was unofficially reserved for off-duty police officers curious to see what new outrages were being committed by the freshman jurist. They called it the "peanut gallery."

Del Rio was many things to many people. To that special sub-category of embittered minority members convinced there was no justice to be obtained in the white man's court, the black judge was a hero of his race. To veteran police officers weary of watching their hard-won collars, usually black, released by his order on technicalities, he was a wild-eyed racist who owed his appointment to his affiliation with the local Democratic Party. His apologists referred to his conduct on and off the bench as "unorthodox"; "colorful." His adversaries, too exasperated to observe the niceties, employed the phrase "criminally corrupt." In all events he was a Detroit original.

Of which, as it was expressed by one of the participants at his disbarment hearing some years later, that city had more than its share.

Charlie Battle, stopping by in uniform on his way to pick up the deputy mayor's dry cleaning, took a vacant seat in the front row of the peanut gallery. That row was almost all cops. Some he knew, others he didn't and drew the obvious conclusion, based on their dress and the way they sat, either slouched on their tailbones with ankles crossed or hunched forward with their arms folded on the railing, that they were plainclothesmen. The one next to him, a STRESS officer Battle had seen a number of times around 1300 and spoken to once or twice in a hallway, sat with his chin resting on his forearms and the thick rubber-fisted grip of a nine millimeter Ruger lolloping from a speed rig under his right arm. Detroit's downtown courts had to be the only ones in the country where the rule against firearms went so elaborately unenforced. Counting the big S&W on the bailiff's Sam Browne belt, his own department-issue .38, and the pearl-handled job the judge was known to pack under his robes, Battle calculated there was enough iron in the room to sink a small rowboat.

Today Del Rio wore a white silk turtleneck beneath his black robes, which together with his glossily slicked-back hair and gold-rimmed glasses gave him the air of a TV evangelist. He drummed manicured nails on the handle of his gavel and stared at the ceiling while the prosecutor began his questioning of the witness on the stand.

Battle tried to get a good look at the defendant seated at the front table, but from his angle all he could see was the Indian's broad back in an inexpensive striped suit and his long hair gathered into a ponytail. Once during Kubicek's testimony, Porterman turned to say something to his flashy-looking attorney, but the lawyer's big afro got in the way. No matter. Battle had already satisfied himself from the newspaper photographs taken at Porterman's arraignment that the man who called himself Wolf was the same man Russell Littlejohn's father had seen climbing the stairs to his son's room. He'd wondered if the prosecution in its eagerness to close the books on every major local crime that had taken place in the last twelvemonth would try to link the Indian to Russell's death; but he was hardly surprised when no mention was made of it. The accidental-OD scenario seemed to have satisfied everyone it was necessary to satisfy.

Anyway, Battle knew who'd killed Littlejohn.

For his star witness turn as the arresting officer in the Ogden kidnapping, Kubicek had bought a new dark blue suit and gone back to his flattop haircut, which he preferred for its clean look and low maintenance, and to hell with his wife's notions about contemporary style. Haircut or not, he felt more comfortable than he had in some time as he answered the gray-haired prosecutor's questions about how he had returned Porterman's fire after the Indian had gunned down his partner without provocation. *Partner;* the dead man had been on loan to 1300 from the third precinct and Kubicek had never met him before his reinstatement. The guy wore squeaky shoes and read aloud from "The Playboy Advisor," with special attention to the stuff on blow jobs. Kubicek would probably have put in for a departmental divorce in a day or so.

"Dave was a good man," he said. "I was proud to serve with him."

"Thank you, Sergeant. I have no more questions."

Del Rio propped his chin on his hand. "Mr. Corbett?"

Theophilus Carver Corbett — honest to *Christ,* the names they picked — walked around the defense table and leaned back against it with his arms crossed.

"You say the defendant fired on Officer Beddoes without provocation?"

355

"Shot him down like a dog in the street."

"Was this before or after a sniper in the employ of the Oakland County Sheriff's Department fired at the defendant with a high-powered rifle from a nearby roof, missing him by inches?"

"I don't know anything about that."

"We have Deputy Kingston's testimony that he fired the shot. Are you saying you didn't hear it?"

"It was windy."

"I see. It was windy. The Detroit ballistics team reported finding evidence that the bullet ricocheted off the steel cover of the pay telephone near where the defendant was standing when you approached him. Surely you heard that."

"It was a heavy wind," Kubicek said. "And I'd appreciate it if you didn't call me Shirley."

Laughter rippled through the spectators, loudest in the balcony. Del Rio, who hated being upstaged, rapped his gavel.

Corbett grinned, appreciating the joke; the fuck. "Did either you or Beddoes identify yourself as a police officer as you were approaching the defendant?"

"Beddoes did."

"Do you remember what he said?"

Kubicek cleared his throat. "He said, 'Police! Don't move!' Then the Indian shot him."

"Those were his exact words? 'Police! Don't move!'?"

Kubicek said they were.

"Can you explain to this court, Sergeant, how it was you heard the exact words Officer Beddoes used to identify himself as a police officer when you managed to hear *neither* the ear-splitting report of a Remington thirty-thirty rifle fired from the roof of a building twenty feet away *nor* the shrill whine of a high-speed bullet fired by that same rifle bounding off a steel box *ten feet in front of your nose?*"

The defense attorney had started walking toward the witness stand as he began his question, finishing with both hands on the partition in front of Kubicek with his face three inches from the sergeant's.

He met Corbett's gaze. "The wind died down for a second."

For the first time since he was shot, Wolf was enjoying himself. He enjoyed watching the big man in the box squirm, enjoyed watching Corbett work. He'd heard the attorney was dangerously unpredictable, a borderline nutcase. It was the kind of insanity that should have been embraced by defense lawyers everywhere.

Now Corbett turned his back on Kubicek and headed back toward the table, winking at Wolf. "How long have you been a police officer, Sergeant?"

"Eighteen years last November."

"In that time I imagine you've had your share of close calls?"

"That's why they pay me."

"Don't be modest. Would you say you've been called upon to use your training and reflexes a number of times in your own defense?"

"A time or two."

"And if you were standing all alone on a dark windy street corner late at night, and a man you never saw before came up to you suddenly with a gun in his hand, how would you react?"

As he spoke, the attorney brought his right hand across his abdomen inside the left flap of his maroon suitcoat. Something caught the light as he turned around.

Questioned later, Kubicek would say he went for a piece when he spotted the gun, but that was just for the record. He'd known it was there before he saw it, was coming up from his seat with his hand around the checked grip of the .45 while Corbett was still turning, his body between Kubicek and

358

the weapon. And then there it was, just where he knew it would be, right at the end of the attorney's outstretched arm with its empty black eye staring right at him.

The .45 was up as well, although not as high, and it bucked twice against his ribs.

By then guns were going off all over the place.

Like every other cop in the front row of the balcony, Battle was up and moving at the sight of Corbett's pistol; but unlike all the others, he was moving toward the stairs leading down to the main floor of the courtroom. A dozen or more speed holsters, spring clips, leather grannies, and drop-releases squeaked, rattled, sproinged, and skidded their burdens into swift-moving hands and then the air exploded and Battle, moving away from it, thought, *Jesus. Marble walls. Holy Jesus.*

Chaos awaited him at the bottom of the stairs. At first he could see nothing for the gangle of arms, legs, and desperate faces swarming toward the exit. The bailiff, taller than most of the spectators by a head, stood in their midst, gesticulating with his gun to keep them herded in the right direction. As the bodies began to thin out, Battle saw Kubicek standing in the witness box and the Indian, rising, behind the defense table with his back still to Battle. There was no sign of the judge. Battle pointed his own revolver at the ceiling, steadied it by crooking that elbow into the palm of his other hand, and started that way.

Wolf saw when the first of Kubicek's bullets struck Theophilus Carver Corbett. The attorney's narrow shoulders hunched, his raised arm bent at the elbow, and the little .25 automatic, the square one that looked like a novelty cigarette lighter, wilted in his hand, swiveling upside-down on the pivot of his finger inside the trigger guard. He continued to crumple in on himself as the second bullet entered his body. In another moment there was nothing standing between Paul Kubicek and the Indian. Their eyes met. The bleakness in the sergeant's remained. And Wolf knew.

Buzzing bits of metal struck the marble behind the judge's bench, crackling on impact and adding puffs of white dust to the blue swirls hazing the air. Kubicek was aware of this, but separate from it, as if he were thinking with two heads. With Corbett down, the cop-killer stood before him, one hand gripping the oak table that was no defense at all, the other stretched out in front of him palm-first, no expression on his face, as if he expected to catch the bullet in mid-air. The arrogant shit.

All the time in the world now. The sergeant raised his arm to the level of his shoulder, sighted down it, just like on the range, and pumped a slug square into the middle of the impassive Indian face.

Silence, sudden and loud.

Andrew Porterman, Wolf, the defendant; it didn't matter what you called him now, what was left of him lay half under the defense table with the upper half sprawled on the seat of the chair he'd been sitting in up until sixty seconds ago, one arm bent over the back.

The STRESS sergeant stood motionless, the big automatic still extended in front of him. Time lay on the air.

Sounds then, desperate pants and scrabbling. Kubicek turned his head. On the floor behind the bench, Judge Del Rio was crawling on his knees and elbows toward the door to his chambers, black-gowned buttocks pointed at the ceiling.

The sergeant lowered the .45, brought it around.

"Guess who, cocksucker!"

The force of the words blasted Kubicek back around. Straddling the center aisle between the spectator seats, Charlie Battle, his

361

.38 clamped between both fists, stared at him with his eyes white all around the irises.

Kubicek raised his vision higher, to the twelve black muzzles trained on him from the balcony.

He laid the pistol on the railing of the witness box and clasped his hands behind his head.

Chapter Thirty

The shoot-out in Judge Del Rio's courtroom was investigated, recorded, and consigned eventually to local legend, where it joined such storied events as the Collingwood Massacre and the death of Harry Houdini.

A postscript, unknown to all but a handful of insiders, involved the discovery of a number of jagged depressions in the marble wall behind the judge's bench, describing a broken line twelve to eighteen inches above the floor, and corresponding precisely with Del Rio's retreat on all fours to the sanctity of his chambers. Since all the bullets fired in the incident were police rounds, the conclusion was that one or more of the officers in the balcony had selected the judge for his target; but the only action taken in regard to this intelligence was an order from the commander of the Detective Division requiring all personnel present on that day to report to the firing range for target practice.

And time resumed its flight.

May, siren that she was, broke sunny and

seductive over the industrial and residential sprawl of metropolitan Detroit. Windows opened against the seal of the long winter, short sleeves came out of storage, and colds spread like mildew.

The worst, after the March mudslides and tempests of April, was to come.

June brought the deadhammer heat associated in southern regions with July and early August. By mid-month the mercury reached ninety, with humidity to match. Storefront windows glared like white steel in the sunlight. Parking meters squirmed behind ribbons of heat twisting up from the pavement. At five o'clock the city's major arteries clogged with stalled vehicles like dead flies in a fixture, while anger grew like a stench.

Two motorists shot each other on Michigan Avenue over a broken taillight. They died twelve hours apart.

In a blind pig downtown, a man refused to put his shoes back on for another man who complained about the smell. He was shot to death for his stubbornness.

A husband on Mt. Elliott Street threatened his wife with a pistol when she protested his gambling. She scooped up a shotgun and blew him nearly in half.

In a similar neighborhood on the northwest side, another man shot his live-in girlfriend to death when she declined to share her welfare check with him.

A tenant in a residential hotel on East Jefferson shot his landlord in lieu of paying rent. The landlord was dead on arrival at Detroit Receiving Hospital.

This sudden seasonal upsurge in the violent-crime statistics of a city already notorious for its homicides attracted the attention of all three national television networks. Camera crews arrived and uncoiled cables in places that were barely acquainted with electricity. This renewed interest inspired United Artists to move up the world premiere of *Murder City* (formerly titled *Detroit P.D.*). The feature film opened the July 4th weekend at the Fox Theater on Woodward, once a grand motion-picture palace, more recently reduced to all-night showings of third-rate black exploitation flicks and quasi-respectable stag films. It shared a double bill with *Deep Throat*.

There were no searchlights or stretch limos in evidence opening night. Neither Mayor Gribbs nor Police Commissioner Nichols attended the event, despite their cameo appearances onscreen. The presence of the Detroit Police Department, however, was unmistakable, particularly when a brawl broke out in the lobby after the first showing and a fully equipped riot squad waded into the mob with helmets and batons. Peace was restored, but when a similar disturbance took place following the eleven-thirty show, a deputy commissioner ordered the theater closed, "with regret." When it reopened a week later, *Buck and the Preacher* topped the bill, supported by *Fritz the Cat*. That night a fistfight over the missing prize from a box of Cracker Jacks was quickly broken up by the ushers.

Wilson McCoy spent this entire period on the second floor of his condemned building on Twelfth Street. When news reached him that Wolf was in custody, he scrubbed the glutinous cosmoline jacket from a short-barreled Winchester pump twelve-gauge shotgun with its stock cut down to the pistol grip, cleaned the big shiny .44 magnum, loaded them, and kept both within reach at all times. Word that Wolf had been gunned down in broad daylight in a downtown courtroom had him carrying the Winchester with him to the toilet. He was certain now the FBI would mount a full-scale assault on the safe house, and to hell with the civil disturbance that would inevitably follow.

He lived on the canned goods he'd been stockpiling since the day he moved in. At night, writhing on his cot through the thick gummy weeks of June and early July with no electricity to operate a fan, he sweated pure sardine oil and Dole pineapple juice. When in all that time no attempt was made to breach his plywood-reinforced citadel, he made a decision. He thrust the revolver into the waistband of his army camouflage pants, covering the butt with his olive-drab sleeveless undershirt, and Went Out, leaving the shotgun behind. His little back-up .22 made a reassuring weight in his right boot.

The heat was brutal. He crossed to the shady side of Twelfth, where the shadows cast by the burned broken buildings lay like a damp towel across his shoulders; but the unaccustomed exertion of walking brought the sweat streaming down his face in moments. On Edison he turned east into the hammering sun, accepted his complimentary *Chronicle* from the glum old man in front of the bakery, skimmed through its pages for his name, failed to find it — confirming his faith that the FBI was stonewalling the media in its fever to spit him on its grill — and threw it into the ashcan at Woodrow Wilson. There the taller of the two brothers he knew from Tino's, the one with the Wilt the Stilt goatee, was slumped in the shade of a graffiti-splattered iron bench left over from the days when the DSR bus still stopped there, but

McCoy walked past without speaking. The feds had honeycombed his old neighborhood with informants; you never knew who you could count on from one day to the next.

Rounding the corner onto Hazelwood he slowed his pace, out of breath now, his clothing soaked through, the accelerated aging cycle of the wanted felon catching up with him at twenty-five. But the tension was lifting. Three-quarters of the way around his fiefdom and no attempt had been made to take him. The magic was still holding. The jackals, sated for the time being with their fresh carrion, were reluctant still to approach the lion in his lair.

His spirits were high when he reached Tino's and took his usual seat in the corner. The wind from the ceiling fan cooled his skin and pushed the sharp-sweet odors of garlic, tomatoes, and hot grease all around. His half-dozen fellow patrons, all but one or two of whom were strangers, recognized him and began to whisper. He felt like Billy Dee Williams.

The owner's big slab face showed no expression at all, although McCoy knew he was glad to see him. Of all the celebrities who had dined there in the past — Aretha, Stevie, Berry Gordy, the Brown Bomber — he was the only one who still came around. The last firefly.

"The Redd Foxx is good today," Tino informed him, gesturing over his shoulder with a long-handled cooking fork. "I got six of the biggest fattest porkers you ever seen hanging in the cold room."

McCoy tucked his red-and-white-checked napkin inside the scoop neck of his undershirt. "Gimme the Wilson McCoy, double order. Bring out three or four thick slices of that garlic bread while I'm waiting, and a big bowl of barbecue sauce. And a bottle of Ripple."

"Hungry man."

"No shit. I been eating out of cans so long I piss aluminum."

The appetizers came, hot and steaming. The garlic made him belch and the jalapeño peppers in the sauce started him sweating all over again; but everything was delicious.

His appetite found its second wind just in time to devour the meatball sandwich that bore his name. He used the last of the bread to swamp the last trace of sauce from the bowl. Then he washed it all down with Ripple. The cheap wine shot straight to his head, filling it with great plans — plans he knew he'd have to scale down in order to fit them inside his little ten-block universe. It was a tight space, full of the same tired faces, any one of which might be hiding a scheme to take him down. But what the hell, it beat prison.

Author's Note

The shoot-out in Judge Del Rio's courtroom is a part of Detroit lore; but outrageous as it was, it occupied center ring only briefly in the circus that was the period.

Between 1967 — the year of the riots — and 1974, the number of homicides committed within the city limits of Detroit increased eightfold, climbing to 801 in 1974, a rate of 44.5 murders per 100,000 citizens.

In January 1971, a police crackdown squad, STRESS (Stop The Robberies, Enjoy Safe Streets), was implemented to bring down the number of violent crimes taking place in the streets of the city.

Upon assuming office in 1974, Coleman A. Young, the first black mayor in Detroit's history, chose as his first official act to disband STRESS, whose high-pressure tactics had prompted hundreds of citizen complaints as racist in nature.

In 1975, the homicide rate in Detroit declined for the first time in thirteen years.

In 1993, two decades after the events herein

described, two Detroit police officers were found guilty and sentenced to lengthy prison terms for the highly publicized beating death of a drug suspect in front of a crack house in the city. Both were former STRESS squad members.

In November 1993, Dennis Archer was elected Detroit's first new mayor in twenty years after Coleman Young, broken in health and bedeviled with accusations of moral and criminal corruption, decided not to run for a sixth term. In his inaugural address, Archer pledged to create a new system of cooperation between government, police, and the citizens of Detroit to defeat crime.

The employees of THORNDIKE PRESS hope you have enjoyed this Large Print book. All our Large Print books are designed for easy reading — and they're made to last.

Other Thorndike Large Print books are available at your library, through selected bookstores, or directly from us. Suggestions for books you would like to see in Large Print are always welcome.

For more information about current and upcoming titles, please call or mail your name and address to:

THORNDIKE PRESS
PO Box 159
Thorndike, Maine 04986
800/223-6121
207/948-2962